SARAMINDA

JOSÉ SARNEY

For
Álvaro Pacheco
Joaquim Campelo
Napoleão Sabóia
Pedro Paulo de Sena Madureira
from the family of ultra good people

SARAMINDA
BLACK DESIRE
IN A FIELD OF GOLD

JOSÉ SARNEY

TRANSLATED FROM THE PORTUGUESE
BY GREGORY RABASSA

ALIFORM PUBLISHING
MINNEAPOLIS   OAXACA

ALIFORM PUBLISHING
is part of The Aliform Group
117 Warwick Street SE/Minneapolis, MN USA 55414
information@aliformgroup.com www.aliformgroup.com

Originally published in Brazil as *Saraminda*
by Editora Arx
Copyright © 2006

English translation copyright © Aliform Publishing, 2007

First published in the United States of America by
Aliform Publishing, 2007

This publication was made possible with the generous support of the
Cultural Department of the Ministry of Foreign Relations of Brazil and the
Consulate General of Brazil in New York.

Library of Congress Control Number
2007937569

ISBN 978-0-615-16478-6

Set in Times New Roman

Cover art by Marco Lamoyi, *Odalisca*
Cover design by Carolyn Fox

CONTENTS

The Setting

Up till the end of the nineteenth century both Brazil and France claimed the territory between the rivers Oiapoque and Araguari, today the Brazilian state of Amapá. The matter was resolved when Switzerland's arbitration recognized the rights of Brazil in an interpretation of the Treaty of Utrecht of 1713, which established the boundaries of Portuguese America.

It is a region of immense forests, unknown and mysterious, with waterfalls along great rivers that run south to the Amazon or east to the Atlantic.

After gold was discovered in the basin of the legendary Calçoene River, prospectors, pioneers, swindlers, heroes and drifters rushed to the region: Creole Frenchmen from Cayenne and Brazilians from Pará and Maranhão. That vacant wilderness came to be a bloody frontier of violence and passion where territory, women, claims and wealth were fought over.

It was in this world and this magical moment between reality and fable that Saraminda lived.

"La Guyane est une terre où la passion est souvent presente."
("Guiana is a land where passion is often present.")
   Patrice Moureau-Lascaux

"Saint Thomas, deep in the writing of his *Summa Theologica*, heard a monk come up to the window and say: 'Look, a flying ox ....' He got up and went to the window to look."
   Antonio Alçada Baptista

1

La Couleur*

Cayenne is forlorn. There is a slight, almost imperceptible breeze at the mouth of the Laussat Canal. The Customs House and the Governor's Palace—silent buildings, symbols of the power of metropolitan France—are drowsy. Opposite them, in the center of the square, is an iron fountain brought from Paris, open, like a flower spreading water, in memory of Tardy de Montravel, who piped in the springs of Lake Rorota. And beside the sea, next to Almond Tree Point, is the prison from where in the silence comes a whispering, a dark murmur from the cells, the sound of suffering and death. These are destinies consumed in rancor and solitude, in dungeons, irons, fevers and tortures. The streets are twisty, unplanned, with puddles of stagnant water, mosquitoes and worms leavening the garbage scattered everywhere. The city, small and abandoned, has houses built of planks with roofs of straw, wood and tin. Everything smells of decadence and distress. Stories are told of convicts or ghosts in the woods where blacks go in search of food. They live off of gathering and from the few establishments that distill rum.

The building that houses the Office of the Guianese Miners and the Mines Service is abandoned and the sea waters that beat against it with their monotonous eddies are bringing down its walls. Night can't hide this collapse of what once was life. The gold has disappeared. So what of Guiana, which was nothing but gold after it was first struck in 1854? The good times are long gone and their memory is only left in the tales told of the euphoric discoveries, when rivers with beds of yellow sand were found, or the fantastic

---

* A term for gold in French Guiana.

explosion in the price of gold after the War of 1870. Hope is almost nonexistent and the only vigor, diffuse, is found in the fragile allurement of agricultural enterprises and a new policy for the natives. Neither rumors nor dreams of new mineral wealth circulate through the city stupefied by despondency. Everything is murky. Guiana is vegetating in a poverty of cinnamon and dyewood.

The darkness covering the streets hides the disillusion. There are no signs of merriment. The doors of the old bars, closed for so long, have faded paint, rusty locks, and lean broken like an old fence. The sidewalks where women went back and forth have disappeared. In that world of silence there is one solitary, stubborn sound, full of melancholy and longing, that comes from Chez Martin, where old Louis is playing an old song from Brittany on a grand piano with broken strings and a cracked lid, salvaged from a ship that foundered on the sandbar at the harbor.

The prospectors who gave the colony its glory days have gone off, fleeing from the times. The blacks remain, descendants of slaves from Martinique and Guadeloupe or from the settlements of runaway Maroni: Bonis, Saramacas, jungle blacks. Even the memories of the battles of discovery and conquest, the time of invasions, sieges and sacking are forgotten. No one remembers the old Guiana, the lair of pirates who plied the Antilles sea and hid there, attacking caravels bulging with gold, copper and silver pillaged from the empires destroyed by Cortés and Pizarro, who sent their spoils to the land of Spain where the kingdom was swimming in wealth, God receiving his share in the golden altars of the Seville cathedral.

Nor did the Portuguese galleons escape pillaging, loaded down as they were with Brazilian sugar, dyewood, jaguar pelts, catamounts and parrots. The corsairs of the tropic sea sought out Cayenne and established their trading posts there. They weren't only Frenchmen from Dieppe, Saint-Malo and Cancale. There were also Englishmen and Dutchmen who carried Chinese, Mandinga, Bantu, Gege and Congo slaves in their holds for the emerging plantations or for hard labor of any kind. All those people left marks that mingled with the strong, dominant black that resisted and tamed them all.

Clément Tamba was one of them. Dark, smooth-skinned, his hair was parted on one side and smoothed down with brilliantine.

He was tall, with a broad face, small eyes, thin lips, an angular nose, long-fingered hands, strong shoulders and a barrel-chest, as if his lungs were always full. His muscular body gave him a look of solidity. He dressed neatly, his clothes well cared for, but his expression was a sad one.

He had always been involved in dealings with the French, supplying wines and game from hunting to the prison, Government House and colonial authorities. He'd grown up in the misery of a wooden hut along with his sisters, mother and stepfather. As a boy he sold sweetmeats of sugar and coconut which he hawked on the street, and as a young man he began doing odd jobs, putting some money together to open a fruit stand, then selling liquor and later fabrics, and finally he had a store with assorted merchandise that included products bought in France, England and Portugal, acquired from freebooters who sailed along the coast and did business from the Orinoco to the Amazon.

But Clément Tamba suffered from a greed for gold, knowing that someday he'd get into prospecting and wealth and perfumed transient women. "I miss the avenues of Paris, although I've never been there," he used to think, calling forth the memory of his Breton father, gone forever. Every time some European customer came into his store he'd beg him, "Tell me about Paris," and he'd stand there listening with distant eyes to the description of gaslights, cabriolets, can-can dancers and women who picked up customers on the rue Saint-Denis.

His forebears were part of the painful memory of the African immigration. The family history went back to the tragedy of the slave ships, in the distant memory of a grandmother, a black slave from Dahomey, princess of a conquered kingdom and sold to the traders who came to São Jorge Fort on the Gold Coast of Africa. In Cayenne she'd been bought by Jacob Biarritz, a Sephardic Jew who took her as a concubine after losing all his religious beliefs and sinking into the desires that tormented him in the solitude of those hot southern vapors. Clément's mother had come from that ruined line. Possidonia Biarritz was a black Jew who had lost her flower of maidenhood in a violent romance at the hands of a soldier from Fort Cépérou, one Augustin Ruppert, a dissolute and brutal Frenchman punished for bad conduct with service in the colonies. He began to drink and would spend the night staggering along the rue du Port, where he would urinate on the corners and shout foul words in Creole. Clément Tamba spent his childhood among his mother's tears and his father's rowdiness, listening to him shouting late into the night, trembling with fear of his brutal treatment. Until one day his father disappeared.

"Where's my father, Augustin Ruppert, who doesn't come home drunk at dawn anymore?"

"He went off to France, chasing after some woman. May God have him die at sea," his mother replied.

Still young, Possidonia Biarritz immediately married a released convict from Maroni Prison, René d'Orville, who'd just completed a twenty-year sentence for killing his wife Edith Mourreau, a can-can dancer. One day, in the Les Halles market in Paris, overcome with jealousy, he hanged her with a rope made from an embroi-dered sheet soaked in lavender cologne. Then he turned himself in to the police, swearing eternal fealty to her memory.

Silent and sad, he was a good companion for Possidonia and had three daughters with her—Marie, Mazi, and Marthe—the last of whom died young. The two older ones went to Martinique and all that was heard of them was news a few years later that Mazi had married an English sugar planter living in Marigot.

It was during those years of solitude and decline that Clément Tamba's head was turned when he saw a golden light shining in the Brazilian Firmino Amapá's story about discoveries in the head-waters of the Calçoene River in the Contestado region, a territory claimed by both Brazil and France.

Clément didn't believe Firmino, accustomed as he was to so many reports of such discoveries that were never confirmed and simply increased the disappointments of those times.

Firmino gave him details of the course of the rapids that had to be followed up to the source of the streams that came down from Mount Salomoganha, on a gold-bearing plateau from where brooks of golden water and nuggets descended, spreading gold along the basins of the Calçoene, the Carnot, the Cunani and the Caciporé. He spoke of lucky strikes, of old pioneer prospectors, of veins hidden in the forest already being worked. He revealed the fact that it wasn't just his secret alone but one shared by many pros-pectors and panners in the region, and that the news had run like a wildfire from the banks of the Araguari to Saint-Georges on the

Oiapoque. Mysterious foreign travelers on the roads concealed their aims without telling where they were going, but everybody knew they were hunting for the new golden highway.

"Clément Tamba, gold doesn't hide, it likes to show off and you can find it right there in front of you. I dreamed about it. I was sleeping on the bank of the brook that empties into the Carnot River and it appeared. My nose was stuffed from so much sniffing. I looked at the clear water and it was shining on the bottom, close to the mountains. There's so much gold in the river beds people pick it up with their hands."

In order to awaken Tamba's curiosity he grew secretive, began to mutter doubtful words that suggested occult things, and feigning reluctance as he rolled a cigarette and sealed the straw with spittle, asked him if he wanted to hear more.

"Do you want to see?"

"See what, Firmino?"

"The genuine article."

Clément Tambá felt that something conclusive was about to happen to him. He remembered the indecipherable dreams he kept having of golden dragons, enchanted princesses, mountain forests that glowed, things meant for children and adventurers.

"Don't tempt me with talk about those visions," Tamba asked.

Then Firmino, in a low voice, as though he were talking in a hiding place, looked to one side and the other, sank into a long silence, and revealed his thoughts:

"Clément Tamba, you're holding your luck in your hands. I don't know why I decided to tell you about these secrets. I came to Cayenne looking for a partner. You need people and money to claw that gold out. Gold doesn't like being left alone."

Firmino concluded his seduction with a request:

"I want you to trust me and take me into your house. Just the two of us, locked up in your room without any witnesses, with your promise to keep to yourself what I'm going to show you, something I haven't shown anybody."

"Firmino," Tamba said, filled with curiosity, "I guarantee on my honor. We can go in. I want to find out what your secret is."

The two went through the gate by the end of the counter right next to the wall and walked through the back, which opened onto a wide corridor leading to the bedroom.

"Here we are, Firmino."

"Lock the door."

Clément Tamba obeyed. The two of them stood a time by the window next to an unmade bed, the mark of a womanless house. They looked at each other with the silence that comes along with questions.

"So, Firmino, what now? Tell me whatever you've got to say."

Firmino was in no hurry. Calmly, without hesitation, he slowly developed the talk, preceded by a tactical silence. He cleared his throat before he spoke:

"Here is proof of a great secret."

He immediately unbuckled his belt and took off his pants. Tamba couldn't understand what was going on and he found the figure that emerged vulgar. Firmino was wearing above his long johns and around his waist, tied over his belly, a broad item of thick leather that had two compartments, both the size of a jacket pocket, hanging side by side, with flaps closed by clasps. In a careful and slow ritual, he undid the two clasps, took off the strange belt, and laid it on top of the bed. From inside he took out two small transparent bottles filled with yellowish sand. He picked them up, one in each hand, and held them up to the bright light coming in through the window.

"Do you know what this is?"

"Let me see, Firmino. Give them to me. I want to hold them in my hands," said Clément coming forward.

"No. No touching, just looking. Watch." He shook the jars. "Take another look, take a good look, the mystery's been revealed."

"Give them to me, let me see them close up," Tamba pleaded again.

"No, just look. It's something to be looked at, not touched."

Clément looked, studying the two objects with closer attention, and fixed his eyes on the yellow light that was growing as brilliant as a star, as blinding as the sun.

"Do you know what it is?" Firmino asked, standing, his lips held close to Clément Tamba's ear as he mouthed each syllable. "*La cou...leur.*"

Clément Tamba held his gaze between Firmino's hands. The two jars were there, hanging down. The words didn't enter his ears, they just buzzed and probed, as if they were going to pierce his eardrums. Clément Tamba was overcome by a great heat, perspiring all over. His eyes were glassy with greed.

"Where did you find that gold?"

"Come with me," Firmino replied, "and I'll show you where rivers of gold run, where you never pan less than forty ounces. The sand is yellow, there's gold everywhere."

Clément saw his destiny. He was won over. It had been bound to happen someday. At some moment in his life he'd find the path to a lucky strike.

"It's *la couleur*! It's *la couleur*!" he said to himself in a voice softer than the one he'd just lost, and he added, "There really is gold on the Brazilian side of the Contestado. It's a new Approuague!"*

---

*Gold was first discovered in 1854 in a tributary of the River Approuague, prompting a rush of panners and gold diggers to the region.

2

The Gold Razor

Clément Tamba came to the end of his life lonely and delirious, a skeleton left over from prospecting on the Calçoene. The years had transformed him.

"I have trouble remembering the star-jasmine tree that gleamed as white as an August moon. At night the breeze would give off a perfume that came into my room, where I always kept the windows open," Clément said, answering what Lucy had asked when she saw him stumble looking for the water jug.

"The star-jasmine tree is dead now, Clément. It withered away and disappeared back into time."

"The light in my eyes has died, too. It was that smell that made you visit me and come and lie down in my perfumed room. Do you remember when I told you, 'Lucy, you're all alone, I'm all alone, you're still beautiful, the same as during the years when your beauty gave a magic touch to the dances in Cayenne. Let's wait out death together.' And I invited you to walk down the long corridor where the boards creaked under our heavy steps. I opened the door. The windows were wide open and the smell of jasmine filled that bed made of rugs as it asked for the body of a woman."

"I don't know why, Clément, but the smell of star-jasmine reminds me of the few times I visited your house on the claim, those dark green trees, the February rains."

"We're old and we're falling apart."

"Don't ask me about anyone, they're all dead now. Everything is dead: friends, plants, time. It's all over."

14

Tamba had a gloomy wooden house that had been rotting away over the years, a rundown shack on the rue d'Estren. The rooms were filled with solitude, a living room with old worn furniture, the scratched table with its boards coming apart, the chairs with torn cane seats, and a glassware cupboard with no glasses or cups. In the bedroom, next to the dirty bed whose mattress smelled of piss, was the agate chamber pot, its rim all chipped by the onslaught of the years.

At the end of that day Clément was groping along over his own shadow toward the corridor leading to his quarters, watched by Raimunda, an old Brazilian woman, the widow of a sugar-cane seller, who had been vegetating there as a servant for over twenty years.

"Death is a tough business, Mr. Clément. Me and you have been waiting for it a long time," she said with a quaking voice.

On that afternoon unlike others, Clément had called her and asked her to bring the key hidden in a moldy bag under the mattress. He also asked her to wind up the music box that played Bach's "Minuet," imprisoned there by the small bolts that held the tin handles and pouring out a plinking sound that followed the rhythm of the tempo. That was the only music heard in the house. The old grand piano that had belonged to Louis and which he'd bought as a keepsake was nothing but dust and cobwebs, standing silent guard over the living room. Everything had been lost. Clément Tamba was the ragged remnant of the solitude that he himself had built up over the years.

"My destiny was to look for my destiny," he would say, his eyes closed. "Lucy, take the key from Raimunda and let's open my safe."

It was the old safe from his store, for which he hadn't found a buyer when he got rid of the place. It had two parts to it. The upper had two fluted columns supporting the heavy gears where the hinges were. The other part was decorated with a quadrangular design edged in faint colors of yellow and pea green, with shapes that folded into loops curling in an array of flowers. The dial with its circle of numbers was symmetrically placed with the keyhole underneath. To the side, all by itself, was the large knob that worked the four round security bars. The lower part was nothing but a closed box with no other function but to support the real safe, which was on top. The brand name was engraved on the rim of the lock: Coffres Smith; Sécurité Totale. It must have weighed four hundred pounds and was the bitter memory of those years. Lucy had her memories, too. She'd come to live with Clément when he returned to Cayenne after the claim was destroyed. She hadn't gone prospecting for gold, but stayed there with her son, who died in Algeria. Her husband had been murdered in a brawl on the loading docks when, doing his duty as a customs inspector, he was placing a fine on a rum smuggler. All alone, the marks of her young beauty still showing, she consented to live with Clément and they had been together more years than they could count.

"Why does Clément want to open the safe, something he's never talked about, this afternoon?" she wondered. Clément had never said what he kept in it. His money was in the night table drawer, along with the bag of gold nuggets, the jewels, and the French treasury bonds he'd bought, whose interest he collected through the agency of the Banque de la Guyane.

Clément wanted to see himself free of the weight of that secret. Up till that day he didn't know what Cleto Bonfim might have been thinking one night in the middle of a terrible storm, the leaks showing the awful shape the roof was in, when weeping he asked:

"Keep this package, Clément. It's a relic that cost me my soul. I can trust you with it. Don't say anything about it. It should be put in your safe. It's an old jewel whose safekeeping can only be entrusted to a friend." And he added, "Clément, I've just learned that France has lost this territory, which belongs to Brazil now. It was a decision made by Switzerland. Tomorrow there's only going to be one flag flying, Brazil's. You're French. They'll want to kick you out."

The blow of that sudden bit of news might have been the announcement of death or of a sacking. Clément Tamba's store, the largest in Saint-Laurent, was French, with the name France de Calçoene and the blue, white and red flag flapping on its pole. In short, he was a Frenchman from Guiana and allied with the rebels who were going up against Veiga Cabral, the guerrilla fighter in the jungles of the Contestado.

"Bonfim, is this news or an order to leave?"

"No, Clément. I'll give you protection. No one will do you any harm here. I only want to give you this object that's a part of my life. I can't stand sleeping next to it for another night. It's been my hell, bad luck, and I want to get rid of it. I can't stand being with it another day. It's been my obsession and my martyrdom. It goes against my conscience, a doubt I want far away from me."

Clément went back to the bedroom.

"You've got good eyes, Lucy. Look through my things for the piece of paper with the combination of the safe's lock."

She opened the bag where he kept old papers. Inside was a yellowed piece of paper with printing on it. *Safe. Combination of same belonging to Clément Tamba, city of Cayenne. No. 11,728. Two turns to the right to zero. Continue and stop at 20. One turn to the left to zero. Continue to 71. Turn back and stop at 14. Put in the key. Give it two turns in the lock and turn knob to open.*

"You can start revealing the mystery that's in this safe, Lucy. Follow the directions."

Lucy did what it said, filled with emotion and curiosity. Clément was thinking about the time he'd first met Bonfim in the Café Tour d'Argent, where they would hold auctions of women willing to follow the life of the prospectors and the road to the diggings. Lucy, her hands nervously trembling and with the emotions of a person confronting the unknown, opened the safe. The top compartment was empty, the steel drawers half-open. Alongside them, at the bottom, where she put in her hands and felt around with her fingers, she came upon a moldy package and took it out.

"Is this here what you're looking for, Clément?" It was a faded velvet bundle with something inside.

"Open it, unroll it."

Lucy unfolded the small bundle on top of the bed. The cloth was old, ravaged by mold and powderpost beetles. She unfolded the ends and the secret lay exposed.

Inside was a gold razor with a blade thinner than paper. It gleamed as though time hadn't passed. The polished gold sparkled in the shadowy light of the bedroom. Lucy touched the razor and opened it. Encrusted on both sides of the handle, on the part that held the blade, were a dozen diamonds and in the center a sapphire, along with a glimmering cat's eye. All the stones lit up at the same time.

Clément asked to touch the razor. His eyes, like some miracle of thought, got their sight back and he recognized the hand of Cleto

Bonfim holding the razor. It was a jewel of mysterious beauty, carved into grooves with designs of birds and curves unfolding beneath mermaids. At the end, almost imperceptible, was the profile of a woman.

His distant look could see her Creole beauty, her body, her dogs, her perfume and her sorcery.

"Put that razor back, Lucy. It has a sad history."

3

A Yellow River

Clément Tamba returned to Cayenne after six months deep in the jungle of the Calçoene River basin, having climbed up the seven waterfalls that served as a staircase for the river in its descent to the sea. It was a river of crystalline waters that came down from the Guiana plateau over those steps as it passed through dense forests, savannahs, swamps and open fields, snaking around hills, following its bed, taking on tributaries here and there, small streams, rainwater that had gathered, and water from other large rivers, the Carnot being the largest. It emptied out into the ocean through a broad mouth of sand and mud, where sandbars and tidal pools formed.

He'd made an agreement with Firmino to look the claim over, return to Cayenne and hire men for work. The arrangement was to set up a company to work the claim, which couldn't be done without labor. In that forest spread, gold was hiding under the mountains and it kept running away, concealed in the headwaters that drained off in every direction. There were few Brazilians in the territory and the French population was even smaller. The news trickling into Belém do Pará had only brought out a few old miners and former prospectors who'd worked the mines in the areas of Roraima and Maracaçume closer by, which were in decline and had almost petered out. Of those who went to the gold fields, like sailors on long ocean voyages, few returned. Illness, the jungle, battles with Indians and against isolation decimated whole groups.

"Gold diggers are the greatest sufferers God has placed on this earth. They live on lies, saying that they've found gold," Firmino would say, adding, "They're people who don't know how to do anything, tired of farming or brought there by chance after the breakup of families, running away from crimes they've committed. Monks and saints don't come to dig for gold." Afterwards, once they were there, with their feet in water day and night, their legs swollen, mosquitoes biting and opening sores, bone diseases came on, bad colds, but they were unable to stop, living with fear, misfortune, violence and death. A suffering that never went away. In order to forget it they only had *cachaça* and rum, dreaming of women and humming tunes. The men there didn't know how to pray anymore.

When he came near the first claim, which turned out to be that of Limão, Tamba, who'd never been on a portage, found a gate made of crossed pieces of wood blocking entry. It was guarded by a man with a stiff leg. In order to make walking easier he would clutch his knee with his left hand. His right hand held a rifle. His look was somber and determined.

"Just where do you gentlemen think you're going?" the guard asked.

"We've come to see the prospecting, because I was the one who discovered this gold," Firmino replied.

"But this claim has an owner, it belongs to Cleto Bonfim, and you can only come in here on his orders," he answered.

And with a movement that must have been quite frequent for him from the natural way it was executed, he raised his weapon as if to mean he was saying things meant to be obeyed.

"Who's Cleto Bonfim?" Firmino asked.

"He's my boss. I came with him as his worker and I'm the gate guard."

"When did he come here?"

"Six months ago. We came from Chiqueirão, back there in Pará."

"How many of you are there?"

"Around fifty."

"And where's Mr. Bonfim?"

"In the shed."

"I'd like to talk to him. Can I?"

"It's not so easy. He's a man who only sees people he knows and that he knows are coming."

"Go tell him it's Firmino Amapá. He must have heard of me."

The guard stood still. He looked up, waited a bit more before talking, and then said, "Wait just a minute."

The man fiddled with his rifle, grabbing the bolt and shoving it up and down, and put a cartridge in the chamber. He cocked it and stopped, held back by the shouts coming from Firmino and Tamba. "Don't shoot, our business is peaceful! Don't shoot! We didn't come here to be killed or to kill anyone!"

The man calmed them down: "I'm not going to kill anybody. I'm going to fire a shot to let the boss know there are people here. It's our warning signal. They'll come right away to see what's going on. You don't have to worry, just wait and they'll be right along. What you can't do is even dream about coming in..."

The shot rang out in the solitude of the forest and for Firmino and Clément it sounded like a firing squad.

A half hour later five men, all armed, came out of the woods from behind the gate to the visitors' rear. Facing them was the only one wearing a revolver, a thin figure with a straggly moustache and goatee. Of medium height, he kept looking down as he spoke without any show of friendliness, fragile in face and body, his head shaved, walking with quick steps, one foot turned slightly inward. He didn't inspire fear but mistrust.

"Mr. Cleto, these men here are talking about wanting to visit the claim. I said they can only come in on your orders."

"And what did they say?" he asked, addressing the worker and ignoring the visitors.

"Nothing."

"I'm Firmino Amapá. I was the one who discovered gold in these parts. Everybody knows that. I came with my partner Clément. We hired the three men that came with us and we haven't come to pick a fight with anybody. I know there's room in every direction here."

"Just who are you?" Cleto asked and repeated, "Are you Firmino?"

"Yes, I'm Firmino. If I wasn't, how would I have known how to get to this place?" And he added, as if he knew Cleto, "Look, Cleto, you got here first, but I want to tell you that discovering this vein cost me too much."

"Sure, I know you were the one who found gold along the Calçoene, that story's all you hear around here. It was a great strike. Every prospector here knows that. Our gold in Pará disappeared everywhere and from what I know in Approuague, too, and it came to hide hereabouts. You can rest easy, Firmino, what's needed here is people. There's gold enough for everybody. João is here to keep out bandits and crooked outsiders. You know how a claim attracts lowlifes. But you've got a right to my friendship. If you want it."

And Cleto invited them to come with him to the shed. He gave them something to eat and then showed them around the claim. There were some fifty men working at the panning, including the guards and Celestino Gouveia, the foreman.

How many years have passed since that distant morning? Clément Tamba was now vegetating there in the solitude of memories in the old mansion, alongside Lucy. Night was coming on and his eyes weren't closing. He'd been waiting to die for more than a hundred years. Everything from his time had disappeared. All that was left were the bitter memories and the ghost of Cleto Bonfim, who would come to poke his spongy memory and evoke his other life, the roughest of them all, the one he'd lived on the claims by the River Calçoene.

"I've come. I'm here. Look at me, Clément."

"I was wary of you that day, Bonfim. You didn't inspire confidence. Your mask-like face told me that a person could expect a trap from you."

"No, Clément," Cleto replied. "I was never a man for killing deer from a blind. I knew there was enough gold there for everybody—the more people panned, the more there was for me to buy. No one could get away from me. I was the only one with supplies, food, tools, medicine and the working force of my men. Firmino discovered the gold, but I opened the path with a machete. I controlled the road. Also, as a prospector I had respect for Firmino's fame, a man of steel, the discoverer of gold along the Calçoene, and this place has its mysteries. I thought then that if he came back it was because the gold had called him. In these gold fields people learn to sense the gold's messages and wants. Everything has its meaning. When you go against the wishes of the gold it will run away and peter out. I knew that the gold of the Calçoene was calling Firmino. Not you. I didn't like your face. I thought you were an adventurer, an exploiter. You had nothing of us about you, you weren't a panner. You had a thin face, the look of a cagey character. But all that passed. We became the best of friends and went on to live our lives together in the same suffering."

And he continued:

"Firmino couldn't take out the gold he'd discovered because it didn't want him to. That's the way gold is. It called Firmino but it killed Firmino. Those six months you and I spent together made our friendship the best there could be between two men. You taught me Creole, Clément, invited me to visit Cayenne. I showed you the Limão valley. You didn't understand anything about gold. I explained it all and you were very sharp, you took it all in. That was where you got rich. I never argued over anything with you. I didn't spend but a short time with Firmino. He was my brother in prospecting and my comrade. A responsible man, no flaws."

"I felt very sorry when Firmino died," Clément said.

"Me, too. But I always respected whatever the gold wanted. I never thought it could be challenged. Gold has always been an enchanted king for me, with every type of power and revenge. It's evil. It got its revenge on Firmino. Gold has the power of God. It brings happiness but it brings misfortune, too. Only the gold knows why it showed itself to Firmino and then killed him. That fever he caught, quicker than any I'd ever seen, took him away in three days. Vomiting blood. But before he died, when hope was gone, he desperately begged to be buried on top of Mount Salomoganha, standing up. It had something to do with people who don't want even their souls to leave a place. He died not wanting to die.

"We did what he asked. It wasn't an easy thing to climb up and dig that deep hole up there on top. There were a lot of rocks. A standing grave in rocky ground isn't an easy thing to make.

"But I ordered them to gather up three pannings for him to take with him into death. I called Raimundo and said, 'Tell the gold in the gully that you people are going to get three panfuls for Firmino Amapá to take into his grave. Say it in a loud voice so the gold will hear you.' Each panning came to more than forty ounces. The king of gold was sending that present to him. When he went into the hole standing, I poured the gold dust and the dross onto his head. I carried it in an oil can and sprinkled it all over. Life's like that. The steak is never for the one who owns the steer."

Clément's eyes grew dim and he whispered:

"Lucy, turn out the kitchen lamp. With less light I can see Cleto Bonfim better."

"You don't need to see me. Time has dissolved me."

"No, Bonfim. When I see you I can see the day I came back to Cayenne with your order for me to set myself up on the new claim. I was already sick with gold fever. My blood was already yellow. I sent word to everyone about my arrival. All of Cayenne heard about it. A lot of friends and acquaintances came by. I remember the look on Linderfo's face, goggle-eyed and red. They all listened to me. In those days my store was on the rue d'Enfer. The big table in the main room had no tablecloth on it. The black boards were polished, nice and smooth, with no nicks or scratches. I helped with the polishing myself, careful not to raise any splinters. I brought out two benches, one for each side of the table. They all sat down. I was standing at the head of the table, speaking. 'Cayenne has been in bad shape, my friends. Things are going to change now. The days of lean cows are over. Our future is going to be different. I've come from the Contestado in Brazil. There's gold everywhere there and not enough people to get it out of the ground. You people can join up with me and go there. I've already got an established claim. We'll be rich, our lives will change and Cayenne will have some life again. Money and riches will circulate like in the old days.' I talked some more, describing the locations, I spoke about the trails, the jungle, the mountains, and I left for my room, letting the suspense build. I left them wondering, silent and curious. I came back with three green glass bottles. They were filled with something that looked like sand. I uncorked each one and, before their amazed eyes, slowly poured that rough, yellow sand onto a white china platter at the center of the polished table and made a pile that grew as each bottle emptied. When I finished, I said with a mysterious air, 'That there is ten pounds of gold! *La couleur*, what's always been the symbol and dream of Guiana. Two months, six men, and panning. The custom there is to put in an aluminum basin and divide it up with a mug. Wait till we set up the *lontanas*, the sluices we Creoles used back in the Approuague.' And with a show of enthusiasm I proclaimed, 'You can believe me if you want to. There's lots of gold in Mapá, which the Brazilians call Amapá,

24

and it won't peter out the way it did here. We Frenchmen have got to go there and occupy the land. If we don't, the Brazilians will get to own it. The land there belongs to France and the gold belongs to its people.'"

Clément Tamba had caught the contagion of prospecting, but he was a businessman, a realist who knew how to look far ahead. He was no patriot and wasn't interested in French territorial disputes. All he wanted was for Cayenne's commerce to grow with a new source of business, a new future starting up.

"What do we care about France? France has abandoned us. The only thing we're good for is taking care of their criminals. They don't like black Creoles and they insult them the way Coudreau the professor did, but we're black Frenchman," said Jean-Pierre, a merchant from the Ceperou district who sold tobacco and sugar.

"The *Metros** will like this business and back us up," Tamba replied, "because we're going to give them a territory one third the size of France, rich in forests and gold, rich in everything. When they just get to see how rich Mapá is…"

And he made a spectacular gesture to impress them all.

"There's so much gold in Mapá that I..." He got up and went to his room again and came back with an old hunting gun that he laid on the table, continuing, "I brought this shotgun along so I could show you how much there is. I picked it up on the way here in a swap with a hunter, and inside, inside it," he repeated, "is a whole barrelful of gold! Even hunters don't have enough good places to keep their gold. They use the barrels of their guns, filled with gold, like jugs for storing gold dust..."

And he took the cork out of the gun barrel and poured the gold out onto the table. He shook the shotgun and with a theatrical gesture whacked the barrel to empty it completely.

Then he got the scale and began to weigh it all. "Eleven pounds, six ounces!"

The next day he announced the closing of his store. He began to remove merchandise from the shelves and made piles of the packages ready to be sold. First the fabrics, hats, ready-made clothes, footwear, boxes of sugar, biscuits from Rheims, Meunier chocolates, tobacco (crimp cut and rough), matches, cigarette paper, condensed milk, boxes of candy, canned asparagus, olives. He regretfully took down the shelves that held things to drink: cognac,

*French living in the metropolitan areas.

Saint-Julien and Saint-Estèphe wines in flagons, Madeira, Muscatel, Guignolet, Contenac, Bordeaux and crates of Syracuse. Then it was turn for the rope, nails, wire, grains and knick-knacks of every kind.

"The next day I closed the store, Cleto, and sold off everything. I went into the unknown heart and soul. There the two of us remained: you, the big boss, and me, the Frenchman."

With news of a new gold strike the boats that arrived in Cayenne had but one destination: the River Calçoene. And the ships coming from Europe didn't waste any time anchoring for new landfalls, they just loaded up with people and merchandise. They followed the open sea to the mouth of the Calçoene and went up it to the first set of rapids, Firmino's, where the village of Firmino stood, named in memory of the discoverer of the gold. Other ships followed the gold route on the Cunani and went as far as the village of Cunani, which was up a high gully, with a small church and a few houses. The majority there was now French and the flag of France flew before the house of Captain Trajano Benitez, a Brazilian who'd agreed to be the representative of France and the delegate of the governor of Cayenne. They weren't only French ships, like the *Belle de Martinique* or the *Guyane* or the *Carsuène*, but also English boats like the *Admiral* and the *Meteor*, and even a Dutch ship, the *Catapania*.

The villages were growing in population and the most important of all was the village of Calçoene, which merged with the village of Firmino, so that the two became one on the left bank of the river, where commerce flourished with shops selling everything and where the currency was measured in gold dust. It was here Clément Tamba established his first place of business and set up his new store, where he bought gold and sold panning equipment and tools, where he formed partnerships, collected commissions, and earned as much as he had ever dreamed of and more. Then he branched out and set up a house in Limão. But he couldn't match Cleto Bonfim.

"You took me to Cayenne, Clément, introduced me to the Société Equatoriale, which ended up buying my gold. I built a house there and got used to enjoying life until that day when we went to the Tour d'Argent to bring back some women to have fun with and make our nights on the claim merry."

"Only you, Cleto, because I don't like picking up cabaret women. I always brought women I knew, lady friends from here, who came and went back."

The door slammed. Raimunda entered. She was bringing a jug of water and mumbled, "Who you talking to, Mr. Clément?"

"Cleto Bonfim."

"Where is he?"

"Here," he said and pointed toward the wall.

Raimunda saw those thin legs and a thin face with a straggly beard take shape.

"Listen here," Raimunda said. "Don't you go talking to Mr. Clément anymore. He don't like talking about the past."

"Go back to the parlor, Raimunda. Let me visit with my friends," Clément muttered.

Lucy came in.

"Don't be upset, Raimunda. Tamba's getting ready to die. Every night he tries to go back to Calçoene. I don't go along because my legs are weak and there's a smell of dead people there."

Tamba closed his eyes. His thoughts stopped with the barking of a dog. Saraminda was naked, bathing in the waterfall.

4

Saraminda

She had green eyes, straight hair that flowed down over her shoulders, the blended skin of African and Indian, and firm breasts with slender nipples that looked like strong, erect straight-grained trees which wouldn't bend in a high wind. Her hips were firm, average in size, the curves outlined and low, as if sliding down along the lines of her body and harmoniously joining her thighs and thickening above her full, rounded legs. Her torso was somewhat long. Her face had a dark beauty, somewhere between clean black and dirty white. She had an enigmatic look that showed in her fleshy mouth, the top lip tilted slightly upward. Her teeth showed through a brief slit, and when she smiled a touch of life came from her face combining that look and that mouth and the charismatic strength of her speech and her smile.

Her skin was smooth, soft and lustrous, like plush, the mark of her Indian blood, which came from her grandmother the Creole Balbina, who ran a brothel for deep-sea sailors, the daughter of a Dutchman named Jansen and a Waiapi Indian woman from captive service in the Jesuit mission.

Balbina had an extensive descent. Her daughter Julienne, Saraminda's mother, was a prostitute in a dockside brothel at the age of fourteen and she left it when she was taken away by a black man from Guinea, a free slave who'd run away from Jamaica and dropped anchor in Cayenne, and with whom she lived until he died during the flu epidemic. A widow with four children who made a living from a stand where she sold fish and game, she fell in love with a Sergeant Descoup, who would take her for long walks in a bean field behind the cemetery, and she would give herself to him with a mature love. Descoup never wanted to visit her at home and she didn't want him to visit her there either, ashamed because of her children, and he because his military superiors might find out that he was the lover of a Creole woman.

Saraminda was born of that romance. Her mother immediately spotted characteristics of her grandmother in her. Saraminda lived in utter poverty until the age of fifteen, when she appeared in Marie Turiu's night spot, the Tour d'Argent, frequented by prospectors and Cayenne bohemians, where auctions took place and there were get-acquainted parties for the recruitment of women who would go off for nights on the claims spreading out along the new gold frontier in the Brazilian Contestado.

On that night Cleto Bonfim, from the Calçoene region, was there. It was a night of grand festivities—the smell of cigarette smoke rising, the brawling of men who ordered rum or brandy, drank and then threw their glasses, the Brazilians wanting hard liquor and the French ordering wine, whatever its provenance, Bordeaux or Burgundy, and the Creoles drinking either one without any preference.

The night went along with quarrels, women and drinks as the music flowed from a saxophone, violin and old piano, the same one rescued from a shipwreck on Cape Orange, played by Jean-Marin, who had been a musician in a cabaret called La Nuit de Lyon on the Rive Gauche in Paris.

Cleto was drunk. He'd gone up against Indians and adventurers and in the end became the owner of the richest claim, which he left every few months for Cayenne in the company of Clément Tamba to pick up merchandise and supplies and deposit the gold he'd extracted from that land. On his return he brought back a retinue of women bought at auction to enliven the nights and chase off the big mosquitoes in the shed on his claim. He had a great liking for women. He was experienced. He knew all the maneuvers and tricks they used to get at his money. He succeeded in escaping from a lot of them, but he paid others for their time and illnesses, and still others he drove off in a rage.

It was a night of great merriment. The wine had already brought on euphoria, the music was frenetic, the tables were lively, and the auction of women was beginning. Marie Turiu, owner of the place and a well-known procuress, started the bidding.

"These pretty girls would like to get to know the gold country. They're open to invitations and offers. Nothing in life is ever accomplished without the happiness pretty women give it." She guffawed, opened her arms, and made her pitch. "Who'll bid for this item, fifteen and with the flesh of a goddess?"

Saraminda came out onto the platform with a firm stride and the air of someone acting in a play. She was something beyond imagination. She stood out from between the other two girls, a French redhead and another pretty Creole. Everyone took notice of her unfettered breasts, her fleshy hips and legs, her smooth and shiny straight hair, and that touch of emerald green in her eyes that contrasted with her dark skin.

She didn't wait for any bids. Bonfim was surrounded by companions, people he trusted, hired thugs and friends. They were men of different types, long-haired and short, all with a steady gaze, armed, and glasses in their hands. As was his custom, Cleto Bonfim had two pounds of gold hanging around his neck, the nuggets stretched out on a thick cord that went down his hairy chest, exposed so that all could see what he always liked to show off. It contrasted with his thin body and the expression from a face where random hairs grew. He was wearing a faded military jacket.

Saraminda, with no thought of past loves, resolute and uninhibited, stepped forward toward the audience and raised her right hand, her forefinger pointing upward, and proclaimed:

"I'm not part of the auction. I belong to Cleto Bonfim. I'm going with him and I want to belong to him. I know where he is and, as far as I'm concerned, the auction is over."

Marie Turiu looked at her, shocked. At his table Cleto was taken by a great surprise. He didn't know that woman and he didn't have any close connections in the city or acquaintances who could tell him anything about her, nor did he consider himself a fellow who was an apt target for seduction. Even with his head all dizzy, he tried to put his ideas in order and make some sense out of what was going on. Was it a coup on the part of Marie Turiu or a prank by one of his friends? Recovering from his surprise, he got up, went to the aisle, and joining in the spirit of the festivities, replied arrogantly:

"I won't accept any woman who gives herself away. I do the choosing and I've always done a good job of it."

General laughter and cheers were heard. Saraminda wasn't upset. She was impressive in her firmness and in the way she'd rehearsed her role. It was something new in those festivities with their primitive gestures and tastes.

"I'm not a woman who's giving herself away. I've chosen. I belong to you, Bonfim."

There was a silence followed by much applause. The drunks came to, turning their attention to every corner in the room.

The kerosene lamp gave off a yellow light that reached the ceiling and spread out over the room. They were all exchanging curious looks that converged on Bonfim. The three-piece band started up again frenetically and to each reply it gave a fanfare.

"Where did you get that idea of throwing yourself at me, woman?" Bonfim asked from the center of the room.

"Don't ask what can't be asked," Saraminda said. "I don't know why, but that's what I want, and," she changed tactics, becoming a timid little girl, softening her voice and finishing with a honeyed tone, "I want to go to your claim, by...your side..."

Bonfim no longer knew by now how many bottles of wine had gone to his head or if what was going on came from drinking. He went up to the stage, looked at Saraminda, and spoke. "If you're after my gold, woman, I'll give you some, but don't try to pull one over on me."

Saraminda looked at him seductively, pursing her lips, and didn't consider herself defeated. "I don't want your gold, Bonfim. Gold is what I am. I've never owned anything and don't know what it's like to own something. But something tells me I should belong to you. That was the mission my destiny gave me. Come."

Cleto Bonfim was puzzled. He'd never seen such a woman, since the initiative had always belonged to men. He'd been told that Creole women had the habit of getting someone and not being gotten. But as he experienced that situation he didn't find it normal. He climbed up onto the platform, took out his famous string of heavy nuggets and placed it around her neck. "If that's what you want, here you go." There was general applause. Saraminda, her breast adorned, began to weep, and he saw from up close the beauty of her bust and skin.

Then she drew back and closed up like a morning glory. Her eyes grew dim, and from her lips, changed as if by magic, came sweetened, unctuous words replete with meaning, like the mating dance of doves:

"Thank you, Bonfim…"

She could have waited for the men to bid for the women with the gold that was bursting out of the Contestado of Amapá in Brazil, but she refused. She offered herself and settled the matter without a price before the auction started, which surprised even Marie Turiu. No one knew how she'd discovered who Bonfim was, that man who when he came to Cayenne bought tons of provisions, dried meats, fish and merchandise of all kinds for daily consumption on the claim, from kerosene to French perfume in cheap vials, jars of vaseline for men to comb their hair on holidays, wines, canned goods, medicines, tools and bags of oakum, sawdust. At night he would visit entertaining places, bars, bawdy houses and dancehalls. That night he was in the Tour d'Argent to watch the *Parade* of women they talked about so much in the city. It wasn't his first time. He was a celebrated customer, always accompanied by his retinue and, invariably, by Clément Tamba, whom everybody knew to be his friend and business partner in the Contestado.

After placing the string of nuggets on Saraminda, Bonfim went back to the table he'd left. The crowd toasted him. The men and women were all excited in the smoke, with drinks, music and seductive pleasures. Saraminda remained motionless alongside her companions, timid, not leaving the platform, with a decision waiting to be made. She didn't look like the woman who'd appeared there a while before. She didn't go with Bonfim.

She stood there motionless, enjoying the stares, hiding her soul.

Marie Turiu then came forward, taking the arm of Lucienne, a Frenchwoman with long blond hair from the homeland, the daughter of a paroled prisoner from Saint-Jean du Maroni.

"Who wants to take this princess so she can get to know the River Calçoene and sing and dance for the gold men? A beautiful woman, refined. Who's the lucky fellow?"

"Fifteen ounces!" shouted Gerard, a young man from Cayenne.

"It's not to spend an hour here, Gérard, it's to travel to Brazil," Turiu said.

"I know, my little Turiu, it's to die of fever and kill whopping mosquitoes..."

"Damn you, don't call down a curse!" Lucienne said.

"My sweet," he replied, "stay here, go to my place. There's something there that can't be found anywhere else in the world—Gérard!"

Everyone enjoyed the scene. The auction continued.

"Who'll go with Lucienne?"

"Come with me," said Zacarias, a gold buyer from Cunani. "I'll give two pounds of gold and two months in my house, with access to wine and love."

"You'll be happy, child. She goes with you, Zacarias!" The lady of the house pounded the gavel.

More applause was heard. Turiu took hold of the mulatto girl Wiabo and introduced her.

"I'm not going to say anything. Look at this pretty Saramaca, a black girl from Guiana. A rare item. What a face, what lips, what hips! What happiness to have this thoroughbred...Who'll bid?"

There was a string of bids and Juvenal, the owner of a general store in Cunani, went to the platform, took her by the arm and shouted, "Two and a half pounds with no set time to return."

Marie Turiu was left alone on the platform with Saraminda.

"Cleto Bonfim," she said, "you still haven't established how much you're going to pay to take this girl, the prettiest woman I've ever seen. Take a look, all of you," and she held Saraminda by the face as if she were going to yank it off like a mask and display it for the audience, "green eyes, the face of Saint Iphigenia, delicate, seductive, magnificent..."

Bonfim, half-staggering, stood up and shouted with the strength he was famous for:

"That woman is already mine. It's disrespectful for you to start the auction all over again. She has a price. I give twenty pounds of gold and she'll come along forever."

Saraminda tightened her lips, raised her hands to her face and wept. She left the stage by a step on the side, walked through the tables to everyone's applause with the band scratching out a can-can, and went over to the group where Bonfim was. He stood up, grabbed her, and gave her a kiss as if they were betrothed. With a soft show of affection, she requested:

"Sit down, Mr. Bonfim."

And she sat down on his lap, ran her hand around his neck, rested her head against his, and whispered in his ear, "Do you know why you paid twenty pounds of gold for me, Mr. Bonfim?"

"I don't want to know because I already do," he answered with a voice heavy with wine.

"Well, then, when we're alone I'll show you. It's a mystery. Any man would give the whole world for it."

The night went on as the piano, off by itself, began to play an ancient song of old Cayenne.

5

A Price to Pay

Cleto was the owner of a big house in Cayenne, where he would spend long periods when he arrived with gold to sell and accounts to settle with his business and export representatives, the largest of which, the Société Française de l'Amérique Equatoriale, dominated the gold market. He took advantage of those times for some night life, ending up at his house where the festivities continued with a few friends and with women who would end up in his bed. It was a place of merriment, bearing witness to the explosion of riches from the new diggings.

When he left the Tour d'Argent with Saraminda, Cleto's ideas were confused. It was the height of the wee, small hours and on the deserted street he was beginning to sense how elusive that woman was. She wouldn't let him go ahead in his usual way, wrapping her up in his desire. Not used to that reaction, his tongue thickened with rum and wine, he complained:

"What is it with you? After all that come-on, aren't you going to light the fire?"

Saraminda wouldn't allow herself to be touched anymore, pushing his hand away from her body and face.

"I'm thinking that I don't know what I did," she answered.

"Take off your clothes, you're a brothel woman, you don't have to think or be romantic, I want to see your breasts," he said, stumbling along.

Saraminda's retort was firm:

"Treat me with some respect, Mr. Cleto. I'm no dirty rag, I'm a woman to be treated with pleasure. I appreciate good manners. I may have gotten into prostitution, but I'm no tramp."

Cleto insisted, his voice husky:

"I bought you at an auction for a high price and I want to receive my merchandise. That's how I am and I don't know how to wait. I pay a woman to be the way I want her. Cut your tricks. I'm getting fed up."

"Well, you can just settle down. If I'm merchandise then you bought me but you haven't paid," Saraminda replied, disguising her fear and trying to find a way out of her indecision.

"You'll collect from me, woman. Do you doubt that Cleto Bonfim's word is worth more than any gold?" And he went on, "Stop being an imbecile. If not, you'll get my whip and twenty lashes instead of twenty pounds."

"It's not your word, it's my fate. And business deals have rules," she argued again. "I'm not accustomed to being beaten. If that's the case, best to call the deal off right now. We can undo the arrangement."

She felt relieved with that hypothesis. She halted, pushed Cleto's hand away, and at the same time steadied him so he wouldn't fall down drunk.

"Don't you know who I am? I'm Cleto...Bonfim! And any deal I've made can't be unmade. My will is made of gold!"

They were just about to his house.

"I don't know," Saraminda replied, "that's your affair. Take a look here, Mr. Bonfim." She opened her blouse and showed him her breasts, squeezing the nipples. "These aren't just any merchandise to be bought like this. They're mine, a rare thing that I won't throw away. Look at their value and treat me in a different way, without any drinking or brutishness."

Cleto opened his eyes wide and saw the nuggets of an intense yellow encrusted on the dark flowing breasts, the same color as the small flowers of a nutmeg tree.

"Is what I'm seeing real?" Cleto babbled, almost falling down.

"Take a good look, Cleto Bonfim."

A cat broke the silence, knocking over some boxes in the kitchen. Saraminda was frightened.

"That's nothing. It's just souls from the other world trying to get a look at you," said Cleto, who knew the noises of the house, going

36

on, "It's a cat, it's nothing. Just an ordinary nosy critter."
Saraminda, immersed in the pride of showing off her rare breasts, took no more notice.

"Look, Cleto Bonfim!"

And the nipples looked phosphorescent, gleaming like gold that had been worked and polished.

His eyes ran around in a circle, following the spinning spark of light.

"I've got things of gold that money can't buy, Cleto."

He leaned forward trying to touch her breasts.

"No, they're not to be touched like that."

"But I want to kiss them."

And he brought his open lips forward.

"Not that way either. Nothing is going to happen here. They're my jewel that only I know how to use."

Cleto thought she was talking about payment.

"I'll pay."

"I'm in no hurry to receive payment."

"What a strange woman." He was still able to put his thoughts together in spite of the crazy state of his head, perceiving in his hallucinations that he was rather drunk.

"Where at this hour of the night can I get twenty pounds of gold, you witch woman?" he said aloud.

"I don't know." She grasped at the excuse to get away. "All I know is what you know. If you can only get the gold tomorrow, you'll only get what you want tomorrow."

"Are those breasts of yours made of gold or am I out of my mind?" Cleto asked.

That night in Clément's house, a long time later, Cleto only re-tained a memory made hazy by the years, turned into a romance by forgetfulness. It was the moment when, as he sat on the bed next to Saraminda she leaned over his shoulder and in a gentle voice said in his ear, "Look, Cleto, I don't want to be a slut with you. I'm all woman. The price you paid deserves respect for a piece of good merchandise. I'm going to say it and you can believe it or not. I want to be with you in the way where a woman has a right to have a man. It's about being a female, not a whore."

"That story bothers me, Cleto," Clément said. "How is it that you tell it to me now after a lifetime of so many years together? You don't know whether these things happened anymore because you're dead? Don't argue with me. You died and your passions died. Don't you remember how I was at your funeral that afternoon, almost at night, and how I cried with my eyes and with my soul?"

"How can I remember if I was the dead one?" Cleto said.

"Well, that day I went to the cemetery and there I heard old Esode's saxophone playing the French song you liked to hear, 'La Routine des Jours.' There were so many people, nothing but weeping all around so that it was like a Lenten litany. That was when the argument came up as to whether you should be buried with around your neck the necklace made of two pounds of gold nuggets that was your pride and joy. 'It can't be done. If they do it, this same day someone will come and break open the tomb to get it,' I thought. 'Who would rob Cleto's corpse?' 'No, it can't be done. The nuggets can't be left around his neck.' There was a parade of suggestions coming from all sides. Then I got my idea. I made the decision and they all accepted it: Send for a mortar and pestle to reduce the nuggets to fine ground dust, mix it with earth and throw it into the grave. There's no thief who could steal that. Night was coming on. A new moon was showing its face. We all began to mix the dust from the nuggets with soil and then you were buried. I remember the shovelfuls of earth on the coffin, the gold mixed in, and you motionless beneath us, feeling the gold accompany you in death. That was the only gold you took with you."

"But what you don't know is that after a few months of rain the gold came down and clung to my chest. It stuck. Look."

He opened his shirt and showed Tamba his chest with golden hair.

"No, old comrade, you're dead. Don't show me anything. That chest doesn't exist anymore."

"I'm here. Show me the razor I gave you. I want to see it."

Bonfim was reaching back into his memory. He remembered the first night with Saraminda: "I'm leaving, Cleto. My house is on the rue Madame Paye. I'll expect your gold tomorrow. It's time for you to cure yourself of all that drinking and pay up the twenty pounds of gold."

In the twilight of his recollection those were the last memories of Saraminda's departure that night.

He remembered that he got bold. He came forward and hugged her, opened his mouth, seeking the other mouth, and was lifting up her skirt, tearing at her blouse, pushing her toward the bed.

"Come on. Now. I want you now…"

"Don't you force me, Mr. Bonfim." She spoke decisively and with rage. "My body is mine. It's not yours. You haven't paid me. There's no force that can make me. I won't give myself to you."

For the first time Cleto felt the power of that woman's mysteries. He lost the feeling in his arms, which became like a scarecrow's. His head whirled. His eyes dimmed. His strength left him. His body was dead meat.

When he awoke the next morning the sun was already high in the sky. Saraminda had disappeared.

6

A Fleeting Thought

"Clément, my dear friend, that woman's smell has haunted me right up until today. Everything I went on to do came out of a desire and a passion the likes of which I didn't know could exist in a man's head."

"Go away, Bonfim. I bought Louis's piano so I could turn my nights into the past. When I wake up in the hot pre-dawn of this here Cayenne it'll be playing all by itself, but it's not Louis playing, it's nobody, it's Firebeard Kemper, the young fellow from Saint-Malo."

"Don't kill me a second time. Don't mention that man. I never want to hear that name again. A filthy, disgusting guy. He stank of treachery. I don't know what the devil it was that led him to our claim. Guiana's been full of criminals and adventurers but that one was the worst of the lot that passed through here. He must have been a leper freed from the Île des Cabris."*

"Guiana is a land of passion, Bonfim, old friend. No one's landed here except with hate, passion or adventure in his heart. It's a jungle of legends and magic spells. It's the suffering from slavery, the brooding over France's ingratitude. It's Cayenne. They think that being Guianese only applies to people from Cayenne. The rest are different people. We're all Frenchmen, born from a night of drinking. But I love Cayenne by the sea, its islands, its woods."

"Not me, Clément Tamba. I'm a Brazilian. You forget that..."

"But Saraminda was French, Bonfim."

"Look, old friend, don't kill me all over again. Saraminda was born in heaven. Saraminda was the only woman who ever existed in Guiana."

*Site of a prison built in 1855 which later became a leper colony.

40

Clément Tamba thought that the years had arranged it so that he could participate in the mysteries of life and death.

"I'm tired of living, Lucy."

Bonfim's shadow was strolling along the corridor.

"I want to set my thoughts free, Lucy," Clément said. "They're prisoners. I've been locked up tighter than the deportees in Saint-Laurent du Maroni prison. I've never released them. They're not secrets, they're spooks, demons handcuffed to my soul, prisoners inside me. They weep, they cry out, they moan, they call for help. I seduced Denara, my Aunt Greba's daughter. I had her. I practically raped her. She didn't want to and did everything to get free from my desire. I stole the gold of the movement to set up French militias. The weapons didn't arrive because I never bought them. I'm going to set my most imprisoned thought free, Lucy, the one that was condemned to death. It's a desire that never reached its end."

"You're not at an age to curse or do penance, Clément. Finish out your days in silence. It's all over now."

"I loved Saraminda too, Lucy."

The piano started playing. It was "Les Miroirs d'Argent," an old song from Brittany the piano played from Diougan's greasy score published in 1847, and which Clément had owned ever since he'd arrived in Cayenne. That voice and dark song rose up clear and melodious in the silence of the night, pouring out slow and sad, as if they were coming from tears welling up very far away in a magic of sounds.

"It's Jacques Kemper singing, Lucy."

The night was receding and coming back. In the mansion on the rue d'Estren, Clément's eyes were befogged by time. No one existed anymore, the hours were different. All those nights he would get up and put his ears on alert, his head tilted first over his left shoulder and then the right, trying to catch the sounds of the forest, the rustle of the wind, the birds, and the silence of the house. How many times had he asked to die, felt tired of living? Over more than a hundred years and the days kept repeating themselves with a destructive monotony. At those times Bonfim's visit broke his loneliness, Bonfim there by his side as he mulled over olden days, extracting nostalgia while he made himself suffer as he recalled the years. But that suffering was all that was left for him.

"Speak, Bonfim my friend," he asked when he held the face in his hands and took a long time browsing through his thoughts, painting in his head the faded landscapes of Vila do Lourenço, the Limão, the Calçoene, the Cunani. "Lucy remembers the arrival of the dead from the battle of Veiga Cabral. That war was what brought me back to this house. The corvette *Bengali* was approaching the Laussat Canal, towing a mysterious barge giving off a great stench that stank up Cayenne, and nobody knew what it was: the rotting bodies of the French soldiers arriving after three days' travel. The city was outraged. There was weeping, lamentation and grief. Everybody wanted vengeance. The richest Brazilians of Amapá were brought along as spoils, wounded and tortured. They were a trophy for Governor Charwein. Lucy was present when they unloaded them. Cayenne was nothing but suffering. The burial took place at night. Candles everywhere and then a movement to erect a monument to the dead. It's there even now, right there at the south side of the cemetery."

Clément and Bonfim fell silent. From far away a French tune could be heard on the piano.

"What's that sound? What piano is that playing?" Bonfim inquired.

"A piano from out of the past. It's playing inside your tomb."

"No, it's Louis's piano, from our nights at Chez Martin."

"Oh, old friend, nothing made me sadder, nothing ripped apart my soul more than that Frenchman, remembering that Saraminda loved him more than me…"

"No, old friend, Saraminda loved all men, but you were the one she belonged to. A woman like that wouldn't have stayed the way she stayed, yours, inside that house in the middle of the loneliness of the claim if it weren't for a great love. You were her man, only you."

"Gold, old friend."

"No, she could have got gold from anyone she wanted."

"But I remember, Clément, the look she gave him on the day she got the dress from Paris. After the dogs she asked me for a monkey as a present. 'Kiss me, Bonfim. I want you to get me a monkey to keep me company.' And I had them catch a monkey in the jungle. First they brought in a marmoset. She turned it down. 'No, Bonfim, I don't want a little monkey, one to sit on my shoulder. I want a monkey that can jump in the trees so I can watch him.' And I had them catch another. I was embarrassed when I told the hunters to bring me some more monkeys. There was a *meriquiná*, then a hairy-monkey, then a smelly-monkey, then a *jupará*, and more. Finally they brought in a spider monkey, the black kind, with long arms and a tail, the kind that wraps its tail around the branches and swings back and forth with its head down. She found it funny. He was a show-off and a mischief-maker. It took a long time to tame the monkey. She called him Nicomedes. They tied him up with a long rope around his waist so he wouldn't run away. With the rope at full length he would leap and swing from tree to tree. Saraminda would stand at the window of the bedroom watching, a big smile on her face, clapping her hands, making smacking noises, throwing kisses, and Nicomedes would be leaping, swinging, giving off howls. The dogs would bark and the monkey would stop, pretending to be scared, and everybody had fun. I felt sorry for myself, Clément, old friend, but I liked it, I liked doing what she wanted. Another time she wanted a parrot. 'Bonfim, get me a parrot, the kind that talks, *sachant déjà quelques mots de créole.*' She knew I couldn't speak French, only Creole, but she asked me in French. And I hired old Ritinha, a washerwoman from Cayenne, to teach the parrot Creole. 'Mr. Bonfim, I've got a female parrot. She already knows how to say *non ka pati, pa ni problem bom*, and *to ka emerde mo*. Which means let's go, everything's OK, and shit. But she'll learn more.' 'I'll go find out if Saraminda will accept a female parrot and let you know.' 'Saraminda, Ritinha has a female parrot, do you want it?' 'Give me a kiss, Bonfim, I want it. But ask her to teach it to say Saraminda.' And I did just that. Four months later the parrot arrived. 'Saraminda, *urupaco, papaco.*' She laughed happily and jumped up and down, while Nicomedes leaped and the Lion of Rhodesia I named Xaxá growled. And after a time, from listening to Saraminda calling Nicomedes so much, the critter said, mixing her languages, 'Saraminda *emerde*, Nicomedes leap.' And without anyone's knowing why, it came out with a curse, '*Patate to maman.*' Your mother's a whore. And Saraminda laughed, happy."

7

Clocks That Don't Run

Night returned and dawn hadn't arrived. It was as if the clocks were balking. The hands were moving in the opposite direction, going and coming, back and forth, with the hours of day and night in retreat. Clément Tamba was exhausted. The weariness of living made his feet drag, dominated his movements and the solitude of his soul.

"Did you love that Creole tramp?"

"No, Lucy. It wasn't love. Inside love there's desire, there's passion, there's friendship, there's affection, there's jealousy, there's everything. When I broke open the strongbox of my love for Saraminda there was only silence inside. Inside the silence was the obsession of going to bed with her. Saraminda was a desire that couldn't be satisfied. Nothing burned into men's thoughts like imagining her naked body on the broad verandah, humming and bouncing her hips."

Night was returning. The clocks were striking hours near dawn. Clément wanted to open the window to see the sunrise, but night halted and went back to being night.

"Put the razor back in the safe, Lucy. I shouldn't have taken it out. The edge of its blade cuts off my thought. I remember when I got back from the Calçoene and had a meeting in my house to recruit people to work the claim. My madness began then. I sold everything. It was a regular holiday in Cayenne. All that was left was that strongbox that Ledério wouldn't sell, I don't know why. 'You don't sell a strongbox,' he said. 'It's like selling your luck.'"

Ledério was a Maroon whose grandfather had worked on La Condamine's expedition. In some strange way he bore in his character the whole burden of the Boschs, the Bush Negroes who'd run away from Surinam and hidden in the jungle. They'd escaped from the slavery of men and been caught by the slavery of the jungle. Sometimes, when he was dozing off, he would speak Taki-Taki, the language of the Bonis. He always refused to be called a Creole and would justify himself by saying, "We fought for our freedom, it wasn't given to us. Not the Creoles, they avoided the fight. They were freed by the law."

"Ledério was alway with me," Clément remembered. "He stayed with me all his life until the day he disappeared in the labyrinth of the jungle. Even today I still don't know whether it was what they call *piaille*, curses someone ordered from a witchdoctor, or whether he just wanted to go back to the jungle like his ancestors."

The door creaked, opening slowly. Cleto Bonfim appeared again. His soul was never free of Clément.

"Bonfim, old friend, you again?"

"Again, Clément. You always draw me out of my peace, force me to mull over my hates and my passions. But I don't know how to leave."

"Did you give Saraminda the gold on the night you slept with her?"

"No, Tamba, she refused to sleep with me, like I said. But I did the next day. I was in good shape then, but I was hooked. I returned after I got the payment. I was living on the rue du Fort, by that big curve that goes around the foot of the hill the fort's on. There she got into my bed, but she convinced me that it had to be different, as if we were betrothed. A strange woman. She wanted to drive me crazy by taking off her clothes and lying down beside me. When I saw her naked my thoughts all centered on her body, which was gleaming. There's nothing more beautiful than a black woman. She was a pale blue-black. Her curves and every part of her body were arranged just where they should be, nothing out of place. She was more than a woman, she was gold itself. Her smile was calm, strange. When I looked at her she was *la couleur*. How much did she weigh? A hundred pounds? I was going to pay twenty. My desire was strong. I was like a tethered horse. I couldn't move, caught by her magical spell. Creole women are so beautiful, Clément!"

Clément began to weep. The broken strongbox that was his

love was opening up once more with the desire to have lived that night. His tears fell slowly. His eyes were closed, looking into the past.

"It was on that day, Clément, that I saw for the first time that she was completely free, even of her clothing. That's the reason for that thing that nobody on the claim understood, the dogs' devotion. In order to conclude my business and meet her demands I went to the Company. The manager welcomed me with his usual bows. I told him I wanted twenty pounds of gold in bars. He was dumbfounded. I always brought in gold, now I wanted to take some out. 'We can give you a certificate of deposit, Mr. Cleto. As much as you want, it's guaranteed. But gold, we just don't have any today. Our shipment to Paris was only yesterday, on the *Dauphine.*' I never forgot the name of that ship. It had the name of a flower. Would Saraminda accept a certificate of deposit? 'It's very, very dangerous for you to go around with gold like that, Mr. Cleto, all by yourself. You know how careful we are. You can take out francs or pounds, as many as you want because you're a big supplier of ours. You have all the privileges and the complete trust of the firm.' The man speaking was Monsieur Jean-Louis Lefèvre. Some time after that encounter he killed himself because his wife Laurence ran away back to France with an officer of the Gendarmerie. She was quite a woman and had eyes of fire. One time at their house I had some Bordeaux and noticed that her restless eyes were those of a woman who still hadn't calmed down her soul. Poor Jean-Louis.

"When Saraminda got back I asked her, 'Saraminda, I wonder if you'd accept a certificate for the gold I owe you, certified by the Company? It's just the same as gold.' 'I don't know anything about those things,' she answered, as if not giving the matter much importance. 'Give it to me and I'll go talk to my grandmother, who's a wise old woman.' A suspicious and knotty woman, but I had no way out. I was trapped in a cage. Something about ancient Africa and the suffering of the souls of the Bantu kings. She didn't want to go to the Société. I gave her the document. It was the longest wait of my life. Not because of the gold, but because of her. I went to the door, looked out at Cayenne. The city looked asleep to me, so beautiful in its sadness."

8

Gold Beneath the Hammock

Balbina was old but she still carried the signs of her days on the
waterfront. Her companion, the Saramaca black Wandero, whom
she'd never married but from whom she bore eight children, had
told her tales of the slaves brought over for the plantations in
Surinam, and through oral tradition the story of the sufferings
during the crossing, the slave hunts in the jungle, and the colonies
of escapees. The owner of the oldest brothel in the city, she knew
that life quite well and had suffered the penury of her years of
decline. Retired because of age and infirmity, she lived in a filthy
slum tenement where she received the visits of her children, her
grandchildren, and her old friends. Saraminda called on her for
advice.

"I don't understand these things, Saraminda. Your grandmother
is old, on the road to death. Where did you dig up that story about
bank gold? In my day they paid very little. It was in fractions of a
franc. No one ever saw anything gold at the house unless it was
thin chain necklaces of fake metal."

"I was auctioned off for twenty pounds of gold," her grand-
daughter said.

"Auctioned off? That used to happen in the days of white slavery when women were bought and sold as slaves, like blacks. I
don't understand and I don't want to understand how that got to
be your lot. But auctioning a woman off to belong to a man is
something new for me."

"Keep the amount I received buried under your cot. It's four pounds of gold and a banknote. I'm going off to the diggings. My fate follows me and I'm not going to free myself from it. If I don't come back buy some houses for your grandchildren."

"I accept the paper, Mr. Bonfim, but I want four pounds of gold brick," was how Saraminda closed her deal with him.

Stroking his goatee, he inquired, mistrustful, "What do you want a gold brick for?"

"That's my business," and she didn't say anything more.

Bonfim did what she wanted. He remembered that day and how pensive she became after getting the gold and the bank document.

"You've paid a lot, Mr. Cleto. Don't you think that our joining together should be more than just a horse trade? I want you to have some fun and happiness, the pleasures of love-making people have when they've become joined together."

"I paid and I want to get something. I don't expect anything more."

"You can have me whenever you want. I'm a kept woman. I'm yours now. I want you to receive my gold body all wrapped in tissue paper, rolled up in velvet, smelling of patchouli."

"That was how she convinced me to buy her an evening gown with beaded embroidery and a bright white nightgown, the most expensive one there was in the shabby shops of Cayenne. I bought it on the rue Lallouette, in the shop that distributes in Guiana the ladies fashion magazine *Le Seul*, published in Paris at 30 rue de Lille, which served as a reference book for seamstresses in the city. How the gown glowed that night, the color of the moon, somewhere between white and blue, her dark body inside it, with her soft voice and her laugh of a person without sin."

Cleto stopped. Clément rubbed his hands. Cleto went on:

"I discovered what love was like. Her hands slid over me, and she said: 'You're so smooth, you're like the skin of an otter. Kiss me, Bonfim,' she asked, like someone praying. And there I was, begging her to surrender, and she was like an anaconda, coiling around me, flighty and still not flighty, all around me like that, whispering. The lamp was at the foot of the bed. The light was growing dim. I couldn't see clearly and I got up to raise the wick. The room was filled with rays of twilight glow. When I looked down at her body and saw her, I was afraid my eyes might be playing a trick on me, so I let them really look. She went quiet. I lowered my head way down and looked right up close. There were the nipples of her breasts that I'd only caught a glimpse of, yellow, like gold ore dug out of the earth, but with a gleam of something worked by the hands of a goldsmith, an artist who made beautiful things. The tips were large, erect, hard and round, glowing like embers. I kissed them. They filled my mouth and melted away. But my lustful behavior didn't stop there. 'Come on slow, Bonfim.' And my cold hands moved down her body, slid along her skin, wrapped around her neck, caressed her shoulders and her sides, and went from one side to the other, up and down, roaming across her stomach. I searched for the skin of her belly in order to squeeze it but I couldn't find it. I freed my hands so I could lead my head along. I didn't try to kiss her. I laid my head down by her neck to discover the pathways to my claim. 'It's better slow, Bonfim, come on slow.' 'I want to see your eyes, Saraminda.' And I saw the green stones, the color of a moonlit night. 'I'm thirsty, Bonfim. I'd like a glass of water. I'm sweating.' 'No, no water right now.' And she: 'It's so you'll relax and let some time go by.' The light in the room was strong. The emotion of the flame on the lamp was frantic. It would quiver, throw off a lot of light, and die down. I don't remember hearing any sounds. I remember my getting the glass of water. 'Drink, Saraminda.' And she tried to cool herself off with the rest of the water and I shouted, 'No, Saraminda, I don't want you all wet from that water. I want your sweat.' And my hands started up again. My urges went galloping along. My hands slid down, covered the paths where they'd already been, but they still hadn't reached the edge of Salomoganha Mountain. I was cold and her skin was warm. 'Come on slow, Bonfim.' I looked inside myself and I saw Cleto Bonfim's look of happiness and fulfillment. My hands were limp, swallows in a windstorm, sliding along down that flow of wet mud. Saraminda had no hair above her woman's parts. My hands touched there. It was like the sides of a *jeju* fish, oily, smooth, and slipperier than flaxseed. 'Saraminda!' I cried. 'Are you Indian?' 'It's something I inherited from my grandmother. She's like that, too.' I was already out of my head, my craving growing into something wild, passion, love, I was overcome by a surprising

49

boundless joy. It was just as if I'd opened a new vein of gold, with no earth, no water, no plants, nothing but gold. 'Mr. Bonfim,' the strong, prayerful voice that was so good to hear, 'You own me. I want you to see the day and night of my eyes.' I looked. They were flashing."

"Cleto Bonfim, you're telling things you shouldn't tell. I don't want to hear about your intimate affairs, your romances, your wild lovemaking. It upsets me," Clément said nervously.

"You have to know, old friend. I can't hold back my dreams, what happened to me, my wild nights of mystery. It's all inside of me, weighing me down. I've got to unload it. Surprises and new things came on like January rains, heavy and strong. Do you know what happened?"

"Don't tell me. I don't want to know. Go back to your hells with your confessions and your knaveries."

"Saraminda was a virgin!" Cleto Bonfim exclaimed.

"You believed a brothel woman was a virgin? You astonish me, Bonfim."

"Not as much as the words I heard her saying astonished me."

"Virginity is more important for men than for women, Bonfim. They make a big thing out of it. It's something that doesn't have much weight or importance for women. They don't know if they have it or not. It's all in their head. But when they make love, even when they're taken, virginity and honor come back."

"Only God knows the mad feeling that came over me, Clément. I was infatuated. My heart was bursting, and I was the one who jumped up and put out the lamp. On that night, with her in my bed, more nestled down than a wild dove, Saraminda was a snake and a little baby tapir. The rain was falling hard in the early morning, an unending rain, cold with nighttime raindrops, waterfalls, herds and herdsmen, waves, winds, and caresses like winds and wild ducks, herons flying and the mouth of the most distant day, pounding, pounding. The torments and the laments of that sweet mixture made happiness wipe my face clean. It was an open, endless green field, all love."

Cleto lowered his head and then quickly raised it and said slowly, "She came in the night. She was a virgin. It dawned. She was a woman."

"No, Cleto, be still, you lewd liar."

50

"It's the truth, Clément. Saraminda surrendered in the flower of her purity. She'd saved herself for me. It was fate."

Clément arose and wept, unbearably upset. Lucy asked:

"What's wrong with you, man?"

"It's the pain of someone who hasn't bathed in a waterfall or ever felt the pleasure of a queen bee."

9

Love On the Trail

"How I remember the trip to the Lourenço claim after she'd come to me. I was living a happiness that was growing and filling with strange things. It wasn't a trip. It never was a trip. It was something completely different. How many times had I gone to Cayenne? How many women had I brought back to Calçoene? They embarked thinking about the return trip and I thought about sending them away. The nighttime lights would pass and their faces weren't the same anymore. The women were ugly, yellow, with teeth that were crooked, missing, and crumbling. None of this can be noticed at night. Marie Turiu took charge of herding them together and prettying them up. She knew when I was to arrive and she would get everything ready for me to have a good time, and I liked bringing women to the claim. It was a sad little game, that playing at having a good time. It was part of my vanity, my sadness, my sense of adventure. It wasn't anything that could justify turning a man's head. A woman became a fragile doll. When she arrived the atmosphere changed, curiosity grew, the men got all excited because women and gambling were forbidden there and their heads were full of it all. But it was all right for me. My strength could impose order or disorder. I could do anything. Me, not my gold. The women came dreaming of a future filled with grams of gold. They were prospectors of a sad joy. They didn't have to go to the panning. They collected in Cayenne. I almost always got sick of them and sent them away. Saraminda's voice: 'I'm yours, Mr. Cleto, you paid for me.' What kind of a story is that? I paid to bring some life to the claim. No woman had ever caught me, tied me down, or had the courage to raise her voice and say no. I am, I was, Cleto Bonfim.

"Everything changed when Saraminda told me I couldn't sleep with her until after she'd got the gold. No woman ever thought that I'd be a tightwad. If it hadn't been for some spell that changed Cleto Bonfim I'd have given her a few good slaps, whipped her with my belt, kicked her, punched her and thrown her out. But I wasn't myself anymore. Those green eyes in that dark body, the yellow breasts, that grassless field, the prayerful voice, the slithering of a snake had bewitched me. "I'm yours, you made me something of yours." Not mine, no. The only thing that's mine is what I want and I never wanted a woman of mine, I always wanted a woman in my gold, not in my heart. I always felt they were like chinaware, a plate breaks and you buy another one. You exchange it, replace it, like a clay pot. But she'd spoken as if she was going to settle down on the claim and stay with me, hitch up for real. It was the drinking bout that had cost me my life. The twenty pounds of gold were nothing. I was born without a gram to my name. The expensive part was my life and that woman sticking to me. But she did give me happiness, and that was something. Me, Cleto Bonfim, I did a repulsive thing I never thought I'd do. Right off, there I was, kissing a woman's filth. But she said to me, 'Look at me, Cleto, take a look at me.' And I looked and it dominated me so much with an urge to fondle her that I kissed her. It was a big fat kiss. She moaned, asking for air. 'Kiss me like you wanted to, Mr. Bonfim.' And she was grabbing my hair, pushing my head down, lowering it. And she was running her hands along my sides and I was catching the smell of her body. 'Who taught you these things if you're a woman no man has ever known?' 'I'm not a stitched-together woman like those girls in Cayenne who try to trick you. I'm the way nature made me. I know a lot of witches who can stitch women together.'

"I didn't like Creole women but I liked this one. I've had lots of women of all kinds. Some of French blood, some Dutch, some red-headed Guyanese black Sararás, ones that followed convicts, sisters, wives or family members. I've had Chinamen's women in Cayenne and women from Marajó island in Pará, short, well-shaped, snub-nosed, with pretty faces, long hair, tricky mulatto women and open half-breeds. Once I tied in with an Indian woman and at other times ones I can't remember. I had lots of them, out for adventure or those down on their luck I brought to my tent. But I got sick of them right off, the bleached blondes made my eyes tired, their gecko skin disgusted me, and a lot of them were nosy, the miners got all hot under the collar. One of those women, Tatie by name, mucked about so much that when she came back a bunch of the men raped her in the woods, eight of them. She was hurt badly. I found out and had every man given thirty lashes punishment with a guava switch to set an example. A woman, even if she's a loose one, should be respected. That was my way. I respect women and women have never taken any liberties with me. I'd always been all man until that day when I got suspicious of Kemper, that repulsive Firebeard.

"I, Cleto, remember getting off the boat at the port of Calçoene. 'Hold my hand, Mr. Bonfim, I want to get into the canoe.' Very carefully I took hold of that hand with short, fleshy fingers and a firm palm that stuck to your own. I was carrying a bought woman in my arms, a woman with no ties to the claim. Me, Bonfim. She sat on the seat at the rear of the canoe. The oars began slipping through the water and we began our trip up to the second set of rapids. There we waited for the water level to rise so we could get through the course ahead of us. There were a lot of boats with supplies, cans of kerosene, baskets and more baskets of dried *gurujuba* beans, sacks of flour, jerked beef, turtle beans, gunpowder, shotguns, barrels of lard, spices and plenty of salt. Some bundles of heavy cotton denim for jackets and pants, ready-made clothes of all kinds. There were also medical supplies, Le Roix laxatives, and Aubert English waters. I'd also bought a large covered chamber pot so Saraminda wouldn't have to go in the woods. I, Bonfim, was lost now. I don't know what got me to buy a pot, but I didn't want her to display her parts, not even to the ground, seeing to her needs in the pigpen where everybody went or over the pit of a latrine with its awful smell and earthworms swarming underneath along with mosquitoes and blow flies. But I brought it along. It was a deep chamber pot, with blue trim, and the cover had an acorn in the middle to pick it up with. In the morning the workers would come to take the filth away, empty it, wash it with boiling water, and later on she got the new idea of washing the urinal with mint water. I, Bonfim, never sat on the pot. I'm no fairy to piss sitting down. I've always been a tough guy and I don't like to lower myself.

"'Cleto, old friend, did you bring just that Creole woman?' asked Astrolabio when I came ashore. 'What happened? You never came back to my dock here except with a whole battalion.' He was my agent, the owner of the store there, my friend, but I was hard on Astrolabio, the bumpkin, a way I'd never acted with him. I cut him off. 'I don't like people taking liberties, old friend. I haven't given you the right to talk about what I want or how I live. I bring in what I want and I don't have to answer to anyone.' He went away. 'O.K. I won't say a word. It's none of my business.' But he was so annoyed I can still remember the face he put on. Saraminda got out, sat down on a stool and huddled. She was like a poor wet swallow perched on a stake. Her hair let the back of her chubby neck show. I saw another good thing in that. Everything about her was beautiful. Her black neck glistened into white. I got the urge to kiss her, kiss her hard, lie down on top of her, but I controlled myself. I wouldn't give them a chance to see what point my animal urges had reached.

"Our men waded out by the dock with the water up to their knees. They secured the boat and were unloading the merchandise in preparation for the trip through the jungle. On days when the river had risen the trail was swampy, a dirty, wet, cold path. The claim was far away, some thirty leagues, more than a week's trek through that great stretch of woods full of jungle surprises. Saraminda didn't ask any questions, I mean, she asked one that left me without an answer: 'Mr. Bonfim, how long are you going to want me?' It gave me a fright. Could it be that she was already thinking about leaving me? How could she be talking about the time to go back? Showing no surprise I answered, thinking of myself as Cleto Bonfim: 'As long as I want.' She fell silent and I was sorry. My answer should have been: 'You'll never leave me.' I was already sure that she'd never go back, that I belonged to her and would never send her away. I wanted her to be mine always. In my head happiness would come when I was auctioned off: 'How much for Bonfim?' And she would say, 'I bid forty pounds of gold and my whole life.' I never should have said what I did. Why did she ask me that? Was it to find out what I wanted, aware of my reputation? Hadn't she told me that she was mine, my piece of merchandise? Why should she have asked that? Then I felt my thoughts change and now my mind was a mass of questions of mistrust and doubt.

"'Have you ever traveled jungle trails, Saraminda?' 'Never, Mr. Bonfim.' What the hell! The Creole girl who'd given me the impression of being strong for adventure, capable of facing up to anything, now seemed fragile, defenseless in these regions. She could ruin her feet, could hear the terrifying silence of the jungle, sleeping under the trees, crossing rivers, brooks and ponds, and fighting off mosquitoes.

"It was a long trip from which a lot of people didn't return. And I, Bonfim, was worried about that Creole woman, who was like any other woman, bringing some joy into the hot nights on the claim. When was I ever worried about a woman on a trip? How many had come, walked, scratched their feet, caught malaria, stayed on the road or gone back halfway through, or maybe hadn't gotten back at all? That was never a worry of mine. But now all I could think of was her, not wanting that she hurt her feet or be eaten up by the big jungle mosquitoes, be afraid or come down with fever; I wanted her to be always happy under my protection.

"That was when the idea came to me to carry her on a bamboo litter like a sick or old person, with mosquito netting and *pindoba* palm fly swishes. But did I, Bonfim, have the courage to speak to the men about carrying that woman on a litter? What wouldn't they think or say? That weakness for a woman was compromising my authority on the claim. 'Bonfim brought in a Creole woman on a litter, all fine and delicate!' It was shameful. And what about recruiting the men? It would take at least eight bearers for eight hours a day of traveling. And two more in case someone dropped out. 'Saraminda, you're going on a litter.' 'Whatever you say. Kiss me, Mr. Bonfim.' Damnable woman. How could I kiss here there. 'Not here.' 'Take me to the back of the store.' Oh, yes, the men were watching suspiciously, but with a smile on their faces and no doubt thinking, 'What the devil is Bonfim doing with that woman?'

"But she was spellbinding. When I came out of it I was kissing her on the throat in the bedroom behind the store, stroking her face, squeezing her body and, afterwards, firm and energetic, giving orders. 'You men get a new hammock. Make a thick, strong bamboo stretcher. Celestino, round up eight good bearers, men with a steady step to carry Dona Saraminda to the claim along the stages by ground.' There was general surprise. Not over carrying her, which was already rather something, but from my calling her *Dona*—Missus. Dona Saraminda. That Creole, a mining-camp woman, *Dona*? Where was Cleto keeping his head?"

Night came on. Everybody went to the mess hut. Cleto and Saraminda walked off to sleep in Astrolabio's house, in the room where he'd been so often during unloading times. Early in the morning on the next day they would be up and on their way by canoe and on the trail in the darkness of early morning, meeting up with the sun along the way.

Saraminda picked up her bundle and slowly opened it by the light of the oil lamp. Cleto was watching. Out of it she took a white cotton hammock trimmed with English linen lace that gleamed as though it had been oiled. It was beautiful and delicate, a rare thing in that lost and distant place. Cleto was startled.

"Where did you get that hammock?"

"I bought it for sleeping with you." She set it up by wrapping strong knots around the hooks in the walls, got undressed, lay down, put out the light, and sighed, "Come, Bonfim."

That was the first night in which she felt the savage heat of the jungle, the damp vaseline of flesh melting in the mists of the forest, a strange thing, the thick sweat from the body of Cleto Bonfim.

10

Days When the Sky Was Wind

"What day was it when my delirium got started, that passion of mine that took over my bones, broke the supports of my head, and turned me into a mushy swamp? It must have been when I put out the lamp. Me, Cleto Bonfim, bewitched by that Creole woman's arms and legs. 'Kiss me, Mr. Bonfim,' and she wouldn't let me sleep. The rain at the diggings, the storms, the thunderclaps. 'I'm afraid of lightning, Mr. Cleto. Move closer to me. Cover the mirror.' Holding her hands as if praying while the death rumble crackled in the sky as flashes crossed through the jungle and the elements growled.

"When it rained, it was always in the afternoon. It would begin when they came, those black rams, growing larger, their dark wool billowing over the horizon. The sun would run away and a sad light would take over, then ash gray clouds, and right after that herds of huge black mountains moving this way and that while the wind kept up as its gusts lashed the trees and dusted them off, their branches swaying as if to break and their leaves flying madly off, carried by the wind, chasing the flashes. The forest was all agitated, birds fled before the black clouds at the whim of the whirlwind. And then the rain would come. We would watch the beast hulking onward and all those sudden scars that join earth and sky together, torrents falling in heavy drops that didn't look like water but an ash-gray curtain, a sheet of smoky drops like skirts or dresses made of water. Then the cloudburst came down in heavy thick blobs, hissing in the leaves with a heavy rustling, like a caress from violent hands, combing the forest, invading it, covering the trees, hiding everything. You couldn't make out a thing anymore, everything was dark, everything was sad, and the thunderclaps came along with lightning strikes that smelled of brimstone. 'Protect me, Mr. Bonfim, I'm scared of thunder, cover me with my silk dress. It keeps the lightning off.' And I covered her, wrapping her feet, protecting her body with my full love, and I asked her not to tremble, grasped her hands, me, Bonfim, a critter wilder than any ant bear, bound up by the bonds of that female who had the smell of rain. And everything was gray and it rained all afternoon and into evening as the caravan of clouds ambled along over our hut.

"'Protect me, Bonfim.' And the open sunshine of morning, me sitting next to her without any urge to leave for work, wanting to stay there all morning, all day, for all time, a dumb ass, just like a donkey on a riverbank.

"'Tell me the story of your life, child, of when you were a little girl.' And she would lay her head on my lap and I'd look into her black panther eyes of green that kept looking at me, looking at me, and her mouth opened, pouring out words that I put together in my ears and played with, trying not to let them run away out of my head, to keep them under lock and key seven times over in chests of lead.

"'I never had a mother's love. The one who showed me affection and tenderness was my grandmother Balbina.' It was the voice of an angel. 'Take me to bed, Bonfim.' It was morning, they were waiting for me at the diggings and me in the hammock, because she had her days when she'd only receive me in the morning and others in the afternoon, and the rest at night. And she'd send a messenger to get me at the warehouse: 'Tell Cleto Bonfim to come here right away, it's urgent.' And I'd go and she'd tell me, 'I've been wanting you, Cleto. Skip everything and lie down with me.' And I would lie down and in that way I burned right down to my roots. The times when her belief in the stars came out were other difficult moments. There would be a new moon or a full one. She couldn't receive me in the waning quarter and I was left to go crazy, but there was nothing I could do. She wanted to follow the teachings of the sorceress she believed in. It was the first time that she talked to me about having a child, but she never filled her belly with one. It wasn't because of me, because I'd got eight women pregnant, from the Chiquerão claim along through Lourenço,

Vila Nova and Aporema. After Saraminda gave herself to me I didn't have a taste for any other woman. I'm not sure if it was a spell or the foolishness of an infatuated man.

"'I don't want you with a mustache, Mr. Bonfim,' and this fool shaved it off. Then it was, 'Let your mustache grow out, Mr. Bonfim,' and I let it grow.

"'I'm going to tell you about my childhood. I discovered my body when I was eight years old. I went to bathe at the well and I saw myself naked. It was only then I saw my little breasts coming along, already showing the yellow of their nipples and, down below, Cleto, I saw that I wasn't the same as other women. I was always deprived.' She'd show herself and tell those stories just to catch me.

"I don't know when I got my hate for her because it was never something that was born. My rage was love, the rage of jealousy. It was when I started asking myself, 'Could it be that Kemper ever touched her body?' The idea was enough to drive me as crazy as a mad dog. I would have to kill her before he could touch her, but I couldn't live without touching her, without her nights, without her prayers. Me, Bonfim, worse off than a dead ox, an old hen, a beached alligator, a dumb cow.

"Me, Bonfim, seeking out the sorceress, taking herbal baths that the miserable witch prescribed for me. Me, Bonfim, who'd rather die of leprosy than lose Saraminda.

"It was on the day she told me about her body that she asked me for the dress."

11

A Wedding Dress

"During the first days the jungle had a scent, a nice smell that got into the shed, with everything covered by a delicate and long-lasting perfume. The first thing her hands did was to put things in order, wildflowers, the sawed planks that served as benches, the decoration of tree branches, and the charm of the small mirror she nailed to the wooden wall where she would spend the day looking at herself, twisting her neck, turning her head about. I found all that simple and nice, something that never ended, and I asked her, 'Are you happy?' 'I am, Mr. Bonfim.' And she would stand there, musing, her eyes on the mirror, just looking at herself. And I began to wonder what it would be like to keep that woman there in those silences, in that lost jungle.

"So what happened one day after she got there? She started to cry, defenseless: 'Bonfim, for the love of God, Mr. Bonfim!' And when I looked at her I saw she was taken by some odd fright, looking at a giant bird-catching tarantula that was taking long, extended, tentative steps near her feet. 'Don't be afraid, Saraminda, I'll kill it!' Me, Cleto Bonfim, working in delicate ways like that, something I never thought I'd do. Me, who'd always been tough and hard. No woman had even given me a tickling."

Clément interrupted:

"Bonfim, old friend, these stories are lost in the past now. Stop it. You don't remember when I got back from Calçoene bringing twelve pounds of gold. Nobody thought there was any gold left in Guiana, but I called everyone together and I had to lay it out on the table so they could see there was gold on the Brazilian side of the disputed territory. Cayenne had eleven thousand inhabitants. It was too small. The fire of 1888 had done away with the business district, the market, the police station and the mayor's office on the Place Gambetta. The business that brought in the most money was the piddling trade with France in perfume nuts, rose water, hulled cacao, annetto paste and shreds, stuffed birds like egrets and others, big white and gray ones. I'd arrived from the Calçoene on Master Francelino's boat called *Fé*, *Faith*, and docked there was the *Meteor*, the ship that made the run to France and whose master was Captain Edouard."

Lucy picked up the old towel and went over to the blue crystal bowl with a fire-baked trim of pink flowers and told him:

"Stop talking to yourself, Clément. These things make me sad and affect my old age. I don't like to hear about the past. The old days are always cruel. You're getting dotty and you keep repeating that story everybody knows, about your coming back to Cayenne with the news of gold."

"I'm chatting with Bonfim."

Next to Bonfim the figure of a woman. Her face was covered and she was hiding in the shadows, keeping away from the light.

"Who are you?"

"I'm Artônia the witch."

"Why have you come to pay me a visit?"

"Because I'm after Bonfim. I want to know who ordered my throat cut, if it was him or Saraminda who was afraid of my powers of prediction. Why did he order me killed? Was it jealously of Kemper on Saraminda's part or because of Bonfim's fear that I'd kill her? The mystery of my death haunts me."

"Go in peace, you soul in torment," Clément said.

"And a few days after she arrived? Saraminda asked for a house, a house, Clément, she wanted a house built, a Cayenne house in Limão, a comfort that had no place on the claim where there was nothing but huts and sheds, tents and lean-tos. 'I want a Creole house,' she begged. 'With painted crossbeams, a wooden ceiling with diamond-shaped carvings, a high porch and wide hallways.'

Right away I thought about building the house. But who here knew how to build a house like that? I sent to Cayenne for a master carpenter, a licensed specialist. She wanted it to be all in rosewood and brazilwood, with crab-tree wood for the smell of its boards, for it to have just one story, for her bedroom to face the forest, for it to be built on a hill beside the waterfall in the stream, and for there to be a downward view, all open, in order to watch all the coming and going on the claim. I hired sawsmiths from faraway places and brought in all the material. And I ordered it built. And she explained how she wanted the living quarters: a porch that went around the house, with doors opening inward where she could hang Venetian blinds to let in the breeze. 'Saraminda, this isn't Cayenne. The sea breezes don't reach us here and all we've got is the wind from out of the woods.' 'You just build the house up there and in my head I'll see the ocean at Cayenne and the breezes will come. I want it painted bright green and yellow and red, just like the house that used to stand on the rue d'Enfer. I want the handrail and the pickets made of rosewood.' I did everything she asked. It took me more than a year to have it ready. She wanted the porch on the side to be all enclosed in the front, with just a single door, in the style of the Creole chapel in Cayenne, and later on she didn't want the porch closed in front, demanded that the door be moved back, that it have a mesh of crisscrossed metal strips, that her room be where the verandah used to be, two windows opening on the down side overlooking the straw huts and sheds. And that's how it was done. She changed her mind several times, put things together and took them apart, modified, and the carpenters were never sure what she wanted.

"The house was hidden in the jungle up there with its clumps of forest on every side, half on a slant so her eyes could take in the view she wanted. In the end it even looked nice. The paths up to it were V-shaped and from in back of the dense forest came the stream, the cool, clear water slipping along, passing almost underneath her window, where birds came to drink and after a little while the dogs would come.

"A few weeks after the house was finished, I told her that she was going to stay there as my wife, the one I loved. 'In that case, Bonfim,' she requested, 'send to Cayenne for a wedding dress. I want a wedding dress. I've always wanted a wedding dress. It's been my dream ever since I was a girl. If I'm going to be your respectable woman, I want a wedding dress.' 'But I'm not going to get married. It's not my custom and there's no priest here.' 'I'm not talking about marriage, Bonfim, my soul is already married to you. What I want to have is a wedding dress, a nice pretty one, hanging on the wall so I can look at it and think about the way I married you and to wear whenever I feel like it. When it gets here it's going to be like the first day all over again.'

"And I, Bonfim, ordered the dress. It came up seven sets of rapids in canoes, protected by wine-palm mats, in a wooden box, a spur of the moment order carried on the heads of Saramaca blacks, covered to protect it from the rain, because they knew it was something precious and that if it suffered any damage they'd pay dearly. And who was there who didn't respect the wishes and commands of Cleto Bonfim, which were those of Saraminda? I remember how happy I was when that white dress was caressed by her hands, carried to her hammock, held out in her arms, receiving her kisses. And she whispered to me, 'Cleto, this dress is worth more than the gold you bought me with.' 'I didn't buy you, that money was a gift.' 'No, Cleto, I won't forget the feelings of that auction.' 'Don't talk about that, child. Just look at the dress.' And the dress had a long organdy skirt trimmed with lace and a garland of orange blossoms made from wax.

"She got dressed with all the ceremony the act called for, helped by Maruanda and me, fluffing out the skirt, straightening the veil, unfolding the linen petticoat, and she asked me not to touch her. She whirled around the room like a little child. Then she grabbed me, danced with me, kissed me, let go, stretched out her arms and took in the air, breathing deeply, spinning around the room. Until she lay down and asked to be undressed. We were alone. We sent the servants away and I was quite willing to do what she asked, and she was falling asleep, so deeply that there was no awaking her. It was a sleep of happiness. I lay down beside her. She was breathing heavily, smiling, but she was asleep. I remember that night, I only know why now, an ominous owl that wouldn't leave the corner of the house hooted, and having the spell cheapened bothered me. I went out to kill it but I couldn't find it. It was hooting and I was only afraid that the sound would wake Saraminda from her sleep. I didn't know that it was an omen.

"That God-damned dress!"

"I don't know what you're talking about, Cleto. Put away your thoughts of death. Nobody knew that you'd married," Clément said.

"I didn't. She only got dressed up as a bride. It would have been better if I had got married, me her husband, she my wife. It's an idea that makes me think that I would have had more of that present that I hadn't had. Even if it was all agony afterwards."

Lucy was washing her hands in the blue glass bowl. She didn't understand how he could be talking to himself, not knowing that Clément Tamba wasn't alone.

"Lucy, have you died now, too?"

"That doesn't make any difference, Clément. We're dead. Cayenne is dead now. It died with us. Do you remember the chanting in the cemetery, the festive lights, the people all praying? It's the nicest day in Cayenne, the day we remember our dead. With the songs and the candles on Toussaint's night and the many-colored flowers. No one's here anymore. Look at your hands."

Clément looked at his shrunken hands. They were wrinkled, the skin all dry, the bones swollen at the joints.

"Lucy, go get my bonds from the Banque de la Guyane."

"The Banque de la Guyane doesn't exist anymore, Clément."

"Then have them book me a passage on the *Belle de Martinique*. I've got to go to Paris to find out about my gold," he rambled on in his confused memory.

"Our gold isn't worth anything anymore, it's nothing but sand."

"That doesn't have anything to do with our lives."

"What lives?" Cleto asked, joining in the conversation.

"The gold in the disputed land belonged to us more than the Brazilians who expelled us, kicked us out," Clément said.

"We discovered the Calçoene gold," Cleto said.

"But we were the ones who exploited it, coming out of Cayenne and taking over from the boats from Belém do Pará, which were nothing but big canoes. We brought ships and sluices to Calçoene, you didn't know what a *lontana* sluice was, you only knew about panning. We brought in *chanquées* and all the other heavy equipment to get the gold out of the deposits." He was repeating the same talk that used to fill the gaps in conversation when they got together on the claim.

"France gave me Saraminda, who never learned to speak Portuguese right."

"The rainy days were so sad. The splashing against the boards of our house...On one of those days she asked permission to take a bath in the water from the gutter pipe from our roof. I sent all the servants away, sent them down the hill, telling them to come back only after the rain. And she took her bath, with the water from the sky running over her body like a waterfall, falling with bubbles from heaven. I was bashful. I hid in the bedroom and wanted to put on my pants. She cried. How had that woman changed so much? When I bid for her and she left the Tour d'Argent she was all feisty, like a swindler, with that hip-swinging of a prostitute. And when she got to my house she changed and came on with a little voice, like she was praying, peeking at me coyly and putting aside the trappings of a low woman, to come into my life. Maybe I've been gullible. The gentleness she gave me wasn't supposed to happen, the confusion that got into my head. She was tearing me apart and when I came to I'd already been bitten. It wasn't just my body, it was my soul. I'd be bathed in happiness just by taking her finger and pulling it over my beard, me, Bonfim."

Cleto raised his voice and shouted, "Cleto Bonfim!" A shout of rage. It was so loud that Clément covered his ears so they wouldn't burst, but Lucy didn't hear anything.

"Cover your ears, Lucy. If you don't you'll go deaf. Bonfim's roar is like an explosion, a thunderclap, the blast of a cannon. It's the cry of a tortured demon."

"What Bonfim?"

"It's the bite of a snake."

"That night Saraminda's green eyes were sparkling in the darkness. She was dreaming on her feet. She started talking about mansions in Paris. She, who'd never been there. It could only have been some spirit who'd come down into her. 'See the Seine. The Louvre. The river as it slips along. The Place de la Concorde, the Place des Vosges...' 'What Seine, Saraminda?' 'The river slipping along. It's going to reach Le Havre, Honfleur, into the sea...'

"She woke up early in the morning. 'Cleto, put me in the hammock and come sleep with me.' The dress was hanging on the wall.

"Her yellow breasts lit up and then her hair swayed over my eyes and I didn't see anything anymore.

66

"It started raining on the claim and the morning was as dark as the end of an afternoon."

The Limão claim was half a league before the Lourenço claim and it was nothing but gold. Each panning produced over a couple of ounces. Nuggets were everywhere to be found. There was even gold in the caves. All the gullies were good. From Vila do Firmino, from the first falls on the River Calçoene, it was thirty leagues, including the trip along the river, facing the rapids at Dead Man's Falls, Ananás, Travessão, and the trail through the jungle, the ups and downs of the terrain where the trees reached up to the sky in a variety of species, the *tonka*-bean, the wild chestnut, the crab-tree, sapodillas, *macacaubas*, soapberry trees, palms of all descriptions, the wine-palm, the *caxirama*, the *anajá, miriti, bacabeira, tucum* palms, rasp palms, and in the swamps water hyacinths, pond lilies, philodendrons, *canaranas*, and great silk-cotton trees keeping watch over the rim.

After the swamp came the Oh-My-God Marsh, Limão, and Lourenço, and then the mysterious Salomoganha Mountain rose up, its base sweating gold. The *tonka*-bean tree is only found where there's gold and the base of the mountain was covered with *tonka* trees and their fragrant beans.

The Brazilians from Pará and Maranhão came in bands, as did the French Creoles from Guiana. Cayenne was closer, attracting more people because access was easier and gold was discovered first off in the river basins of the Cunani, the Caciporé, and the Carnot, substantial streams that flowed down from the foothills of Tumucumaque, running in an easterly direction on their way to the ocean. The French were already acquainted with the mysteries of working mines, used to working the River Approuague during the fever of the strikes that brought about the rise and fall of Guiana and the explosion and the exhaustion of the gold.

It was in the Brazilian Contestado, the disputed area, an immense jungle between the Oiapoque and Araguari Rivers in the Calçoene sector, that the French Creoles immediately established their village, the Limão encampment, where Saraminda wanted to live. Cleto lived in a different village, Saint-Laurent, later called Lourenço, an encampment perched on the crest of hillocks surrounded by valleys interspersed with gullies, all gold-bearing.

"Me, Cleto Bonfim, a Brazilian from Cametá, the gold king of Calçoene, head man of Lourenço, accepted living in Limão—in the midst of Creoles. I built a house. My shed in Lourenço was still my workplace but I lived in another house, mine and Saraminda's, in the middle of all of them because they were her people. 'I don't speak Portuguese, Bonfim. It's better for me there where the language they use is mine.'

"When I did what she wanted, she said to me, 'Thank you, Cleto, for making me happy by living here, behind the hill, beside the trees, in a big house that you built with sweet-smelling wood, a hardwood house, so that everybody will say that it's the prettiest, that it's yours, that it's better than the ones in Cayenne, and that it looks like the ones in Paris. Kiss me, Cleto.'

"And I, Cleto Bonfim, kissed her and drooled like a fool. 'Thank you, my angel.' And she became one with her prayerful voice, that whisper like a flowing stream, and I fell. How many pounds of gold went into the carved boards, the decorations of the master carpenters I'd sent for? Everything to kill me."

"But I thought my house was nicer," Clément said. "It was small but it was pretty, done in good taste, the best kind of Creole house. That's where I spent the best days of my life. That's where I saw Li Yung the Chinaman take out that thirty-seven pound nugget for me to hold onto. It was dirty and his hands were shaking from the weight. He told me, 'Keep this for me here, Mr. Clément.' Nobody stole anything. We all knew that no one came out alive from any thievery. Nobody went against the laws of men. But, Bonfim old friend, on the day I left Limão and saw my house in flames I wept. I wept inside and out. It was cruel. People developed a hate for France. We'd been abandoned by France."

Cleto Bonfim remembered how thunderstruck he'd been on the day he found out what Saraminda had been up to.

It was a Friday. Across from the shed the hen came out flapping her wings, cackling, running away from the animal that was trying to bite her. From behind came a pig, the short-legged kind, with whitish markings on a black skin. The half-breed Terêncio who was nearby ran off, afraid of being dirtied by the animal's grunts. The pig pushed his snout along the ground, dragging himself along, smelling and trying to find something to eat.

"How come you don't lay out some food for the animals, Taíta?"

"Look, Bonfim, there's not enough food here for so many people, why should there always be some for the critters?"

It was a dank morning. Dark, low clouds brought on a feeling of dampness and suffocation. Terêncio went back to the bench where he awaited orders. Cleto Bonfim was pensive, not saying anything.

"Why do I have to talk? All I want is to think."

Taíta asked him what he wanted for lunch. He didn't answer. She spat on the ground, cleared her throat, and muttered, "If you don't want to talk, don't talk. Now I can make lunch any way I please. It might even be pork dung with string beans."

Cleto wasn't saying anything. When he went into the house he saw it. How could it be? He was horrified, not understanding anything. He looked again and again and didn't understand. He turned his head toward the window and saw the limb of the *sororoca* tree growing outside with its thin green leaves. Farther on was the large silk-cotton tree, with brown nuts and a flock of striped seed-eaters leaping from branch to branch. He looked back inside. The long verandah, all bright with the sun's rays passing through the windows and, in the middle of the room, Saraminda, naked. He couldn't believe his eyes. Naked, totally naked. "The woman's gone crazy!" How, with that view in his head, could he talk to Taíta about lunch as he chased away the pig who was waltzing into the house?

"Taíta, kill that pig, cook it up, and serve it to the men."

"So, you did say something. You haven't lost your voice."

She had complete freedom. She'd been with him in pantry and kitchen ever since she'd arrived in Calçoene. She was from Alenquer, in Pará. She was used to cooking on claims and didn't know how to do anything else.

"I want to meet that woman you brought, Bonfim. They say that she's beautiful and that you're foolish."

"You mind your own business, Taíta."

And Saraminda, naked in the middle of the room, in his head.

"Saraminda, you can't do that. What are people going to say? Everybody's going to find out."

"I'm all hot, Bonfim, the heat suffocates me and I think about dying."

"That word made my heart beat faster. It was like it had dropped down into my belly and was throbbing like I was pregnant. Saraminda dead? The word came like a crash. 'This house is so far away from everything and I'm so alone that I need to be happy. It's my Indian blood.' What a strange woman, what a round, curvy female! And, starting with the new house, starting with that crazy day, Saraminda turned Indian and went about naked, and she would go to the window naked, and her hair grew longer, blacker and blacker, and the nipples on her breasts became more yellow. Her green eyes looked greener. I never got used to it. The days went on and she was there naked, in front of me, and me afraid that she'd be seen and that the news would get to be the main topic of conversation on the claim."

"Bonfim, old friend, I heard talk about Saraminda that was going about the claim, about her being naked. Everybody knew about it, but I never asked you. It was something not to be believed. I suspected that was the reason you had two thugs guarding the two paths leading up to your house and gave orders that no one was to go up there. But tell me what Saraminda was like."

"No, that's my secret. It can't be described anyway. I can only say that it was hard on me, very hard."

And he sobbed.

"But people don't cry in death, Bonfim old friend. Lucy shouldn't see you like that."

"I remember the fat pig grunting and rooting. The ground was dirty, all muddy, and Taíta asking about Saraminda and me thinking about her and her body, the way God had put her on this earth, with a nice smell all around her. It was better that way. I worked with her in my head and kept accounts better, had more strength, more pleasure, more drive.

"The pig disappeared. Taíta came out with the leftovers from the meal. The hens ran toward her. A *uirapuru* began to sing in the distance, something strange because it only sings at dawn while building its nest. The song got closer. It made our mouths fill with music. I went out of the house, trying to find that song trilling in the air and I went along beside the pigsty. An unbearable stink of rotten dung made me go back and I lost the direction of the *uirapuru*'s song."

12

A Sapphire Ball

I fooled Cleto Bonfim. I wasn't a virgin. I'd had seven boyfriends and seven times I went back to being the virgin I was born. On the night I gave myself to him I was like I'd never had a man before. I was almost a child. I was fifteen but life had taught me how to be a woman. I was attracted to him, something like a bird and a snake. And in those places, at that age I was already a full-blown woman. I liked Bonfim because he valued me. He gave twenty pounds of gold for me and the men in Cayenne only wanted to give me five francs. But I never got to know for sure if it was love, if it was all about wanting to have people like something that belonged to you, that you couldn't lose, to make them feel jealousy and hate for you, people whose side you couldn't be away from for a single hour, who made you long to hear their words, catch their smell, want their body, and get pleasure from them.

On the day I spotted Jacques Kemper's blue eyes and saw that sapphire ball in the white of his eyes my body trembled, my soul lifted up its arms and then I started to lose sight of the light and my virginity began to come back again. I took out the dress from Paris and looked at it, at the embroidery sewn around the bodice and it was of a blue just like Jacques Kemper's eyes. But I decided not to give myself to him. I wanted him, but I knew that if I gave myself to him I'd never get out of that prison.

"Mrs. Bonfim, the Société Equatoriale sent me here to bring the carriage that Mr. Cleto ordered and they made me the bearer of this present, given to you in the name of the firm and of French fashion."

I couldn't catch all the words. His accent was different and I spoke mostly Creole, the language of my people, born in the fields of black slavery and work, with bits of traditions and journeys, a language of love, in which words are a tenderness and a caress. I answered *Sa ou té, mèrsi*. I repeated *mèrsi*. Thank you. I was so perturbed that my head was spinning. His blues eyes were burning me. Bonfim didn't suspect anything. He only said, "You're pale."

When I came to I was in the hammock, and Bonfim was fanning my feet that were in a pan of warm water. I had fainted.

"Where's my dress from Paris?"

"It's right over there, on the bench."

"I want it in the hammock with me…What about the Frenchman?"

"He left already."

He was wearing a coat and tie. His fire-bright hair glowed in the dim light of the verandah. He wasn't like the men in work jackets on the claim. He was a slim man from Cayenne on a starry night. For me Limão was a rain-colored day, rain that never ended and poured down in the morning, in the afternoon, and at night. I was living the life of a prisoner of the jungle and the gold. I went on to be a slave of my own fate, running away from myself. Ghosts would rise up at night. The jaguar's growl would strike my ears just as though it was underneath my window. I could feel the animal's claws scratching at the tip of the hammock. It was during that time that I dreamed my grandmother had died.

"Saraminda, I came to tell you that I was buried today. Your gold is underneath my hammock."

Lorette stole my gold. She took it the day after my grandmother died. But she held onto the paper and later, on a trip I took to Cayenne, she gave it back to me. But my grandmother hadn't died on the day I'd dreamed of her.

"Lorette, you robbed my dead grandmother. I left orders for her to buy houses for you people. Where's your husband Roger, who came to visit me on the claim?"

"He ran off with a Saramaca and went to live in Rémire Montjoly. I stole from you because I knew you'd never come back from Calçoene. Our grandmother Balbina told me the story of the auction."

"So why didn't you come with Roger, who knew where I was, and tell me?"

"Because I'd already broken up with him and shacked up with our cousin Koron."

I began hating her. Not because of the gold but because of Koron. He wouldn't take me one day when I wanted to have him. I never wanted to live with him, but he was the only man I ever had the desire to give myself to on my own. I never knew whether out of love or just want. But I never forgot Koron. For me he was the memory of a clean sheet. Lorette dirtied it. She was a slut. I never forgot Koron. Afterward I found out that he went to live in Surinam and said, "Saraminda died."

I didn't soften my voice in order to change the way I was. I didn't want Bonfim to think I was a coarse woman, and I wasn't. I was a child. On the day of the auction at the Tour d'Argent I tried to find out who was there and decided on him, Cleto. I didn't want to fall into the hands of just anybody. That's why I spoke to him like I was praying. But I didn't do it so he'd get all worked up. I wanted him to get sick of me fast and send me away. When I saw what I'd got myself into I wanted to run off, get out of that hell. How many times did I think of asking, "Give me my freedom Bonfim, send me away." But he hung onto me tight, coming after me with a love for a woman I never knew existed in a man. I'd say something and he'd think I was singing for him and would leap on top of me, whether it was daytime or night and he'd only let me go when his strength gave out. It was like a jaguar in rut and a howler monkey in the rain. I'm not saying I didn't like it. At first I'd be bored, but then I got addicted and my strength gave out, too, and I'd take to sleeping in the afternoon and hiding in the early morning.

"Where are you, Saraminda?"

I'd be all curled up in the bags of packing cloth and hiding in the shadows. He'd come over with the lamp, "Where are you, Saraminda?" I'd be inside the clothes closet, under the bed. It was to make him think I'd run off. He used to think it was a game of hide-and-seek, but it really was a wish to disappear. He would act like a little boy in the dark of the bedroom.

"Meow, meow, my little pussy cat..."

And me, "I'm here, don't come near, little puppy dog, don't come..."

And sometimes he'd pound on the chamber pot or the corner of the bed. "Come out my chestnut filly." And I would join in the game and answer, "Come here, my black stallion."

Sometimes I'd remain silent. He wouldn't know where I was and I'd say, "Close your eyes, follow my smell," and he'd play blind man's bluff. It was a real addiction. Until he'd find me and we'd stay together until dawn.

Afterward I began to ask him for things so he would refuse me and I could leave. I pretended I was sick of the food and would beg:

"I miss Creole cooking, Cleto. I want to have a *bouillon d'aouara** with fresh vegetables, the meat of a young pig, and get them to kill an ox so we can have some good beef. I like to smell the smoke it gives off and the taste of food that's been cooking for seven hours."

And he'd send them out to get some red manioc to make mush and put it in the stew. And I'd ask, "Get some green and red peppers, the best there are, send to Vila do Firmino for them." And then I'd pretend to dislike things: "I can't stand any more grilled deer or tapir liver or peccary meat or roast *paca* or meat and manioc meal. I'm sick of it all."

"What would you like, Saraminda?"

"An alligator tail brochette, fried with tapir fat and cognac, a *hoko* bird, and roast *cochon bois*."

The food on the claim, of which there was a lot, always came from hunting and fishing. Dried *gurijuba* fish that came from the coast and chunks of *pirarucu* fish. There was no lack of rice and beans, and freshwater fish were abundant in nearby lakes and rivers.

He would guess and give me everything I asked for. "What good are all these things if what I want is to go away?" And I'd say to myself, "Don't ask for anything more, just ask to leave." But I knew it wouldn't be possible for me to go away. He'd kill himself but he'd kill me first. He'd have it done or he'd cut my throat himself.

Cleto wouldn't let me leave that place. He was even jealous of the *jatobá* tree where I liked to stand and hug its thick trunk.

"Cleto, let me go to the store to weigh gold the way the Creole women in Limão do. The merchandise on one side of the scale, the gold on the other."

*A typical dish of French Guiana, which has for its base the paste of the *aouara* palm tree.

There was no money, everything cost gold. A couple of pounds of tapioca cake, one gram.

"Let me get out of all this silence, be next to you at work, getting the gold, looking at the merchandise."

He'd let a smile die, and he'd stay that way.

13

A One-Night Spell

I, Clément Tamba, loved the territory of Mapá. We were "the blacks from Cayenne" there. Guiana was famous for being the home of political and criminal deportees. They still talked about the hundred sixty priests banished by Robespierre and put ashore on the island of La Mère or on Goat Island, where political prisoners were dumped, wearing their dirty cassocks and with no other clothing, left there to die. Guiana was a dry guillotine that lacked the spectacle of the Place de la Concorde. And Jeannet Odin, Danton's nephew, was sent there to govern it. He brought down so much suffering on our people that they write his name in the sand and spit on it.

When the news of gold in Mapá arrived all Cayenne took on an air of adventure. Everybody left, men and women, seeking their fortune.

I was one of the founders of the settlement of Limão, where I set up my sluice system with people from Cayenne. The Brazilians were in Laurent, which they called Lourenço. Then I started bringing in merchandise and stores to trade for gold. Nobody worried about the price of anything, there was too much gold. Five ounces for a canvas hat; ten for a shotgun. Beans cost two grams and sugar five. There was no such thing as money. It was there that we tried to hang onto the land, take it away from France and Brazil, while the governor in Cayenne had a plan to expel the Brazilians. A mistake. Jules Gros—an adventurer with lots of ideas, a dreamer—called for me to set up a republic on that tract of land, make a new country. A meeting was set for Vila do Cunani on the bank of the Cunani River. Jules was a political fellow who knew all about important things. He would be President of the Republic of Cunani. And there in the middle of the jungle, with twenty houses and fifty men, we founded that republic. We had stamps printed and money coined. We designed a flag, and we informed the nations of the world of our action. The President of the United States, Grover Cleveland, even sent the news of our Republic of Cunani to the American Congress in 1876. I still have today in my strongbox a stamp, a coin and a flag from Cunani. It would be good for France because she could unburden herself of Guiana and its Creoles.

The Brazilians considered it a toy republic. We had nothing, only the mind of Jules Gros, whom they called a ragtag adventurer. We gave him some gold and he went to Paris, where he set up the Embassy of Cunani and spoke to the press.

"Where is your Republic located?" they asked.

"It's on the greatest gold strike in the world."

But we didn't want anything to do with politics. What we wanted was the gold that had brought us to the lands of Mapá, which belonged to the Brazilians. The gold brought on the urge to take over those uninhabited lands—the few people who lived there were dying of scurvy, malaria and venereal disease.

On the night I made the trip to the meeting about Cunani, I went to Bonfim's house. He knew nothing about politics or what a republic was. I'd been to school, but Cleto only knew how to count, sign his name and read letter by letter. It was on that night that I saw Saraminda in the state in which she had come into the world. She half-opened the door leading to the parlor and stayed in view in the lamp's dim light, naked, her body reddish in the glow. Cleto had his back turned, he didn't see anything. I saw. She did it on purpose, having thought about it, so she could watch me and pretend to hide like some jungle creature.

I got all hot. She was a young girl but she was all female woman. She was something different, with a spell about her. After that vision all I could think of, day and night, was sleeping with her. It wasn't that I wanted to steal Cleto's woman, it was that I wanted to be a man for Saraminda.

"I saw his eyes eating me up, not with the look itself but with desire. I was possessed by the sin of being the woman Cleto had taught me to be. He liked whores and I wasn't any whore but I got to be one. And men made me be desired. I began to like leading them on, being asked, offered, and they all fell, without being afraid of anything, into my game of betraying Bonfim. The claim had two kinds of gold, me and *la couleur*."

"Speak, Saraminda, say something about what you want. Did you want me?" Clément asked, imagining her present.

And he heard, "I wanted you at my feet. You were the head man and I wanted the big men at my feet. But I only found pleasure with the little ones. I almost drove Celestino Gouveia crazy. But the only one I loved with any kind of love was Kemper. It was the ruination of his life, but I loved him. I'd never known love. And I was never able to be me, I never managed to be the same woman. I had the voice of a nun, but I wanted a voice that could say everything I wanted to say, the voice of a devil, a voice of hell, a voice of pleasure. I would speak, I didn't want to be held back. But I wanted to be a woman and fulfill my sin with the fire of my flesh. It was a kind of mystery."

Saraminda didn't want me. I wanted her. She was now toughened up for seduction, free of affection. She was an animal, a tapir in the jungle howling and bellowing in rut after the male. But I wanted her. I was possessed by the devil. How could I get to her? It was impossible. She had everything, she wanted everything, and everything was given to her. The things people wanted on the claim were things there on the land. The claim was a prison. No one could escape from it. There were no bars but there was the grip of the gold. I never found out if Saraminda was hungry for gold. Gold was the trap that sealed her fate. Gold had been burning people ever since God hid it mixed in with earth. Saraminda was gold and she was earth.

"I want you. Throw everything away and be with me," I told her between moments of fear when I took a chance and went to her house one afternoon when Bonfim was in Calçoene. She was naked. Standing. I was trembling. She was like an Indian, as if there were nothing between us. She was silent at first, but then she asked, "Kiss me, Clément Tamba."

And I kissed her.

"Clément Tamba, a lot of time is going to pass before you can go to bed with me. Don't think it'll just be days. It could be years."

And right there she showed herself to me, all of her, like a waterfall on the River Calçoene. I fled. I went down the road to the settlement and I got there with the feeling of having been saved from a fire but with the flames still burning my face and my private parts. It was so painful for me to see what was going to happen. Poor Cleto Bonfim. Poor me, who never reached the waters of the River Cunani.

When Veiga Cabral came to tell me to lower the French flag, France was no longer part of my soul. I was only thinking about Saraminda. Killing Bonfim, lowering the French flag, and taking Saraminda away.

The rue Lalouette, which passes through the center of the Place des Palmistes, was deserted. Cayenne looked like an abandoned citadel to me. But I wanted to have a big house for myself there. The one I had built was the affirmation of my pride. I bought a large plot from the lawyer Ronjon on the rue d'Estren, which had big trees with their crowns close together in arches as they touched each other, with a flat, partially wild ground and a ditch to drain water off over which I built a small bridge as the entrance to my piece of land. It was a Creole house, but it had a great deal of Limão about it. The original vegetation was still intact. I opened up some space for gardens and plants. It had a lot of bedrooms, rooms that stood for the times of my life. I began to shut them all up, throwing the keys away so they would never be opened again. I was finally left with the parlor, waiting there for death, listening to Louis playing the old songs from the crossings from Brittany and Normandy. There I was, locking up my last vestiges. The years weigh and while away, pass away. Gold passed away, Mapá passed away, I passed away.

"Clément Tamba, old friend," Cleto begged, "don't reveal your secrets or your betrayals. Keep them in your soul. Veiga Cabral came looking for me that night when I got to Limão. He said he was going to Cunani to arrest Trajano Benitez, who'd betrayed the Brazilians and had accepted being the delegate of the governor in Cayenne and wouldn't fly the Brazilian flag anymore. He asked me for weapons, gold to buy them, and I gave it to him. Not for my own sake, but so as not to get mixed up in things I didn't understand. He said you were the spokesman for France in Calçoene and I didn't go along with that, but he told me, 'Clément belongs to gold, to *la couleur.* But I'll get him.'

"I gave him a firm answer: 'You're not going to do that, Cabral. I'm against it. I've got my army, too. There's no France or Brazil here. There's only gold and our friendship.'

"Veiga Cabral backed off, saying, 'If he's with you, I'll leave him to you.'

"That Veiga Cabral was a hothead. A short fellow, shifty-eyed, short-tempered, always angry, feeling trapped, with that mustache and its drooping tips. His heart seemed to be made of clay. All he talked about was his mother country, Brazil, and there was no stopping him. He had his hand on his holster and the defeat of the French in his head. He was always going on about the French being in the Contestado: 'I'm going to kick them all out!'

"'Cabral, old man,' I tried to say. 'They're our brothers. There's gold enough for everybody.' But he raged on and kept repeating, 'Anyone I can't kill I'll castrate.'

"A possessed character, that Veiga Cabral!" Clément said. "He was the one who got the whole region up in arms and then took over Jules Gros's republic. He enacted laws, said that anyone who took his mother's name in vain would get three years in jail and anyone who raped a virgin would get death. He wrote manifestos, turned out ordinances, and awarded titles."

"He also asked about Saraminda. Celestino Gouveia told me," Cleto said.

"'What about Bonfim's woman? They say she's an Indian and goes around naked with a pack of dogs.'

"'She's a respectable woman. She has her woman's ways and wants,' was what Celestino answered," Cleto ended.

I went back to Cayenne after everything was all over. All over for me. The Calçoene region I'd helped tame, watched grow, and got started no longer existed. None of them were still the same people. The adventure, the pleasure of being an adventurer had disappeared. The men were just like any other men, full of ambitions and fears. The railroad I saw built was being discontinued. It could have kept on running but the Société Equatoriale was no longer the Company. I wanted to see myself free of the suffering that was rearing its head, the fear and the fighting. I no longer had any desire for gold. My wish was to open up new diggings that had to exist somewhere in that endless jungle. Maybe at the foot of the Tumucumaque range, which in my imagination was sitting on gold. That was where the rivers with the yellow sand were born.

We were threatened with having to abandon our homes and return to Cayenne. Charwein, the governor, didn't really want us expelled. He sent soldiers to occupy lands, protect the Frenchmen, and put an end to the Brazilians' squabble. But he didn't like Creoles. He liked white Frenchmen. Everything went wrong. The Brazilians reacted and sent our soldiers running. How many of them came back dead? Nobody knows. The widows howled, pulling their hair, insulting Charwein. They'd killed a lot of Brazilians on that invasion. Those of us who stayed on the claim didn't know what was happening far off in Vila do Amapá, which was sacked. Everybody became our enemy. Our lives changed. Before it was just gold, now it was the curse of politics. There were two sides and we'd always been just one. The way people can change. I got to seeing the Brazilians as a pack of devils. They used to be my friends and now they looked on me as the enemy. Their faces were changing in my head until the day I said to myself: "I'm leaving. I'm going back to Cayenne." I don't know how I dared to say that. The truth was that I didn't leave, I was kicked out. People who always accepted my weights in buying gold, my prices, and my merchandise began to mutter, mistrust me, argue, and my life was becoming hell. Bonfim knew this. I told him I was leaving, that I wasn't staying on any longer. I began to guard my bottles of gold, putting them inside casks and hiding them, stored away in the bedroom of my house. It was a beautiful house, with open verandahs, pots of ferns all over. Birds came to feed on the porches and drink at the water. I had a feeder made specially for them that always held corn, seeds, fruit. And *guriantãs* came, doves, flycatchers, thrushes, kingbirds, ant birds, *vivis*, oilbirds, *japims*, and when I awoke before sunup I would have my cup of coffee sitting on the verandah, waiting for the first light of day. It wasn't to see the light, it was to hear the birds, first one, two, then ten, and then all the birds there were in the entire jungle, their songs disappearing in the leaves and in their own mystery.

It was then that I saw there was no way out. My servant told me, "Clément Tamba, you know Raída, that flame-haired half-breed woman of Doriques? She ran off, she's gone, they say Joaquino from the Taquaira gulley claim took her."

"And what did Doriques do?"

"He said he wasn't going to chase them."

"It had to come to this," I answered.

Everything was coming to an end. I'd met Raída when she came to the claim on a lease. She spent a month in my bed and then Doriques got himself a sweetheart. She got the hots for Joaquino and ran off with him the way she would have run off with anybody. The Calçoene claim was dying. That day was when I felt it. On a new claim a woman doesn't run away. She doesn't have the desire or the courage. Gold makes her stick.

14

A Legend of Blood

The diggings came awake at three o'clock in the morning for the task of getting rid of water, draining the work holes so that they would be dry when daylight came. There was always a lantern to one side and cans getting filled and poured out so that by sunup the sand could be panned in the empty pit.

The first sign of movement from the human anthill was the red glow in the darkness from the coals of the fire under the trivets for boiling coffee water, which would be poured into the dented iron coffee pot to last all day long. Everyone had his own pot, in the big barracks as well as in the huts for a few people. Those lanterns were the first light. A glimmer would be seen here and there, then others, and then still more farther off, first in the sleeping quarters and then on the road to the ravines.

They all moved at the same pace. When they got up, coffee and manioc meal or rice couscous, and once their bellies were lined it was picking up a can, a pan, a pick, a shovel, their other tools and the inseparable bowie knife, starting the day.

Many of them worked in a system of sharing, splitting the gold and the upkeep. For them it was group work, feeding the large and small sluiceways and *chanquées* that the Creoles had brought from the mining operations in Approuague, with boxes that sometimes had a zigzagged and sometimes a straight trough, continuously taking on gravel with the gold catching in the mesh and landing on the burlap that was burned on Saturdays in a general cleanup when new cloths were put on.

When they left they took along wood for heating up the pot on the fire where their lunch and dinner were cooked—beans and jerked beef, flour, and sometimes dried fish.

A goodly number carried their bottles of cane liquor to drink while they gambled in the barracks, a way for the gold to get drunk and put in an appearance. Another thing it liked was blood. It was the general belief that when a vein petered out it was because the spell cast by the gold was in need of some misfortune.

Celestino Gouveia was Cleto Bonfim's foreman. When Cleto opened up his works and bought the claim, he brought him along as his strong right arm, in charge of the forty-three men recruited as workers. Some of them were fugitives and troublemakers from Marajó Island, Balique, and Santana. Others came from Santarém, Viseu, Carutapera and Gurupi. His job was to keep an eye on them and keep them in line, the people working the digs, operating the washing, slaves to ambition. "Without a strong man and a tough foreman there's no getting gold out. Gold likes violence," Alexandre, a pioneer in the goldfields of Roraima, used to say.

Celestino Gouveia never felt the least shadow of fear. He was almost an animal. He had his trusted men and together they kept watch over the teams of workers. He checked out the veins in his riding breeches and boots, with a whip in hand and a weapon at his waist, day and night. For every thief they caught they would get half of what he'd stolen. It was the local law. Customs on a claim are created by the clock, by fear and by blood. Laws are invented by the adventure.

When production on the claim went down, Celestino was the one who got all stirred up, nervous, violent, and then he would explain how gold liked blood:

"Soil that's got gold in it can only be opened by the color red. When I was working on the Maracaçumé claim in Maranhão such a heavy spell was cast that the gold disappeared and we had to cut the throats of three men in two days in order for production to come back. I never saw a claim peter out like that," Celestino told Cleto Bonfim.

The claims in Calçoene weren't asking for any blood. The bleeding always came from clashes between groups and the constant plots and homicides that were almost a daily custom in those frontier lands of greed.

But Celestino was obsessed with that legend, which fit well with his violent temperament. That was why he was feared and why his presence brought on terror. Cleto, on the other hand, was easygoing. He took care of weighing the gold, maintaining the keys to the iron chests, and checking out the daily tally and addition. Celestino was a battalion of guards all by himself. There was no one better for the job, which invaded every daily aspect of that world of vengeance, misery and magic. Cleto was well-mannered, discreet, subtle in his instructions and commands. Celestino helped him by being silent and loyal.

"Celestino, when the claim is shut down and we leave, you're going to have to hire a whole string of donkeys to carry off the gold of yours that I'm holding. Our deal wasn't by halves, but it's still good at ten percent," Bonfim said.

Celestino's eyes gleamed. He felt like a privileged partner and, even more, the recipient of the friendship and trust of his boss. And in that way a strange tangle of ambition and blood came together with the wealth and work of the enterprise. In his searching he liked to discover ravines where production was going down as his immediate thoughts went back to the gold's desire for blood. He always made them open up ravines that were undergoing a scarcity of gold.

"The Ponta Negra vein is giving out. The Cuvasco alluvium is finished."

He would take inventory with his head in his hands and then squeeze them together in anxiety. It was a ritual that would get him all excited.

"Celestino, you're the person who knows how to make production increase. I have trust in what you can bring in," Bonfim would answer.

Then Celestino would begin his demented ritual. He would stroke the switchblade he carried in his pocket. Night was coming on, casting a deep shadow over the long huts where the workers' hammocks were lined up in parallel rows for the dirty, sweaty gold workers, their bodies battered by the daily tragedy of looking for wealth. Celestino was sniffing out his victim. The madness of looking for an anonymous throat took over his soul. Not even the face should be seen. Celestino waited for the predawn. He sneaked among the hammocks in a hut where everybody was asleep. There was a smell of dirty bodies mingled with the suffocating heat for which night was no improvement. Lying in wait, he sought out his prey. He would stop, catch the shadow of some crossed feet. Finally he caught sight of a whole body, in shorts. The man was snoring, his head tilted slightly out of the hammock. Celestino passed by like a shadow. Fatigue didn't permit those men any insomnia. He took out his knife, opened the blade. Somebody coughed. A sound of broken twigs came from the deep woods. He heard a deep growl, like the grunt of a pig. His quick hand flew through the darkness. A first and then a second quick stroke cut the throat and the knot on the hammock as it fell to one side and dumped the body on the ground. He knew how to stay hidden. There was no light as the lanterns were far off and few. Sneaking out now, slipping away like a monster, protected by the darkness, he reached the jungles whose hiding places he was now master of. The next day gold would appear.

In the morning the news ran through the ravines. They all knew the tragic rituals.

"It was the phantom of the gold that came looking for its share. Production will increase," Celestino told Cleto.

Everyone fed on his own superstition. The next day a pound-sized nugget was found.

"It's a reddish yellow color, just like the blood the gold was looking for. Last night it came hunting for its share," said Juventino, a gold digger from Pará.

Cleto cleaned off the nugget.

"What's the name of that guiding spirit?" he asked.

"I don't know."

15

A Trip on the *Gazelle*

Jacques Kemper was from Cancale. He picked up the nickname Firebeard on the Calçoene claim. His affected accent, his mixture of words in Creole, French, and Portuguese, his blue eyes and blond hair made him a strange creature in those parts. He never understood why life had brought him to the hell of Cayenne as a pawn in the ambitions of the Contestado, that bloody frontier of Amapá where men ran about waving the flags of France and Brazil in search of gold. It all started in Paris when he was hired by the Société Française de l'Amérique Equatoriale.

Paris was like a house inhabited by emptiness whose rooms he was unfamiliar with. When he arrived from Brittany his days were all struggle and misery. First at the home of his Aunt Lucille, a cleaning woman on the Metro, with her three children, two cats, and a husband who smoked cigars all day long. When she took him in she showed no signs of love or protection.

Jacques Kemper was no longer a child. He was fourteen and there had been no way for him to stay in Cancale, having become an inconvenience for his family. After the death of his father he was hit by his mother Charlotte's new marriage, which forced him to realize he was now an orphan. He was transformed into the prey of a sadness and rebellion that didn't disappear even on warm summer days. He couldn't get over the disgrace it was for him to know that a stranger was sleeping with his mother in the room that had once been his father's and all the other things those torments put into his head. His only source of affection was his sister Annie, who wouldn't let him run away, wander off, leave, or roam about in a desire to escape that torture.

"Stop snooping around in our room, you damned brat," his stepfather told him when, victim of those ills, Jacques went into his mother's room looking for intimate things with which to feed his jealousy.

"I don't have to obey you. You're not my father," he answered.

He got slapped around and that only settled his decision to go away. That beating changed his life. He never forgot that pain in his soul.

"I'm not staying here anymore. I'm going to run away. You're no good for anything," he told his mother.

"You've got to obey André. He's taken the place of your father. He's nice to your mother, your sister, your grandmother."

"No. He's not my father. I hate him. I'll kill him."

Charlotte saw the depth of the abyss separating Jacques from his stepfather. His eyes showed nothing but rage, his hands trembled, and so she decided to send him to her sister's in Paris. Maybe he could study and start work there, and forget about André.

In Paris when he was eighteen, he fell in love with his cousin and was thrown out of his aunt's home. He went through some more youthful romances and got the reputation among girls as a sly seducer and woman-chaser. He was famous for always going out with a group of friends and enjoying the company of the lovely young women in the cafés and along the paths of the Bois de Boulogne.

Now, ten years later, he worked for the Société Française de l'Amérique Equatoriale of French Guiana, headquartered in Paris, as a jack of all trades. Starting as an office boy, he was now in the firm's administrative section. He was on excellent terms with the boss and enjoyed a certain prestige, delivering correspondence to the post office and banking houses and taking care of errands that arose. One day in January, when it was snowing in Paris and everyone was calling for heat, the boss called him in.

"We've got a job for you because of both the confidence we have in you and your wish to rise in the company. Our branch in Cayenne wants us to send our greatest supplier of gold, a certain Mr. Bonfim, a coach with gilt ornaments and gold trimming, the work of an artist. He's a man madly in love with a woman and, like all women, she has her whims…You know what women are like, always full of crazy ideas. She wants a French coach in that corner of the world…"

"But I've never driven a coach," Kemper said.

"Yes, but we're taking care of everything and you won't have to drive or even see the coach. It will be crated up and well-protected, and will be your traveling companion. This is of the greatest interest to us. The frivolities and passions of a Brazilian. We very much need that man, who's made us a lot of money. He's an old customer with a very good file. Enough to say he sells us more gold than anybody else. We're going to put on a great show to please him and we can't ship the coach just like any other piece of merchandise. We thought, therefore, to send it with lots of pomp along with a representative of the firm to show him how much we appreciate him as our customer. So the coach will be delivered to Mr. Bonfim and he'll be satisfied and grateful. It will be ready in a few days and you'll board ship in Le Havre on your way to Cayenne. It will only take a couple of months. You'll return and receive special gratification for the trip and the extra service to the firm, with a right to keep getting ahead."

"But I've got to think it over a bit," Kemper pondered. "How can I go off to Cayenne? I've never traveled before."

"Kemper, you're a young fellow with drive and you've got the confidence of our firm," the boss said. "Your mission will be to show Mr. Bonfim our consideration for him, to leave him all puffed up with vanity, and the best way to strengthen our ties with him is to please his wife, who, everyone says, has a great deal of influence on his life and is the reason behind everything he does on that claim."

"But my job will only be to go along with the coach?" Kemper asked.

"No. You have to do deliver it, present our respects to Mr. Bonfim, as well as…," and Mr. Foucaud smiled ironically, "present to his wife a special gift to show our esteem, a dress we had made at the Maison d'Amour which will be an elegant offering from our firm. A special item, with sequins, embroidery and ruffles...things for the vanity of ladies...with poor taste."

That day fate changed Jacques Kemper, because, surprise of surprises, when he reached Cayenne he received the news that his journey didn't end there but that he would have to push his way along the little-known pathways of the Calçoene River claims.

He boarded the *Gazelle* with the dress they had delivered to him in a velvet-lined case wrapped in several layers of cardboard which he was to guard in his cabin like a work of art, something so beautiful that it couldn't travel in the baggage hold or be away from his ever vigilant watch.

The coach was being shipped in a strong crate, complete with iron plates on the corners to avoid any jolts and with lots of instructions, not only for boarding but also for unloading. Kemper traveled to the port of Le Havre where, after being taken through the city and already getting used to traveling, he reached the pier, went up the gangplank, and was shown to his quarters by the stewards.

The ship weighed anchor at night and as the lights of the port disappeared Jacques began to think of his trip as a kind of reward, a vacation to get to know new places, returning to Paris richer in prestige. When he got back, his status would surely be different, something higher.

He felt happy as he leaned on the rail thinking about how life was generous to him, how the winds of fortune were blowing his way. Guiana and Cayenne were faraway words that said nothing but which inspired and suggested everything. He had tried to find out what the region was like and all he got were bits of information about its exotic nature and its use as a prison colony, a place for punishment and suffering. He put all that out of his mind. He was only going to spend a short time there, but he would add some colonial experience to his life.

"Are you going to Cayenne?" asked a lady on in years who was passing on the quarterdeck, wearing a dress closed at the neck and with her hair pulled back.

"Yes. That's where the ship is going, no?"

"Yes, but it stops at Martinique, where I'm getting off."

"I've never traveled on a ship before," Kemper confessed.

"I have two nieces, one who lives in Cayenne, named Laurence, and another traveling with me."

"Yes," Kemper said, not wishing to prolong the conversation.

Then a girl came by, with long and curly fair hair, a thin nose, well-defined lips, and a face that suggested no frivolity.

"This is...," the lady said, then asked, "What's your name?"

"Jacques Kemper..."

"Genevieve," the girl introduced herself.

"Very pleased to meet you."

"I'm going to Martinique, my home."

The lights of Le Havre could no longer be seen and the ship began to roll more. Everything had been left far behind and the departing whistle was accompanied by growing waves.

16

Cayenne Heat

Kemper reached Cayenne on a Saturday. The ship docked at Île Le Père or Green Lizard Island. Then it moved on to the port of Cayenne, where Mr. Lefèvre, the local agent of the Société Française de l'Amérique Equatoriale was expecting him. The passengers went off to their destinations. He remained on the dock with his black wooden trunk that was reinforced with metal bands and iron corner braces. The largest metal plate, in the center, had the keyhole cut into it. It took two turns of the key and this he kept on a small ring hanging from his belt. On top of the trunk he had placed the package with the carefully wrapped and reinforced box that contained the dress for Mrs. Bonfim. He was never far from it during the trip, keeping it under the bunk in his cabin. He sat down on the trunk and took in the view of Cayenne. The city was small and the people poor. In his head he imagined Madame Bonfim as one of those Parisian ladies with a wide-brimmed hat, elegantly made up, wearing a long dress with a narrow skirt, her hair dropping softly off to one side onto her shoulders. Then he practiced how he would greet her. He didn't know how to kiss a woman's hand. He was just an employee of the Société. Mr. Foucaud's instructions never left his head:

"Be careful with the coach and the dress. Don't let them out of your sight. Mr. Bonfim is our main supplier and he has a lot of pull with the Brazilians, so we want him always treated well. Our business is gold, not politics. He gives money to the agitators in Amapá and controls them. His wife is French and has great influence over him."

Kemper knew the value of those instructions and that information. They would never leave his head. He wouldn't leave the dock until the case with the coach was lowered onto the cargo pier. He would have to see its unloading and accompany it to the firm's warehouse. His first feeling of distress came when he didn't see anyone there to meet him. A dock worker appeared and asked if he didn't want him to take his luggage. He said no, because he hadn't seen the rest of the cargo unloaded. He asked the mate, who'd come off with him, about the rest of his things. "We won't be unloading anything. It's Saturday. Tomorrow's Sunday, nobody works. Only on Monday. We're in Guiana, Mr. Kemper! What the devil have you got in that box you won't let go of?"

"A dress."

"A present for your sweetheart, that's what it is," the mate said good-naturedly.

Kemper got himself all ready for the disembarkation. His superiors had ordered a white linen jacket for him, something appropriate for the equatorial climate, polished shoes, a high-necked shirt and a brightly colored tie. He felt like the owner of the firm himself done up in that attire, not at all like his normal wear. He was used to a wool jacket that he never took off on the cold Paris days when he went to the office early in the morning and which he invariably wore every day. But now, even in his white, light clothing he could feel the unbearable heat. He was perspiring, exposed to the sun, standing with the dress by his trunk, when Mr. Lefèvre appeared, accompanied by his wife Laurence.

"Are you Mr. Kemper?"

"Yes. I'm pleased to meet you. Charmed..."

"I'm a bit late, but I've come here to meet you. The employees of the Société stay at a boarding-house near our office on the rue de la Liberté. That's where you'll be going." And he immediately called over a man of color. "Jean, get his luggage and take it to the company boarding-house."

Kemper held onto the box with the dress. Mr. Lefèvre advised him, "You can let him carry it. He's quite trustworthy."

"No, Mr. Lefèvre. Mr. Foucaud's instructions were for me never to let go of this package."

"Around here people don't even carry gold themselves. You can let him take it."

Kemper hesitated: "Mr. Lefèvre, my instructions are not to let go of this box."

"What's in it?"

"A dress."

Laurence smiled and showed an expression of curiosity. Then she asked, "A dress? All that care for a dress?"

"It's a present for Mrs. Cleto Bonfim."

"Mrs. Bonfim? That *piranha*? That's impossible. The Société Equatoriale is losing its sense of shame," she said.

Mr. Lefèvre turned red and retorted:

"Don't say foolish things. Mr. Kemper was sent by the firm and the firm knows what it's doing."

"This is ridiculous," Mrs. Lefèvre said. "A man crosses the ocean to bring a dress for Mrs. Bonfim."

"I'm also bringing a coach," Kemper said, trying to show that his mission was something greater.

Laurence ended up laughing:

"Well, now, that makes it even worse. A coach? Also for Mrs. Bonfim?"

She spoke with an affected tone, stretching out her words. "How ridiculous! Utterly ridiculous!"

Jean cut in, "Are there people to take care of the luggage?"

"We'll see to that ourselves," Lefèvre interceded.

Kemper headed for the hostelry. Even though he'd never traveled on a ship it hadn't bothered him that much, only for the first three days a slight light-headedness. The ship didn't roll all that much. Most of the passengers on the *Gazelle* had disembarked at Martinique.

Kemper looked at Laurence. She had blue eyes, the same color as his own. She was dressed quite in Parisian fashion, in a long skirt with a narrow waist and a high starched neckpiece that covered her hanging hair. Mr. Lefèvre treated her with a certain arrogance that had a touch of anger in it, as though he was upset about something. She had the look of a difficult woman, with a furtive gaze but with a touch of glamour in her expressions and her speech.

"Where are you from?"

"I'm from Cancale, but I've been living in Paris for over ten years."

"I'm from the Riviera, from a very small and beautiful city, Saint-

Paul-de-Vence. That's where painters like to spend their holidays and make use of all their experience."

A brisk, light breeze, hot and thick, moved across Kemper's face. He smoothed his hair. Laurence said to him:

"You'll get used to that breeze, it blows all the time in Cayenne. Heat and humidity never leave us here."

Jean was now carrying the trunk on his head and had the box with the dress under his arm. They walked along the rue du Port, continued on down Louis Blanc, taking Christophe Colomb, turning onto the rue Malovet and reaching the rue de la Liberté, then the Boulevard de Cayenne, passing by the Place des Palmistes with its row of tall trees at whose end stood out the irregular houses, simple buildings by people who put their nostalgia for the homeland into the overhangs and the tiled roofs. Laurence couldn't help remarking:

"It's a mistake to think that Guiana is France. The climate, the fevers, the miasmas, the jungle, never knowing for certain what's going on, all of that is something people forget. All we think about here is France, and these people aren't French. Look at the types. They're blacks, Indians, every kind of commonalty."

"Laurence, stop talking," Lefèvre cut her off. "Don't say things like that to Mr. Kemper."

"I'll tell them to him and they're the truth. If you'd ever told me I would end up living here I never would have married you."

Seeing the uncomfortable position Kemper found himself in, Mr. Lefèvre changed the subject.

"Do you see that house? It belongs to Clément Tamba, one of the gold men and also a client of ours. You'll be seeing him in Calçoene."

"Where is Calçoene?"

"It's the gold-mining region," Lefèvre answered.

They reached the boarding-house. Kemper went to his tiny quarters. He took off his clothes and decided to rest. "You're having lunch with us," Mr. Lefèvre had told him when he took his leave.

Now, without the breeze that was blowing outside, he felt an unbearable heat. What clothes would he wear to go out? There was no other solution but to put on the ones he'd just taken off. It would be torture for him, imprisoned in that suit, frightened now by that sun and infernal heat.

"Mr. Kemper, we have a custom of drinking wine and not perspiring. The Saint-Julien has that virtue."

Laurence began to laugh again. Mr. Lefèvre's face tightened. "Come on, Mr. Kemper. You've got to show me the dress that you brought. You know that we women are curious and it must be a monument to bad taste. I'd like to see that tramp wearing Paris clothes in the backwaters of Laurent. I never had the courage to go there. They say it's loathsome, that it stinks all over the place."

"Don't keep saying such things, Laurence," Lefèvre said sternly.

Kemper remained silent. He would never open the box with the dress that had been entrusted to him.

"Let's organize your trip, Mr. Kemper. On Monday we'll unload the coach and figure out the best way to get it there. There'll probably be a ship sailing for Calçoene this week, the *Meteor*, which is in port if I'm not mistaken. I'll send one of our most trusted employees along with you."

Jacques Kemper's first night was horrible. Between sweating and dreaming he couldn't get any sleep. He had the feeling that he was still at sea and the voices he heard were Laurence's, saying "Open the box, I want to see the dress."

He would have to spend a few more days in Cayenne waiting for the ship to leave. He didn't know anyone there. At the boarding house there was only an employee of the Société who, down with malaria, had come for treatment. He was convalescing now and his eyes were yellow from the horror of the quinine he was taking after a few days of hovering between life and death. Kemper listened to his story with fright.

"The fever comes. You ache all over, your bones, your ears, and your eyes. Then it goes on to give you a hellish sweat. Then it comes back at the same time next day with a chill that makes your whole body shake and there's no blanket that can be enough. And that's the way it goes along all day, all night until you get to feeling that your body is losing its flesh, with nothing left but skin and bone and you haven't got any strength at all."

Kemper couldn't hide his fear.

"Could it be that by going to Calçoene I'm going to catch a fever like that? Can my organism, with no resistance to these diseases, give out right away and die?" he asked his companion. "How does it feel when you start getting the illness?"

"You don't feel anything. By the time you come to realize it, the fever's already set in. There are two kinds. The devilish thing is not knowing which one you've caught. One, which kills you right off, or the other, where you can escape death. Monkey fever is the one that does you in right away. But it's rarer."

Kemper grew more interested, taken by the danger of his coming trip. He never thought that it would involve his health. "Why the devil did I agree to bring this rubbish of Mr. Bonfim's?" he wondered.

"And do you get it in Cayenne, too?"

"You do, yes sir, but less than on the claims. This place here isn't all that healthy either. They still talk about how in the seventeenth century twelve thousand settlers on a certain Choiseul mission died. Fevers, typhus and other unknown sicknesses. And the convicts? They die right off. Tropical diseases are terrible, especially for people who come from the home country with their bodies unprepared for them."

Those words sounded like a death sentence to Kemper's ears as he began to feel his body aching from head to toe.

"And do medicines have any effect?"

"They have some and they're what's kept people safe, thanks to the discoveries of Fonsidar, who's done a lot of research on the sickness. The best medicine is Flavoquine, but it does your liver in. Then you've got to take a restorative and Indian Cholagogue for two months."

Kemper wasn't enjoying the chat at all, but Bizane, his sick companion, went on with his involuntary sadism, "The worst is typhus, which has killed a lot of people. It's a dysentery fever. Your hair falls out and the suffering is hellish. The only cure for it is God's grace."

Kemper almost fainted. He got an urge to go back home, even knowing that he was four thousand miles from France, twenty-two days traveling on the high seas, and with no guarantee that he hadn't been infected. How could such a thing have happened to him, someone who had no connection to Guiana or knew anything about it, whose only wish was to grow old in Paris?

Laurence invited him to get to know Cayenne and they went out together. It was a way for him to leave his fears about his health behind.

"Madame Lefèvre, have you ever become ill here?"

"Not much, nothing serious. For my part I get along well with the place. As far as health is concerned, that is. But it's had a bad effect on a lot of people."

Her words calmed him a little, but the last part opened the door for his fears to come back in.

They walked through the old city, looked at Saint Joseph's Point, and remained for quite a while on Government Square. The main building was the former Jesuit college, a two-story structure with a rather steeply sloping roof. At the entrance was the shield of Guiana. Laurence, all gentility, nothing like the aggressive woman at lunch, explained:

"Look at the shield of Guiana there. First the date, 1645, then the three *fleur-de-lis* on a blue sky as a way of linking Guiana and France, or saying that it's French. Underneath there's a canoe filled with gold, that ruination of men and women which fills the soil of Guiana, its main wealth. The canoe slips along on a red background that displays all the minerals there are in the colony. Below that are three giant water lilies, *Victoria regias*, a pretty plant that grows in swamps and rivers, suggesting the beauty of the forests and the fields of this huge territory."

Kemper was listening to that while his mind was far away, thinking about fevers.

"Mr. Kemper." Laurence was speaking louder now and he woke from his apathy. "Take a look now at the backwardness. Do you see what they put there to hold the shield, clutching at it with its long claws? That lazy creature which eats only ants. Two great anteaters." And she added, becoming once again the woman she had been the day before, "A most fitting symbol for the place: laziness and ants."

Years later Kemper would recall that conversation which had expressed the feelings that the colonial functionaries, who all considered themselves exiles, held of Guiana. But Guiana held a fascination and a mystery they didn't understand.

At the end of the afternoon Laurence brought him back to the boardinghouse. But she didn't stay by the door. She wanted to go in and there was no way for him to stop her. The rooms were in disorder, his clothes tossed at random onto the bed and on top of an old chair. The couch, the only piece of heavy furniture, was up against the wall next to an ironwood table. She sat down there.

"Mr. Kemper, I'm quite curious. Women are always like that, especially when it's a question of fashion. You're a handsome young man. You've got a manly bearing and eyes that people see and can't forget."

Kemper was disturbed. He felt a shiver, trying to figure out how far she wanted to go. "This woman represents a danger. She goes from being serious to being vulgar, and now she's coming out with this. Nothing like this has ever happened to me. No woman has ever seduced me."

He looked at her and all he could say was:

"Thank you."

Then he thought, "What if Mr. Lefèvre were to come by? With this woman sitting there alone with me? What's going to happen? 'No sooner does he arrive than he becomes my wife's lover. I'll kill him.'"

Guiana had become a land of absurdities for him.

"Show me the dress you brought from Paris, Mr. Kemper. I thought about it all night long. I want to see it, Jacques."

The intimate tone startled him.

"Madame Lefèvre, the instructions I brought are very strict. I cannot betray the trust of my employers. It's my job. How could I open that box? I don't know what's in it, and I have never seen the dress. How can I open it?"

"Kemper, you can't deny a woman's curiosity its pleasure. Not a woman like me...I'm not leaving your room unless I see that dress!"

"Madame Lefèvre...Laurence, please."

"All right, I'm going into the bedroom and put it on. Attack me if you want, slap me, stop me."

Kemper was left not knowing what to do. Laurence headed into the bedroom. He followed her. She saw the package on the chair and began to open it without hesitation.

"Madame Lefèvre, don't do that. Don't make me go get your husband and ask him to come get you."

"You can go. He'll find me naked on your bed..."

Kemper couldn't believe what was happening. Later on in his

life he began to be convinced by the idea that there was magic in that dress.

"Well, I'm going."

"Go ahead." And she began to get undressed.

Kemper left the bedroom, sat on the couch, not knowing what to do. Through the open door he could hear the sound of the box being opened and he imagined that Laurence was already undressed and he sensed that she didn't just want to see Mrs. Bonfim's dress but put it on. Until then his life had gone along without any such kind of anguished wait.

The dress had a long pleated skirt that fell from the waist with plaits down to the hem, around which was a strip of lace and embroidered fringes. It had a jacket in an elegant bell-shaped cut, divided into two flanges, also with lace, that fell like stoles down to below the waist, with two rows of satin-covered buttons and tiny embroidered stitches on the sides. The lace blouse underneath rose up all white in contrast to the other bright colors and was closed at the throat with a neckpiece of silks and frills that matched the cuffs of the long sleeves. It was a dress whose lack of hooped skirts highlighted its slim shape. Decorating the fabric were pearls and sequins. It was a pretty piece of modern French *couture*.

Laurence came back into the living room, dazzling. She was a different woman. The dress that Kemper was taking to Mrs. Bonfim gave her an enchanting aura, like a starry sky. The sequins and pearls sprinkled across the bodice and skirt filled the room with light. Kemper forgot about his troubles and was fascinated.

"Give me your hand, Kemper."

She moved slowly around him, as if levitating, possessed by the pleasures of vanity and bewitched by her own body.

"I never imagined myself dressed in clothes like these. They were something in shop windows as far as I was concerned," Laurence said, whispering into his ear. "See how beautiful a happy woman can be, Kemper. My husband is a pig. Come help me out of this dress which is going to be fouled by Mrs. Bonfim. Take one of my dresses to her and leave this one for me. She'll never find out, that Creole tramp."

Kemper stood there motionless in the living room. She began to take off the dress, loosened the waist, unbuttoned it, lifted it, pulled her shoulders forward, slipped out of one side and then the other and was pulling softly on the long sleeves. She let it drop to the floor and delicately withdrew her legs. Kemper helped her. The body of a mature woman appeared, nicely outlined and held by her long stockings, with a slight, almost imperceptible fleshiness at the stomach. The still firm breasts, the long hair and the high heels produced a slim silhouette that was sensual and provocative.

Laurence took Kemper's hand, drawing him slowly to her. He pretended to resist. He could smell her perfume from close up and his eyes ran over the curves of her body.

"Look at me without the dress on and see how pretty I still am, Kemper. You'll see me even prettier in just a minute."

And she led him slowly into the bedroom. She was carrying Saraminda's dress slung over her shoulder. Her own dress had been tossed onto Kemper's narrow single bed. She placed what she was carrying on the chair near the wall, over the seat, letting it drape down both sides. She closed the door.

Kemper was motionless, pale. Laurence took the initiative of putting him at ease. "Let me undo your clothes," and her hands slipped over his chest, twirling the short hairs. Then she took off his shirt with care and caresses and asked him:

"Undo my brassiere. It's easy...the small hooks...like that..."

Kemper never felt at ease. It was all so strange. Laurence lost all her inhibitions and took the lead the entire time.

"Where are you going to put the dress that's on the bed?" Kemper asked.

"On the floor," she answered, "with my stockings and panties."

He saw her lying there, mature, rigid, not showing any affection.

"We've only got one life, Kemper. Don't think about anything. Think about this moment. There's nothing better than a woman given over to an impossible and unexpected love."

A bell rang on the street. There was a knock on the door. Kemper shivered. Laurence sighed and, almost without speaking, said, "It's nothing, someone collecting empty bottles...Lie down...your sweat's driving me mad."

Kemper watched night fall lightly over Cayenne and took Laurence to the door.

"Now I'm going to put Mrs. Bonfim's dress back in the box. It looked beautiful on you. I never thought such a captivating woman could exist in the heat of Cayenne."

"I'm coming back tomorrow, Kemper, so we can take another look at the anteaters on the shield of Cayenne." And she smiled.

17

The Presents Arrive

"Clément, old friend, it was only later that I began to put two and two together and got to know the path of suffering. I, Cleto Bonfim, was the prisoner of that passion, a prison with no limits. The Frenchman brought the dress but she didn't want to try it on. She was fascinated with just looking at it and touching it. She took it out of the box, examined it, smelled it, and sighed as though she'd come across some magical perfume, so she smelled it again and made me smell it. Then she lay down and did the same thing she'd done with the wedding dress; she took it into the hammock beside her, and the dress was pink, which contrasted with her dark coloring, and I thought it had the look of having been worn, but it was pretty. Then I looked at the size and it seemed to me too big for Saraminda. But she couldn't see anything and wasn't paying any attention to the defects. For her it was the fascination of a dress from Paris, a present that she considered a present from Kemper and not from the Equatoriale, because she really didn't know just what the Société was. I sensed all that when she told me, 'That blue-eyed boy came all the way from France to bring me that dress without even knowing me. Who told him I was here?'

"'Saraminda, that man is a delivery boy for the company that buys and sells my gold and he's traveling under their orders. They wanted to please me and in order to please me they have to start with you. He also brought along a calash I ordered for you.'

"'Good Lord, Cleto Bonfim, are you giving me a carriage to go around in?'

104

"'Yes, Saraminda. It's being unloaded at the port at Firmino, waiting for shipment to us. But there aren't any roads for it here. They'll have to be cleared.'

"'What's a calash like, Bonfim?'

"'It's a two-wheeled carriage with a canvas top, leather seats, drawn by two horses…'

"'Am I going to have a carriage with two horses?'

"'You are, Saraminda, one with doors embroidered in gold and golden wheels.'

"'And how can I use it on these roads?'

"'I'm going to have them open up a road just for you and no one else to ride on. It'll go from our house to my warehouse. You'll go and come in the shade, dressed in those clothes from Paris.'"

"That's a lie, Cleto. No calash ever came. A cabriolet arrived, something no longer used that they sent to trick you. They knew that here in Laurent there was no road for horse-drawn carriages."

"Better than any carriage was a landau I'd ordered for Cayenne, and even today everybody can hear it trotting on the streets, drawn by a team of white horses, and the people in Cayenne would go to the door to see it, clap their hands and say, 'Hurray for Clément and progress in Cayenne!'

"And I ordered a sedan chair like a throne for her, too. It came with the coach and the Frenchman didn't know about it. I sent for everything that a society lady in Paris would have. I wanted her to be a goddess. I liked that thing of Saraminda's they called a litter very much. A little house with two windows, one on each side, with curtains, and inside velvet cushions, red with yellow fringes. It was mounted on two gilded beams with padding on the ends to make it more comfortable for the two men who carried the litter, one in front and one in back. And I, Cleto Bonfim, sent for a goldsmith and had him engrave the name *Saraminda* in gold on the outside, on both doors. I did that but she wasn't satisfied and asked me to have him engrave *Love of Gold* underneath. And I asked 'Why love of gold?' and she answered simply with that voice of hers, 'That's me.' And she asked me, 'Kiss me, Bonfim.' And I kissed her.

"After she got those things, the dress, the chair, and the coach..."

"It's not a coach, Bonfim," Clément interrupted.

"It was. In the letter it said *coach*."

"That was a cabriolet. They tricked you and collected a lot more gold than it was worth," Clément spoke again.

"My friend, if that's so I'm going to kill that man in France and I'll start with Lefèvre here."

"You're dead, Cleto, you can't kill Lefèvre He's dead, too."

"Then I'm going to kill death. Let me go on. After she got my presents she locked herself up in the house and put the chair on the verandah and later on went to the bedroom with the dress. She spent a whole day and night like that and wouldn't have me. She was crying. I could hear her sobs with my ears cocked toward the door and I implored her, 'Have me, Saraminda,' and the answer was the silence of her sobs. She should have thanked me for everything and loved me all the more. She did just the opposite. In the morning she opened the door and appeared. Her naked body was more beautiful than ever and then she asked me: 'Where's the Frenchman who brought me the dress?' 'He left this morning.' 'Send for him any way you can. The dress he brought me is torn in back. I don't like that. And a dress that came from overseas.' 'Show me.' And she went to get it. It had a cut, which didn't look like a tear but as though it had been done with shears. There were no shreds, just a straight line. And she repeated, 'Send someone after that Frenchman.' And I sent Celestino Gouveia off on my saddle-horse to gallop after him and bring him back any way he had to. I didn't know that it was a trick, one of her well-known plots. She's a bandit, that woman."

"Don't say that about Saraminda, you scum. Saraminda is everything to you," I said to myself.

"Around noontime Kemper was back, having been ordered to come. Saraminda was in her room. I had everything closed up because she couldn't be seen in the state she was in. Only I had the right to see, and I saw. I had all the doors locked and she was to have contact only with the two housemaids that she herself chose, the Saramaca women Gedina and Maruanda.

"He arrived. I looked at him with great anger and said, 'Dona Saraminda wants to send the dress back. It's torn!' From the very beginning I didn't take to his face. It was too flabby for my tastes. I saw the Frenchman begin to tremble. He turned paler than fresh whitewash and could only stammer, making it hard for Maruanda, who knew French, to translate. 'I was just following orders. I never saw the dress…' At that moment Saraminda's voice could be heard: 'Open the door, Bonfim, I want to talk to him.' 'No, are you crazy?' And I started to go into the bedroom but she was already coming out, wearing the dress, the skirt dragging, too large for her size, half baggy at the waist, and said right off, 'Look at this tear here at the back of my neck, Mr. Frenchman.' I, Bonfim, boob that I was, didn't suspect anything. What she wanted was to see the Frenchman and he was shaking. And when she appeared he opened his mouth round in fright and could only babble 'Oh! Oh! Oh!' with the mouth of a baboon. 'Say something, Frenchman. See what Dona Saraminda is talking about.' I was mad as hell. I wanted to slap him around. A man without any manners or upbringing, sent on such an important mission and with such responsibility, from Paris to the gold fields of Calçoene, and the fool acting like that. I gave him a push. I don't know if he'd seen the tear or whether he closed his eyes, but he answered, 'I'll take it back to the Société Equatoriale and they'll send another one.' 'No, Mr. Frenchman. That's not necessary. You're going to darn the tear,' Saraminda put in. 'I, ma'am?' Kemper said, hesitating. 'I don't know how. I'll take the dress to Cayenne and bring it back fixed.' 'No, Mr. Frenchman. The dress is here in this house and it's not leaving.' I didn't know that what she wanted was for the Frenchman not to leave, and the tear in the dress was the motive for keeping him there, a lame excuse that I, Bonfim, swallowed whole like a frog swallows a fly.'

"But my old friend, did Kemper have to sew up the dress?"

"No. She started reeling him in and he was called in every day to be there morning and afternoon with a woman from Limão hired to do the job. He was made to inspect and help out. The fellow was a regular slug. He didn't even know how to thread a needle. And Saraminda was devilish, never satisfied. She would find defects everywhere, doing and undoing, with the Frenchman present, which was what she wanted. Oh, Clément, old friend, you don't know how I was burning up not knowing if he was involved with her during those days, whether he'd seen her naked and whether they'd gone to bed together. Goddamned filthy, stinking, dressmaking Frenchman…"

"Don't say that, old friend, he must be dead by now…"

"Dead for you. For me he's my everlasting rage. He saw her

naked, old friend. I'm sure of it. No one had the guts to tell me, but from the way she was in heat, which I didn't see, she'd given herself to him. And to that boob, mind you, that sluggard, whiter than a gecko, foolish, with the look of a spook, his eyes bugged out with fright. Clément, old friend, I remember that one day it was raining a sad rain, it pounded against our house as if someone was knocking at the door and the dogs were barking far off, barking and barking, during the daytime, and I've carried those howls in my head, howls that I'd never heard on a rainy morning or in the daytime. It was then that she asked me for the first time to send for five more dogs to keep watch over our house. And I sent to Vila do Firmino for them. And she asked, 'Don't let that Frenchman leave, Cleto. He's a spy come to have a look at the gold and he must be in the pay of that Société or whatever it is to rob you. It's a trick. Try to find out. Have him arrested. I've got a feeling. Always keep him near you.' I believed her, I, who saw in that Frenchman only a piffling little person without any capacity for being a spy. So he didn't leave because I'd arranged things by giving orders that he wasn't to leave. The spy that she'd discovered was the love she had for him. And I didn't see it. Right under my window, flying in my face, it was a snake that had wrapped itself around my leg, and I didn't feel it."

18

A Prison of Dreams

I never got the mystery that hides inside a man who's desired by a woman. Men are the easiest marks, prey just waiting to be caught. I would play with them. I knew how to seduce them, bring them up to the desire that's never satisfied, but I never surrendered myself. I never felt like surrendering. I always wanted them to try again. They were dirty, smelling from work, and they dripped with gold. My loyalty to Cleto was my not wanting to go to bed with other men, but I did other things. I'd play with them the way I'd play with dolls. I got pleasure out of showing myself, and out of the secret of letting them see me naked but closing their eyes out of fear. With Clément Tamba it went further. I let him kiss me, grip my flesh, feel the heat of it, fondle my breasts, and I was on the brink of giving in. But I would resist and not resist. I got a kind of seduction in knowing what I'd feel like after having him. I was afraid of being disgusted by him, by someone I liked, a friend of Cleto's, like a brother. But Tamba was a man with good manners, educated, pleasing, with touches of refinement and a gentleness toward women. I was happy when, knowing how I liked animals, he sent me a fawn that had been weaned, small and with the white spots beginning to appear on its brown skin. I gave it milk drawn from a cow-tree in the woods. The critter grew and with love I got it to eat out of my hand. And when I went into the back yard, wherever I went, it would follow me. Tamba would keep coming back with the excuse of seeing the animal and I knew it was a cover-up. Bonfim was afraid of getting jealous of me. Jealousy is something that grows in people like manioc. It grows at the roots, forms tubers, keeps on growing, draws the green out of the leaves and then dries up. When jealousy is pulled up the plant is dead. I've never known what it's like to be jealous. In the brothel all the men belonged to all the women and all the women belonged to all the men. Some women enjoyed the status of mistress. I quickly began taking on fewer customers, not because of my habit of not enjoying it, but as part of a plan. I was thinking about getting away from all that someday and having a man of my own. Not because of any love, but to belong to one man, because all women had to belong to one man. I'd never known what love was. That's why when I did see love I was scared. Why am I lying to myself, saying that I never belonged to Tamba? I did, in the backyard, inside the chicken house, the only way it could be, just a little, not taking too long. I didn't let him have me all the way and I was happy. I ran off, I'd only let him have a taste and I went running out and Clément was left all crazy worked up with his urge and begging:

"Come back, Saraminda."

I remember his foolish, drooling face. But I wasn't planning to do things any other way. He wanted more and so did I, but I wanted to respect Bonfim. I was careful about that with Clément. With other men I did and didn't just for the hell of it. With Tamba I had Cleto in the middle. There were people close by and I didn't want them to think about me the way they thought about my reputation, without ever having seen or proven anything about me.

I told Bonfim that he should let me be me, that he should let me be wanted by men, but that I belonged to him and only to him. I think all women tell men that they're the best loves in their lives. They swear to be faithful but never can live up to their oath. He accepted me that way, afraid of losing me, and was deceived until the day I called him back and said, "Jacques Kemper's not to leave the claim anymore, Cleto. It's not a question of his being a spy or anything like that. It's just that I've been wanting him."

I thought that under my spell he was going to suffer and kill me. I wanted to die. But he didn't understand and got desperate. He set five men to watching Kemper, had a reinforced shack built made of wild jackfruit trees, and held him there. I think he'd planned to kill him but changed his mind after I said, "If Kemper dies I'll kill myself."

Then he got scared and began to cry and I felt sorry for him.

110

"I'm not going to kill him, but I'm going to send him packing back to France. Under guard from here to Vila do Calçoene, to the Firmino docks where the ships tie up and put on a ship there to send him back to his own country."

"I'll kill myself then, too."

So Cleto decided to imprison him and I agreed, but with one condition: the jail would have to be in the backyard of the house and every day I would go see that he was alive. I wanted a crew of bodyguards to protect him, along with my dogs, who numbered more than five by then. I told Cleto that Kemper knew nothing about me, that I'd never talked to him about things between men and women, but I really couldn't keep my mind off him.

"Do you dream about him?" he asked.

I lied, "No, I don't. For me he's a pet animal that I want to keep tied up like a dog."

Cleto was happy when I mentioned dog. He answered, "He's a dog, a dog, a dog."

But I didn't lie saying I didn't dream about him. All my waking life was thinking about him, seeing his blue eyes entering my body and getting into me all over, turning me blue, changing me into light, satisfying me without satisfying me, just wanting to want. I was suffering. My nights were nothing but insomnia. But I never stopped receiving Bonfim. He owned me. He'd paid twenty pounds of gold for me. I'm not saying it was just for that, it was also because he'd got me into the habit. At those times I never thought that he was Kemper, but I began to ask Cleto to take a bath before he came to me and to put zinc oxide under his armpits and tree extract on his hair so the smell would be his, Cleto's, and not make me think of Kemper's smell.

I only went out in the little chair once, right after my throne arrived, along the pathways of the claim. I wanted to see the thirty-seven pound nugget that Li Yung the Chinaman had found. I got myself all prepared then, put on the dress from Paris, prettied myself up all over, got into the litter, lowered the curtains, and the two Saramaca men who worked for me carried it and I went down the slope by the house, along the paths between the quarries with the ravines below. The men all left their work on the claim and came to the edge of the path and I pulled the curtain back a bit, watching them. Bonfim was going in front and a bodyguard brought up the rear. They'd thought I was naked and I came close to shutting down the whole claim. When I got to Clément Tamba's zigzag sluiceway, I wanted to stop.

"It was near here the nugget was found," he said.

I saw then that the men realized I wasn't naked. We went into the shed. There was a dark room full of small kegs with jugs of gold and a strong door of *lignum vitae*, shut with a reinforced padlock and a keylock. Clément Tamba came to meet me.

"Thank you, Bonfim, for bringing Saraminda to see the Chinaman's nugget," and he took my hand like I was a queen and brought me into the dark room.

He showed me lots of respect. There was a long narrow table and two scales. When the door was opened it let in some light and you could just make things out. Clément Tamba lit a lantern and held it as high as his arm could reach and I saw the dirty stone, reddish in color, porous and half-covered with little holes.

"Is this the nugget?"

"Yes, Saraminda."

"It doesn't look like much, so ugly. It's got the look of dead gold."

"But it's the biggest nugget that's ever shown up in all the claims along these rivers, Saraminda."

I didn't think it was gold, it was so ugly, and then I got to understand that the beauty of gold is in men. That was when I got it into my head to tell Tamba:

"You and Cleto have spent your lives chasing gold and this Chinaman finds the biggest nugget and is going to have his name on it? You two should take it away from him."

"Take it away how, Saraminda?"

"I don't know. That's up to you people."

Outside you could hear the gold workers' loud talk. They were all waiting for the moment when Saraminda would come out. Clément felt a momentary urge to keep Li Yung's nugget, but he resisted the temptation. He wasn't made for that; that was something Celestino Gouveia would do.

I took another look at the nugget. I reached out my hand and pinched Tamba, adding just to play:

"Forget about it, Clément. It's ugly, fit for a Chinaman."

But that wasn't the only time I went out on the throne. I would go every day. I would fix myself up in the afternoon and get into it in the backyard. The Saramacas would take me to see Kemper, to see if he was still alive. My deal with Bonfim. I'd keep my distance, circle the prison. My heart beat hard every afternoon, looking at the trees that knew where I was going, that space that separated me from him. I'd get there, watch from a distance through the bars of the small door and see his shape. I didn't let him want for anything. One day I found out that he'd asked, "How many years have I been sentenced to?"

"Cleto's the one who knows that," Gedina answered. "Maybe twenty or so."

"Just because of the tear in Dona Saraminda's dress? I wasn't to blame for that." Then Kemper got to singing songs from Brittany in the hours before dawn. They came on mysteriously, from far off in the silence of the night, hitting my ears and sounding like pleas of love. When I began to hear them I got disgusted with Bonfim and began to think about it. Evil had penetrated my heart. I wasn't myself, and I wanted to free myself, free Kemper, and free myself from Bonfim by killing him.

Why did I have to kill Bonfim? I belonged to him, he appreciated me, he made me the most famous woman in the valley of the Calçoene. He knew all about the stories going around and the tales they were telling about me. I wouldn't have the nerve to kill him.

"What are they talking about, Gedina?"

"The beauty of your body, your eyes, how your dogs are possessed by the devil."

"My skin, do they know what it's like?"

"No, they don't know."

"My Indian blood, my bare parts, have they ever made remarks about them?"

"No, Dona Saraminda."

"So spread the word, Gedina, say what they're like, talk about my breasts. Let those people go on imagining. I'd like that."

"But I don't talk about you, ma'am."

"Well, start talking. Keep on looking, Gedina. Look at me so you can tell them."

"God spare me! I'll never tell anything of what I see."

"Well, you just describe me to anyone who asks what I'm like."

And I stroked the dog Tupã, scratched his belly, and he lay down and rolled over. I spoke:

"Talk, Gedina. Say what I'm like. Look at me."

"I won't look, Dona Saraminda, it's too much beauty for my head."

Bonfim gave me everything. All I had to do was ask and he gave. But he also collected. I'd thought that happiness would be getting out of the brothel. But it wasn't. Bonfim didn't give me what I knew women needed: a man they have a passion for. Now I was seeing that he was ugly. I didn't like his goatee. So I realized I didn't like him. He'd got me stuck in the jungle surrounded by rotting people, their legs swollen from the slosh of the water, yellow with fever, dropping from sickness.

Almost all the claim was at the base of the mountain below which the mystery of the water and the gold is hidden.

When I got there I looked at the valley; thousands of people, just like ants, hunting for gold. Cleto had more than five hundred under his orders. They all worked on a commission basis. Of the gold they collected, thirty percent belonged to them, five percent went to Celestino and his men who kept watch over the work, and the rest was for Bonfim. But they all worked with tools that belonged to Cleto. Only he could be the owner, a way of enslaving all of them. He owned the scrimmers, shovels, hoes, machetes and sluices. Accounts were settled at the end of the week, but the gold was weighed every day in the owner's warehouse.

At four o'clock on Saturday afternoon the claim closed down. They all went to wash their clothes, which weren't pressed because there weren't any irons on the claim. So with their washed clothes they went to the settlements and the bars. There the *cachaça* flowed amidst the dancing and swaying and everything else. But they didn't take women to the huts because they were all open. They did it in the woods, like animals. An evil-looking bunch, the lot of them. Bonfim always said, "Diggers are people who've got accounts to settle. Where there's plenty of drink and plenty of women a lot of things can happen. They lose their heads and then desire, greed and jealousy take over and bring on trouble. They kill somebody and run away to the diggings. They steal and they run away to the diggings."

But there's no law or authority on the claim. If someone commits a crime he's punished right there, and the punishment is death. And the men, dirty, sick, syphilitic, smelling of gonorrhea, full of cooties and crabs that get into their scrotums. When they got too skinny, hunched over and yellow, Bonfim would say to himself, "He's got a dose of clap." And he'd send them to Vila do Calçoene for a shot.

The women used dishcloth gourd tea to induce abortions and not get their bellies full. Some of them would have remains left over and would take Agua Inglesa to clean themselves out and even so a lot of them died. Even when they were sick the men would mount them with that damned urge that gets hold of them on the claim because there are no women around. In their sad state any woman would do. She could be old, ugly, pretty, young or a whore. Otherwise all that was left to the men was to beat their meat.

The life I had in me when I first got there was gone. A kind of sadness was growing inside that was killing me. I was a prisoner. The impenetrable jungle, mysterious and endless with all its dangers, hanging heavy on me. The vines that twisted around one another, all sizes and thicknesses, hung down from the trees, swinging, looking like something alive. The land snakes and the ones in the swamps, with the black alligators and the anacondas that wait along the paths to the gold veins and when someone trips on their journey wrap around him, crack his bones and swallow him, covering his body with a scum they lick onto it, opening their mouths, dislocating their jaws, and taking in any living thing. And how scared I am of the rattlesnakes that bite and make people start to piss red, the color of wine! Even the sweet things can kill you, from the booze that gets you drunk to the thorns on the *iruparipina* plant that are more full of poison than a snake's fangs. Poisonous plants, the *andá*, the *timbo*, the *cunambi*, the sandbox. There's danger all around.

The claim was one great big case of loneliness. When you look at it, it's like something out of this world. Gold hasn't got any smell. If it did men would go sniffing around and find out where it is. The smell came from the soil and the soil was filthy because of the gold. The gold disgusted me. I'd have given everything I had to go back to the brothel, get five francs and nothing more. But Bonfim and his craziness got me into the habit of being a regular woman and that made a slave of me. I was already starting to wait. I was already beginning to hurt. All my desires had gotten deep into my body like rheumatism, and I couldn't resist. But I was a regular swamp of silence, stagnant water, fenced in with no way out, destined to rot there, full of two-toned caladiums and being just another purple flower with its roots in the rotten-smelling muck. I had to hold a handkerchief with camphor to my nose. It was around that time, in the middle of all that darkness, that I saw Kemper's blue eyes. And they opened up a window for me to go back to being alive.

I wanted to go away. Why kill Bonfim? Go away and take Kemper along. But how could I go away? I had everything and I had nothing. I couldn't even get to the end of the road that leads to the Oh-My-God Marsh to pick up the trail to the dock at Vila do Calçoene. How could I escape from a prison that's surrounded by nothingness, emptiness? And what about Kemper? He'd be the first to die. Bonfim wouldn't have to kill him, or Celestino either. All that was needed was some half-breed under his orders to cut his throat. Just thinking about it made me scream, cry, pull my hair, and Gedina found me like that.

"Dona Saraminda, what's come over you? By the Holy Virgin!"

And I dropped to the floor of my house and only then did I feel that I wasn't Saraminda anymore but a poor calf tied up and on its way to the slaughterhouse. It was then that I thought about the Paris dress and I got suspicious that it might be bad *juju* someone had ordered against me. And I said to Gedina:

"Go bring me a can of kerosene because I've got to make a bonfire."

But first I got into the dress, stroked it, kissed it, saw Kemper's eyes and I spent hours dressed up, sitting on my *maçaranduba* stool. Then I undressed, went into the backyard, and laid the dress out like a woman lying down. I was seeing myself there with my own eyes, there on the ground, wrapped up in my death. I went to get a sheet. I covered it all up and stayed there mourning myself. In my head the flames of displeasure flared up and I felt relief in my soul, as though I'd been sleeping in a spell.

"What a pretty dress, Saraminda. It's wonderful, more splendid than the purple Lenten trees at Easter time. See how it shines. It's got all the colors of the night. No, Saraminda, why burn it? Keep it. It's got nothing to do with your fate. See Kemper's hands sewing

116

up the tear, his eyes looking away, looking at your breasts, thinking about your body. Don't burn Kemper, Saraminda."

"No, I'm not going to burn it anymore. It's mine. It might have brought me trouble but I want to get dressed in the trouble that came from Kemper's hands. This dress is him. It crossed the ocean. It came from Paris."

I was talking to myself. The woodpecker on the trunk of an *anajá* tree called me out of it. He did it again, moved quickly, stopped and pecked, calling attention once more.

"What the devil's going on, Saraminda?"

It was the voice of Bonfim.

I woke up out of my delirium. My dress, my spell. Now I wanted to die dressed in it, lying in the coffin, clutching with my hands crossed over my chest the breast of that dress that wasn't the dress. It was the present that Kemper had brought me from Paris.

"Nothing, Bonfim. I'm seeing what it's going to be like when I die. I want to be buried in my dress from Paris."

But I was really saying that I wanted to be buried with Kemper. He didn't hear that. A thrush was singing on a branch of the bean tree that was full of small beans. On the ground was the wild maracock with its red flower. Zeca the rooster crowed. A gust of wind broke off a dry branch that went rolling across the yard. Bonfim asked me again, "What's this all about, woman?"

I woke up and fell asleep again with my eyes open, sunk in my delirium. All of a sudden I became afraid. I looked at Bonfim. He seemed to be reading everything I was thinking, and I was going to ask him to forgive me. His hand lifted up a heavy club to split open my head with all his strength and the pieces of my betrayal would appear on the ground, the chestnuts of my perdition.

"What's this all about, woman?"

I grabbed everything, dress, sheet, and ran to my bedroom. Bonfim was standing stock-still.

"What in hell is eating you, Saraminda?"

117

19

A Caged Breton

Why has my fate come to this end? I left Cancale, abandoned my mother so I could get away from my stepfather. I flew the coop. Could this be my punishment? I loved my mother but I was jealous of her. My father was dead and I felt that by having another man my mother was betraying my father. I abandoned her out of too much love, not out of hate. I couldn't remain in that house. I was afraid I'd kill my stepfather. My mother saw that. There wasn't room for both of us. Paris was a place of relaxation and happiness until the day Foucaud sent me to Cayenne. From the day I arrived I sensed that the women in these parts have a mystery about them. The tropical heat was already getting into my soul. Then there was Cayenne and Laurence telling me: "Look at the shield of Guiana here…two great anteaters…with their big claws grabbing everything" and "I'm not leaving your room until I have a look at the dress." The afternoon at the boardinghouse, the smell of that woman, the fervor of her desires, the wild madness of her ways, and my not knowing what was coming, afraid of fever, but what would kill me would be the spell of those females. My arrival on the claim, the noble impression made by the River Calçoene, its banks alternating between jungle and plains, rapids and waterfalls; the wild animals, the tapir, the jaguar, the possum, the armadillo, the otter, the *agouti*. The nights in the jungle with the birds singing all together at dusk, their voices getting louder, coming down out of the trees and going back up again, blending with the sunset and the oncoming black cloak and, in a flash, all of it ceasing at the same time in a contrast of sounds, from clamor to silence, a silence so strong that nothing can be heard, not the wind, not the water, not the plants. The solitude of those nights in the middle of a lost world made of dead leaves hurts the bones. Then the shock of the claim, the destitution, an army of men digging in the earth, cracking rocks, tossing remnants into sieves, and everything dirty, the smell of muggy armpits and the deafening buzz of the drive for *la couleur*.

The difficult trip bringing the coach and the dress, going up the river, dragging the canoes over land to get past the rapids, proceeding on land, carrying loads and then putting them back on board, taking them off and putting them on, alternating between river and trail, covering the distance up to the mountains that rise up after the Grand Dégrad. My introduction to Cleto Bonfim.

"Mr. Cleto, I'm Jacques Kemper. I've come in the name of the Société Française de l'Amérique Equatoriale to bring the shipment of the carriage for your wife and I'm also the bearer of a gift the president has sent out of respect for you, our customer: a dress from the Maison d'Amour for Madame Bonfim."

How many times had I already gone over those words written by Mr. Lefèvre, already with Mrs. Bonfim's name, afraid of making a mistake.

My surprise when I saw Mr. Bonfim, skinny and lean, with a goatee, and around his neck that string of long nuggets, his eel eyes, an ignorant and crude man who didn't even say hello and immediately began to say coarse things in Creole only half of which I understood.

"Leave those things here. I'm waiting to see that cabriolet or whatever it is. You can take the dress to my wife when we go up to the house. Take off your jacket and stay in shirtsleeves, that's no way to dress for a man here on the claim. This is a place for real men and not dandies."

I'd prepared myself for the mission, to be a person of importance, the representative of the Société Equatoriale, and I'd made an effort in that heat to bear up under those clothes, which I'd carefully packed on the trip, following rivers and roads that I never thought existed.

"Have a seat and wait for me."

I sat there from eleven in the morning until four in the afternoon, watching people come in and go out, weighing gold, receiving vouchers, and he didn't even offer me a glass of water or have them give me something to eat.

"You'll sleep in Celestino Gouveia's hut tonight. He's my foreman. You can get some grub there."

What a rude man. He didn't know what manners were. He only knew how to be rough.

When I got to the house and happened to meet Dona Saraminda I could see that she was a seductive woman. A different, strange type. She had provocative eyes that I didn't dare look into. They were green, her face was dark, her hair straight. A bewitching woman. And already afraid of Bonfim, I became even more afraid of his wife.

"What's your name, Mr. Frenchman?" she asked with that soft voice smoother than perfumed oil pouring over my body.

"Jacques, Jacques Kemper. I've brought this present for you from President Foucaud of our firm."

"Have a seat, Mr. Kemper."

"Thank you. Here's the consignment, Mr. Bonfim," I addressed the husband. "My mission is completed."

And I handed over the dress. Then she ordered, "Open the box, Mr. Kemper."

Cleto Bonfim was a different man now. In her presence he was about as high as the floor. He was smiling, looking into her eyes, following her reactions as I undid the wrapping. She was watching my movements closely. And the most unexpected moment in my fate arose. I untied the wide pink ribbon and began to take out the greenish paper decorated with red and yellow flowers. Then the box appeared, lined with white taffeta and in it, wrapped in tissue paper, was the dress rolled up.

"Open the paper, Mr. Kemper."

I was overcome with horror and fright when my eyes saw a different dress, not the one I'd brought. Laurence had switched them! She'd gone back to my rooms and pulled her little trick. The she-devil.

"Oh!" was all I managed to exclaim and I felt the blood rising to my head, my eyes growing dim, my hands trembling, and I was taken by a panic that was burning my body and my soul.

"Oh what, Mr. Frenchman?" Bonfim asked, waking me from my stupor.

"How beautiful!" Saraminda said. "Take it out of the box, hold it up, let me see it."

I don't know how I managed to do it. It was a red dress with a lace neckline, long, round half-sleeves with edges in light blue ruffles. It was one piece, with a round skirt over two starched petticoats to keep its balance and a bodice decorated with cheap sequins. At the waist there was a set of bows at the end of a long stripe that came down from the neckline and stopped there. Saraminda, who'd never worn any fancy clothes, was delighted. I could see right away that it was too big for her and I remembered seeing in it the crazy Mrs. Lefèvre who'd brought about this calamity. My fear was that Saraminda would notice that it didn't have the smell of a new dress, of having come from far away, or that it wasn't a work of art. But she understood nothing about dresses and was quite happy. She looked at it, ran her hands over it, and, in one of those moments, her hands slipped across mine as though she was giving me some kind of woman's signal. And her green eyes invaded mine with an expression that I didn't know but which burned like fire.

"May I leave now, Mr. Bonfim?"

"No, Mr. Kemper, have some coffee and Pilar cookies, made in Brazil," Saraminda said.

I don't know how I got the coffee down. Bonfim didn't scare me anymore. My fear was of Saraminda. Early the next morning I began my trip back, part of an expedition which, like so many each day that left or returned, was taking out gold and bringing back supplies. When we were at the Oh-My-God Marsh, trying to make our way through the sludge, a troop of horses could be heard. One of them carried a brawny half-breed with a huge moustache, a wide-brimmed hat, a revolver at his waist, and the booming voice of a bad man: "Where's the Frenchman?"

"Here I am, what's the matter?" And I thought, "I'm done for."

"My boss Mr. Cleto gave orders for you to come back with me."

"Has he got something against me?"

"I don't know. It has to do with a package you brought him."

I immediately thought of the dress. "They found out that the dress I brought isn't new. Dona Saraminda must not have liked it and she's sending it back." I saw at once the complications in my life that were gathering. "The very least of it will be my ending up in Maroni Prison," I consoled myself, so I wouldn't think about the beating and the death I'd get from Bonfim. "Can it be that he's jealous of me and didn't like his wife's ways when she was near me?" What was for sure was that I went back.

Bonfim greeted me by shouting, "You brought my wife a torn dress. Who ordered that insult?"

"I never saw the dress. I'm just an employee of the firm assigned to bring an order. My boss wanted me to accompany the coach and he had me bring the dress. I never saw what was in the box," I said, lying. "I think it must be a defect from the store that sold it."

"Well, you can talk to Saraminda and explain it."

I was afraid that when the dress was returned, Mr. Foucaud would see the item, realize it was another dress, and I wouldn't be able to explain the switch.

Saraminda came out of her room, looked at me, broke into a happy smile, and acted the way she had when she'd faced me the first time.

"The dress is torn in back, Mr. Kemper."

She called me over and showed me the place, quite close to the opening that was closed with cloth-covered buttons and looped buttonholes. I knew nothing about dresses and she was talking to me as if I were a dressmaker. "See, here, right here," and her head almost brushed against mine.

"If you're not pleased, ma'am, I can take it back and the Société will send another. It won't take long. We want you to be satisfied. I don't know how to explain this defect. The fashion shop that made the dress is the best in Paris."

"No, Mr. Kemper. I want you to darn the tear here at home. The dress isn't leaving."

Now how could I get that done? Then with a certain male feeling I was sure that it was an excuse she'd concocted. She'd cut the dress herself and had me sent for, so I wouldn't go away. What a devilishly tricky woman. As if Laurence hadn't been enough, now this other one wanting to lasso me, in the middle of all those violent people, right smack in the heart of the jungle, fenced in by the hell of that mining claim.

Cleto Bonfim settled it:

"Fixing it is women's business. Arrange things with her. I'm going to the warehouse."

And he warned me:

"Get it fixed right, Mr. Frenchman, everything Saraminda wants, if not…"

And he left.

"Look here, Mr. Kemper, right here…"

It was Saraminda starting to show me the cut as soon as Bonfim went down the stairs, and she bent over in an attempt to reveal her unfettered breasts, with nothing to hold them back onto her smooth and shining chest.

"I've seen it already, Dona Saraminda. It's a simple job that won't leave any mark."

"Maruanda, go to the kitchen and get some coffee and Pilar cookies for the young man."

Maruanda went off. Then she said to me with the singsong voice of a breathless siren:

"Look at me, Mr. Kemper, with your blue eyes."

I've never told anyone the other business. Saraminda went into the bedroom and came back with an article of clothing:

"Look, Mr. Kemper, look how happy your present has made me. Now I know it came from you." And she showed me some panties, cream-colored lingerie embroidered with pale flowers, pink and lilac.

"Thank you very much. You came to make me happy," and she lifted up the item and smelled it, as if it were a flower.

I became quite perplexed. I couldn't figure out what was going on. "Laurence," I thought. "She not only switched dresses, but she put in that intimate article to complicate my mission and get a laugh at the Société's present." And I shook even more.

Saraminda drew closer. The east wind was blowing through the window, carrying a smell of cinnamon. Then, after a short sigh, she spoke:

"Kiss me, Mr. Kemper, kiss me. I'm crazy for you."

I almost fainted. I didn't say anything and I didn't know if I had enough breath left to do so. "Kiss me, Mr. Kemper…"

"Put the dress back in the box, Dona Saraminda. I'm going to take it back."

What if the Saramaca maidservant should come back? What if

she'd seen what Saraminda was up to? What if she'd heard what she said? What if Bonfim had begun to suspect that tale about the torn dress? What would happen?

"No, Mr. Kemper. That dress is like gold for me. It's a present from you."

"No, ma'am, it's from the Société."

"Société? Who's the Société? Kiss me, Mr. Kemper... Kiss me..."

Maruanda came in. Saraminda turned cross.

"You stay in the kitchen. Come back here only when I call you."

Outside on the living room verandah was the helper Zerido, whom Cleto had left with me.

"Don't talk so loud, Dona Saraminda, there's someone on the porch, the boy Mr. Cleto told to stay with me."

"I know, but I'm talking in a low voice."

And she opened her blouse all the way and showed me her breasts. Good God, that sight will stay with me until the day I die. They had yellow, gleaming, phosphorescent nipples, like gold. They didn't make you want to touch or even kiss them, but to kneel before them.

"Kiss me, Mr. Kemper..."

I wanted to run, to disappear, my throat was dry. I'd lost my voice. Going out onto the verandah I told the boy, "Take me back."

When I got there Bonfim asked me, "What did Dona Saraminda say?"

"That the dress is torn and I'm going to sew it up."

"Did she give it to you?"

"No."

"You're a damned fool. If you're going to sew it up, where's the dress?"

"She has it."

"I'm going to get to the bottom of this story. Zerido, take the Frenchman to spend the night at Celestino's place. I'll talk to him tomorrow."

Night was already falling. I walked to Celestino's place as if it were the last night of my life. I don't know what happened. I didn't see Cleto Bonfim anymore. That same night I was made prisoner in a room with walls of upright boards through which you could see everything going on around, guarded by two men who would go with me when I went through the clearing in the woods to the trench where I took care of my needs. Then I found out that the guards weren't there to stop me from running away but to make sure that nobody would kill me, in line with the agreement Bonfim had made with Saraminda.

The days passed without my knowing what was going on, not even the reasons for my imprisonment. I can't say that Celestino Gouveia was cruel to me. Quite the contrary, he was the only person who felt sorry for me at that time. He would visit me and try to find out what had happened. I was reluctant to tell him about the tear in the dress so that Cleto wouldn't find out that I was telling secrets about him. At that time he still hadn't felt jealous of her.

"Bonfim is a hard man, Mr. Kemper, a difficult person."

"Do you know why I'm being kept prisoner, Celestino?"

"I don't. They said that you brought some orders that Cleto had made for Saraminda in Paris and that you'd stolen half of them."

"Me, Celestino? I brought the carriage he ordered and a present they sent for his wife. I delivered everything."

"Then it's something else. Maybe it has to do with accounts with the company in France, business affairs, and he's holding you as a hostage. I believe you. I don't see that you've got the face of a thief."

Stories were going around about my imprisonment all over the claim. They said I'd been disrespectful to Cleto and he didn't like it, that the carriage was ugly and he'd decided to hold me there until another one came, and—the most worrisome version—that I hadn't shown Dona Saraminda respect, telling her that she didn't know anything about fashion.

What's certain is that I spent two weeks there. One night they came for me. I thought it was to kill me. They took me to a different prison, through the clearings in the woods. It was better, next to a water hole, even though there was an outhouse that stank everything up. But the walls were made of crossed boards and you could see from the inside out and from the outside in. A hammock had been hung from the braces; beside it were a pair of slippers and a chamber pot. When dawn came I saw the sunlight entering faintly. The maidservant arrived early, bringing coffee and some Pilar cookies.

"Where am I?"

Only then did I find out that my prison was in the woods behind the house of Bonfim and Saraminda.

20

A Note In Rounded Letters

One night right after my arrival in the new jail the maidservant Maruanda called to me. It had grown completely dark and the only light came from a small kerosene lamp I kept lit in the corner.

"Mr. Kemper, Mr. Kemper..."

"Who's calling me?"

"It's me, Maruanda. My mistress, Dona Saraminda, sent me to say she was the one who wanted you kept prisoner here, near her, that nothing bad's going to happen to you and that she's only waiting for Mr. Cleto to go on a trip to Vila do Firmino by the Calçoene docks so she can come visit you. She told me to tell you that she never wanted anybody the way she's wanted you."

"What kind of trick is the lady planning for me?"

"It's just what I told you, Mr. Kemper. And Dona Saraminda knows what she wants. She's got plans for you. I'm going to unlock the padlock and give you a note she sent. She said for you to read it, give it back to me, and for me to burn it in the lamp."

Maruanda came in. It had been so long since I'd had the smell of a woman that in the half-light I thought she might be capable of breaking my solitude. I looked at her eyes. She was around thirty and had kept the pretty, delicate face of light-skinned blacks.

At that moment I thought about escaping for the first time. Running away, getting out of that senseless tangle and going into the forest, without knowing where, loose, to die in the midst of the dangers there, but free of that anguish. The maid looked to be a good accomplice. I needed to seduce her, ask her for help, make her a partner in my adventure. But could I trust her? It would be a job that called for time and all my skills.

"Sit here, Maruanda. I'm so alone," I told her, letting her know that I was flirting.

"Here's the note, Mr. Kemper."

I opened it, hoping there would be some clue about my getting out, the conditions for my release, the reason for my imprisonment. There was none of that. It was a message written in childish, round letters, one line: "Kiss me, Kemper, kiss me, Kemper, kiss me, Kemper," and an addition, "Three times." I folded the paper, more confused than ever, and gave it back to the maidservant, who went over to the lamp and burned it.

"Maruanda," I asked her again, "sit here."

She sat on the floor.

"Tell me about your life. I need someone to talk about something, anything, even just a few words."

"I can't stay very long. Dona Saraminda always knows everything and I'm going to have to tell her everything."

"That's fine. Tell her everything. Tell her that you gave me the note and that I cried. Lie to her. That I said I only think about her, that she's the most attractive woman I've ever seen, that she's enchanting. For her to get me out of here, send me to Cayenne, and for her to come later so I'll be with her there."

"She knows all about everything and she can see things. Nobody can trick her."

"All I want from now on is not to be left all by myself, not knowing what's going to happen to me. And starting right now I'll have a reason for watching time pass, waiting for night to come and for Maruanda to talk to me. Tell me about your life."

She told me, "I was born in Maroni, right near the Saint-Jean prison. I heard stories about the rotten luck of prisoners, the poor devils who came to die in Guiana. My father was a prison guard. A person sentenced in France for up to eight years would serve his time, spend eight more years free in Guiana, and then go back to France. A person sentenced for more than eight years served his time here but couldn't go back to France again. They were freed, but none of them went back. The prison would fill up when the ships with criminals arrived, but they'd soon be empty because a lot of them died of fever, sickness and filth. I could never get up the courage to look at those people. My father died of a fever he caught there, too."

"I don't want to listen to the sad part. Tell me what Cayenne is like."

"I came here brought by Mr. Bonfim. I worked for him. When Dona Saraminda became the lady of his house, his mistress, he brought me over to be her servant. At first he'd make me his woman when he came in drunk. Then he didn't want me anymore. Saraminda liked my work and made me her maidservant. She promised to give me a house in Cayenne and a couple of pounds of gold. But she's a depraved woman. I never saw anything like it. All day and all night. She wants to grab every man she sees. But she doesn't go to bed right away, she turns hard to get, they go crazy wild, the way it happened to Mr. Bonfim. She acts that way because she's a different kind of female. All you have to do is look at her breasts. If she was like us she'd have taken a lot of beating by now."

"When did you come to the claim?"

"When I got here Mr. Bonfim already owned the whole works. He's always been in this business. He came here by portage from Roraima and had already been through a lot. But hunting for gold is a mania. People get rich, they stay at the gold vein and never quit. They're never satisfied. They dig out the gold and then they always want to find a new claim. A dead claim is the most horrible thing in the world. It's nothing but a big hole, dry brush, and leftover gravel, and the ghosts of diggers who've died."

"Do a lot of people die?"

"As many as die in Maroni Prison. The gold has an owner. Every day the men have to give *cachaça* to the gullies. Then the gullies get drunk and let you grab the gold. From so much drinking they gullies peter out and so does the gold. Then the claim dies and it's nothing but bad luck. All kinds of things happen on the claim."

"Fights?"

"A lot of the men end up dirt poor. The misery on the claim isn't just the gold, it's the loneliness. It's a living tomb. We rot away in the holes they've dug *la couleur* out of. Every digger lives a life of suffering and once he's in it he can't get out. When they tell stories about their good luck they're lying. The one who makes money isn't the one who digs out the gold, it's the one who buys it.

Mr. Bonfim began to buy gold and he's got more money than he's got room for. What good is it? He eats what we eat, drinks what we drink, lives where we live, and he works harder than we work." She stopped for a moment and then went on: "He left Cameta as a child, went down one river and up another until he got to Roraima. He went to a dead claim. The only thing left were the holes there full of greenish water, everything else mud, and the jungle growing in between the piles of stone and what was left of the ravines, with a broken cross here and there, the sign of someone's death. There's no name and if anyone should holler to scare away some lost soul, some spirit, his shout would run across the clearing and go into the jungle, blowing along, sounding like the wind. So in that mania of his for gold, Mr. Cleto, along with some companions, went about opening a claim there in a strip by the border with Venezuela. The claim was producing, but from what I heard him tell, there were a lot of Indians around. Every day the Indians would kill a digger with an arrow and every day a digger would kill an Indian with a bullet. They decided to abandon the claim and go portaging through the jungle. Mr. Bonfim was born with the gift of gold. Gold doesn't stink and it can't be tracked by dogs, but Mr. Bonfim's nose seems to be able to sniff out gold. People like that live caught up in the jungle, with no set direction, looking for gold. He only carried a *terçado*, a long iron tool to dig into the ground and expose the soil, an iron bowl, a jug of ointment, the gold pan and a shotgun, gunpowder, flour, salt, and quinine and nitrate pills for fever. That was how Mr. Bonfim got to the claim on the Chiqueirão, in Maracaçumé, in Maranhão."

Maruanda interrupted her story:

"Look, Mr. Kemper, time's passing and Dona Saraminda's waiting for me. I'll tell you the rest later."

Kemper had listened to every word of the Saramaca woman as if he were reading an adventure book. It had been several weeks since he knew what talking was, much less reading. He'd seen no books anywhere there. He looked at Maruanda again. His eyes passed like a ray of light over her body. The semi-darkness filled out her figure and he undressed her in his thoughts.

"Come back tomorrow, Maruanda. You've given me so much pleasure. I liked talking to you. Don't forget to lie to Saraminda. She's got to be on my side."

"She's not on your side. She's on top of you," she replied in a mischievous voice.

Kemper didn't sleep. He heard the first birds singing with the sounds of the night and only by morning did he become aware of his insomnia and get up, pondering his fate. That was when he heard the heavy, thunderous bark of Leão, Saraminda's most faithful dog.

21

A Love for Dogs

Her liking for dogs began when Saraminda had finished her house. From the start she hadn't wanted to be all alone with her maids and the guards.

"I want you to get me a dog, Cleto, an animal I can pet and love. Not one of the kind they have around here. I want a special dog for myself."

So he sent to Vila do Firmino for a dog, purchased from an old settler. It was skinny, with upright ears and half a tail, Quati by name. He was considered a good watchdog, barking a lot and not tolerant of strangers. The reports about him were good. Quati arrived held by an old rope that went from his throat along a stick two feet long which in turn was attached to another cord at the other end and held by the person leading him. This system was to prevent him from going into the woods and it made controlling him easier. Quati arrived from the trip panting. Saraminda wasn't pleased when she saw him.

"I'm not too fond of the color gray."

"Dona Saraminda, when he gets older and fatter he'll change color. He's a good dog, you can trust in that," they said.

Saraminda ordered him bathed, tied up in the backyard and fed, and then she made her decision.

"That name Quati is an ugly one. Change it to Tupã, thunder. A *coati* is a little critter with a bony behind and when it farts it whistles worse than a human being." And she finished her orders: "After you give Tupã a bath, bring him here."

An extraordinary thing happened. When the dog got next to her he stopped, lay down, shook his front paws, lowered his head to the ground and began to snore.

"Let him sleep, he's tired," she said.

When she made a movement to get up, he awoke and went with, following her everywhere. He was docile, but when anyone came close to her he would go into a rage and would only calm down when Saraminda shouted, "Tupã, stop!"

Even Cleto was careful with him:

"Ass-kissing mutt. All he does is suck up to Saraminda."

Sometime later Saraminda made a request: "Tupã can't be left all alone, Cleto. I want you to buy me five more dogs."

And Cleto began sending porters out after dogs. Everybody on the claim was talking about Dona Saraminda's mania and how she wanted dogs and more dogs. The five dogs arrived and she asked for another five and then five more. Vila do Firmino didn't have any more dogs of the kind Cleto wanted so they went to get them in Cayenne and Belém. Cleto hired a dog specialist who began to scout out places seeking to buy them.

Saraminda had gotten news of an old retired ship's captain in Cayenne who was the owner of the most beautiful dogs in the city—greyhounds, mastiffs, bulldogs and a pair of Belgian shepherds, one white and one black. She went on obsessively and wouldn't talk about anything else.

"Cleto, now I want you to send for a dog that's not a local one, but a thoroughbred, and I know there must be some in Cayenne."

Bonfim made inquiries, sent people, and finally did everything to acquire the captain's dogs, paying a pound of gold for them. That was when Clément Tamba chided him, "Cleto, old friend, stop this foolish business with dogs. Do something about Saraminda."

"Clément, my friend, it makes her happy. All women have got some kind of desire. Hers is for dogs, that's better than some other kinds."

Her dogs had names that only she knew how to choose.

Saraminda told Cleto, "I want the biggest dog in the world!"

Cleto sent a messenger to Cayenne carrying a letter asking them to find out from France for him which was the biggest dog in the world.

"Look, my love, here's the answer. The biggest dog in the world is what they call a Rhodesian ridgeback, an African lion dog."

"Cleto, send for a Rhodesian lion dog. I want a Rhodesian lion. Kiss me, Cleto, kiss me!"

Saraminda would stay in the yard under the trees with her dogs all around her, stroking the head of one and then another. The waterfall where she bathed was a mile or so from the house. It was on the Saringuê Creek that came down along the forest slopes, landed on the stones, and from some fifteen feet high leaped onto a dark slab where it split into small streams that came together down below on the way to the diggings, furnishing water to break up the gravel that fed the sluices.

Saraminda would always go there before lunch, around ten in the morning. She would take off her clothes and go under the waterfall with the dogs all around guarding the banks, alert and on watch. No one came near.

Saraminda began her bath with her hair. She would put out her hand to test the water temperature and wet the back of her neck, then the soles of her feet, keeping her body dry. Then she would put her head under the waterfall and move her shoulders from one side to the other. After that she would turn around, stick out her buttocks, and let the water fall hard on them and run down her thighs and legs. It was like a dance. Only toward the end would she turn around to face the falls, letting the water drop between her breasts, which she protected by fanning out her hands so the water wouldn't sting. Then she would spread her legs for better balance, put her stomach forward, lift her head, and watch the water massage her flesh. She exposed herself completely, as though she wanted the water to strike her daringly, and when it seemed like it was done she would withdraw her hands from her breasts and place them under her private parts. Then she would spread her arms with her hands open and move her body forward and backward, absorbing the pleasure of the bath. She would drop her head back slowly, her eyes looking up at the tops of the trees and the sky, her eyelids half-closed to protect her from the brightness. The dogs would bark and she would keep her eyes closed, resting as if she were asleep among the dogs and the song of the bellbirds. She never allowed anyone to go with her. It was a solitary ritual, all by herself, finding delight with her body.

When she came out of the waterfall Saraminda would go to the bank of the stream to a platform where there was a tub made of a barrel cut in half. In it she placed the boiled herbs she had brought from the house in her Marajo gourd, painted black and decorated on the rim with a design of flowers and leaves in red. She filled the tub with water, mixed in the herbs, and then opened a small basket that held basil, *pipirioca*, lavender, sweet fennel, rose petals, rosewood chips and cloves, putting them all in.

As soon as the leaves gave off their perfume, she would slowly draw out the water with a delicate touch and slight gestures and pour it over her head and whole body. The aroma clung to her all over. She adored her scented bath.

On other occasions she would vary the mixture, mingling patchouli and mint with the same herbs in a bottle of alcohol for two weeks, time enough for it to ripen. Once her body was dry, she would pour the contents of the bottle over her head, sighing and enjoying the scent of her flesh, more secret than the odor of the night.

Afterwards she would sit on a stool which had been made from the trunk of a thick tree cut cylindrically, and she would let herself be caressed by the breeze, by the heat, by the light, by the mystery.

Everybody knew about her bath, but no one would risk watching her and being devoured by the dogs.

Only once was she disturbed. The dogs barked and ran to the foot of a large *tamboril* tree with a broad crown. Up there was Clément Tamba. Saraminda came over to see what was going on. The dogs stopped barking and she looked up into the tree and saw Tamba, who was embarrassed. Saraminda, lit by the rays filtered through the crown of the *tamboril*, said, "Clément, if you wanted to see me you didn't have to take such a risk. You should have asked me and I would've shown myself."

"Save me, Saraminda. Call off the dogs."

"No. You come down. They won't do anything to you."

In the solitude of her body she was like a beast of the jungle. Her Creole flesh was smooth, starched, without any folds or wrinkles. It wasn't the deep, opaque black of the Boni. In her the Breton, Jewish, Indian and Bantu blood that had mingled over the centuries was concentrated in her eyes, had thinned her lips, lengthened her neck, and given her good luck and a seductive air.

Clément came down, trembling, unable to enjoy the sight of Saraminda's nakedness.

"Kiss me, Tamba, and be on your way. I don't like your spying on me here."

The dogs went off barking, their eyes turned toward the sun. The splashing of the waterfall mingled with Saraminda's sighs.

Clément left by the path filthy with creeping plants and Saraminda returned by the wide road, tugging on Tupã's leash. The other dogs trotted along in front, among the chickens that flew off and the tortoises that slowly crossed the yard that had been cleared of *cueira* and tamarind leaves.

In the house of shadows the milling of memories fed the phantoms.

"Clément, old friend, did you ever see Saraminda naked?"

Clément Tamba lowered his head and began to weep. Lucy heard his sobs, which filled the old planked corridor, and saw his hands over his face, almost in despair. She asked him:

"Why are you crying, Clément?"

"I'm tired of living. Look at Cleto Bonfim here. There's no end to him."

"Did you see Saraminda, Clément?"

"No, I never saw her," and he began to cry again. "Let's not talk about those times, Bonfim. I suffered too much. That fellow Cabral made me abandon my house, everything that was mine, and made me a fugitive from a place that I'd cleared, that I'd worked and fought for. I didn't want any Brazilian land. I wanted to live there, but Cabral was a fanatic. We French should have killed him. But we didn't love France and France forgot us."

"Answer me again, Clément. Did you ever see Saraminda?"

"I saw her, Cleto, if you must know, I saw her. She was as beautiful as a moon goddess covered by dark clouds!"

"You betrayed me, old friend."

"No. I even thought of taking her away from you. Forbidden love is a curse, old friend. But it wasn't like that. It was desire, an animal thing. It flew off with the wind."

"Cursed be my old friend Clément! I can only stand hearing these things because I'm dead."

"No, Bonfim. I never had Saraminda. She wouldn't let me. She didn't like men. She only loved Kemper and she only had affection for Nicomedes, Xaxá, and her other dogs. It's no use now. All that's left is our cursed loneliness."

"Look at the point I've reached, Clément old friend, me, Cleto Bonfim. I ordered a dog brought from Europe, the Rhodesian lion. They told me they'd have to look for it in Africa. That critter gave me more trouble than all the others. The people of the Société collected for their trouble of hiring a ship to bring the animal here!"

"I remember when the dog arrived. He had the look of someone important."

"Clément, we got to the port at Vila do Firmino two days before the *Catupania*, the Dutch ship bringing the dog, tied up."

"'What's a Rhodesian lion like? Is it like any other dog? Anything like the German shepherd Ferote?' she asked.

"'I don't know, Saraminda. I don't think so.'

"The dog wore a wide collar made of orange-colored leather that was almost its own color. The strap had a shield on it with silver inlays. No one knew what it was, but then they read it and saw it was for the Association of Rhodesian Ridgeback Breeders, with headquarters in Brussels.

"It was then I made a deal with a leather worker in Cunani, a first-rate craftsman, to make collars for all the dogs, thick ones like the one that came with the Rhodesian lion, a long set of reins twined together into one piece. Saraminda was triumphant. She would go out proudly pulling her pack of more than twenty dogs.

"When she went out onto the claim with her thoroughbred dog, all activity stopped. Everybody came out and no one knew how it was done. It was amazing how that woman could lead such a big dog, which she'd only just gotten to know and was now docile and would stop when she ordered it to, lie down when she ordered it to, and stay by her side, affectionate, tamely following her orders; it had sleek, dark, orange-brown skin, a broad face and strong jaws with jowls hanging down on both sides that gave him a look of fear and ferociousness, which he only showed once, enough to inspire terror. Saraminda and the lion were like old friends. He behaved toward her the same as the other dogs. She arranged a festival for his arrival.

"Clément, old friend, I, Cleto Bonfim, invited everyone on the claim for the presentation of the dog. We built a platform, do you

137

remember? He climbed up on it with her and she was all full of pride, and I was happy. I had *cachaça* served all around and the other dogs barked all night, but they didn't fight. It was a day for fraternizing. It looked like the feast of Saint Lazarus, when dogs aren't strangers to each other.

"On that day he showed what he was there for. When Saraminda was getting off the platform Fiapo, a digger working for me, made a move to help her and took her arms. The Rhodesian lion didn't like it and lifted himself up on his hind legs, showing how huge he was, with such a loud growl that everybody stopped talking and a silence hung in the air like a message of intimidation: no one was to touch Saraminda.

"She felt the devotion and loyalty of the dog, and was touched. She cried and said, 'Kiss me, Cleto.' And I kissed her."

22

A Friendly Visit

Maruanda slowly approached in the dark and reached Kemper's prison. Night lay heavy. She whispered between the boards, "It's me, Maruanda."

"I was worried. Why didn't you come yesterday?"

"Because Dona Saraminda wouldn't let me. She prohibited me from seeing you and said I could only come with her permission. But I came. I'm afraid of the dogs. But when she goes to bed the dogs stand guard by her room and won't leave."

"Did you tell her what I told you to say, Maruanda?"

"I told her, the whole lie. She doesn't talk to me about her things and her love affairs. I never saw a man as dumb as Cleto Bonfim. She does whatever she wants to with him. She's got all kinds of wishes and he takes care of them. Her thoughts and her urges. No one knows yet whether she's given herself to the whole claim. But there's a lot of talk."

"What do you mean? Is she like that?"

"She's the most flighty woman God ever put on this earth. But it's dangerous to have her. The story goes around that she has his throat cut later on. There are a lot of tales, but you never can know the whole truth. She doesn't leave any traces."

"What about Cleto?"

"He's bewitched."

"But you were telling me his story and..."

"I said that he stayed in Maranhão, on the Maracaçume claim. There wasn't much gold there and he came to Amapá, portaging until he got to the River Calçoene where Firmino had discovered gold. He's had a lot of luck and connects with the gold. He kept going up rivers until he set himself up here on the side of Salomoganha Mountain, mother of the gold."

Maruanda felt a strange urge to tell the story of Cleto, a man that she admired. She spoke as if she'd taken part in his adventure.

"People came and he put them to work. They all made something because there was more than enough gold. There was gold in every stream. He took money he earned from his own diggings and bought other people's claims. Until Clément Tamba arrived and went back to Cayenne to bring in the French Créoles and all the people from there. He got to be Bonfim's good friend and he learned a lot with him. He's an educated man. They organized the claim, ran things, and were in charge. Gold here is still putting in an appearance all around."

Jacques Kemper thought that once he was free he would get into the gold business, but right now he couldn't do anything.

"Is that how it is, Maruanda, that anyone who wants to can go prospecting?"

"Anybody. What's needed are people. They come in every day, go halves, and learn how to get out the gold that never ends. Haven't you seen the barrels they take to Calçoene? Inside are jugs full of gold."

"No, I haven't seen anything. They haven't let me see, I don't even want to see. What I want is for you to get me out of here," Kemper said, scratching a mosquito bite on his leg.

"It'll be hard, Mr. Kemper. There's only one way—join up with a portage, hide in the middle of some diggers leaving here because they got into some trouble over a woman or a fight and are off to try and find a new claim. They always find one."

"What are they running away from?" Kemper asked.

"Fights. They start to think. They're afraid of getting their throats cut or they're always out looking for something new. Here if there's an argument," the Saramaca woman said, "the fellow's marked out, so he disappears, if not he's dead. It's like I said, fights over ravines, women, work or alcohol."

A shot rang out. Something far off, nothing to worry about, some hunter shooting. Shots could be heard all the time there. The report dissolved into the darkness. If it wasn't a hunter maybe some drunks. An animal made a noise outside, the scratching of claws on bark. It was a possum hunting hens in a backyard. Maruanda fell silent. She thought it might be something else. But it really was a possum. The hen gave a stifled cackle.

"He caught it."

"Caught what?"

"The hen."

Maruanda became worried. She got up and went to peer into the darkness. She saw an elusive shape that grew larger in the obscurity.

"It was a possum all right," she said to Kemper. The shape melted away. Silence returned. She was nervous all the same.

"Don't leave, stay a while longer," Kemper asked. Maruanda was silent, thinking. Kemper took her by the arm, tried to pull her. She shrank back, trembling.

"Who do you think it was?"

"Nobody. Just a possum."

Kemper pleaded again, "See if you can arrange to get me into one of those escapes."

"It's not an escape. It's something that two or three men want to do, joining together to leave. They leave of their own free will, they're not running away. It's because they just don't want to stay. They're marked and sworn."

Maruanda couldn't forget the noise of the possum, but she went on:

"I'll see if it's possible to set you free. I won't say anything about my arrangements. I'll set up the trip and you'll go along. It'll be something different because you've been locked up by Saraminda and Cleto. It's got to be a real running away. But I'm going to take a chance. It tears my heart to see you in this situation through no fault of your own. I'll get you into a portage."

"If you're afraid, so am I. Lie down here, stay beside me."

Maruanda lay down in the hammock. She'd bathed and her body gave off the odor of woods and water. Kemper stroked her arms, a skin with the feel of mature flesh. Her breasts drooped delicately, dislocated from the muscles that held them up. Kemper remembered his affairs in Paris, lots of them with mature women who sought out youths. Maruanda was crushed with fear. Fear of Saramanda's or Cleto's reaction when they found out about her plot with Kemper. But she overcame her fears. Her desire was greater. Her attraction to the Frenchman with the blue eyes was churning inside her. The Creole women on the claim didn't have to be begged for love. They suffered from loneliness, too. Kemper knew when women had been won over. He also had fears and desires. He didn't confess them but he coupled with her like an animal and she accepted him. He turned off the lamp so nobody could see them through the frets and they were accompanied by darkness all through the night. In the hammock Maruanda followed her urges and only left in the pre-dawn. Her body was exhausted and her look was sad from the joy of not having slept.

Around that time Cleto went to Calçoene. It was the time of a full moon. Maruanda arrived and told Kemper about Saraminda's plans.

"Just hold on because Dona Saraminda is only waiting for Cleto's trip to come here. She's all worked up, getting everything ready."

Two nights later a different movement, a dull humming and the barking of the dogs. Saraminda had given orders for all the dogs to be with her. The men that Cleto had left to guard me during his trip ran into the woods when they saw the loose, howling pack led by Leão. The dogs surrounded my prison in teams. Maruanda came with her, carrying the key to the padlock. They opened it and Saraminda entered. I remained motionless, in silence. The moonbeams lit up the floor. The fretwork in the walls showed the yard and the shadows of the trees. She came in naked and with a domineering sensuality was grabbing me and wrapping around me like a snake, willowy, slipping around my neck and whispering:

"Kiss me, Kemper, kiss me, Kemper."

And I kissed her. I kissed as I had never kissed before, a kiss with no time to end, while I took in unwilling and greedy breaths of air. The woman had witchcraft. I changed completely, I didn't want to run away anymore, I wanted to remain imprisoned there, without letting that moment ever pass out of my entire life, there with her, waiting for her. And if that's what's called the desperation of love, I loved Saraminda with desperation. It was as if the light of the moon had covered up my soul and that woman was the moon itself, wrapped in clouds and going through its spells and mysteries, "Kiss me, Kemper, Kemper, kiss me," and everything was heat, sweat, torment, pain, pleasure, hate, fire. "Kiss me, Kemper."

She wrapped herself around me, went on caressing me until dawn and I was with her.

"Have me, Saraminda, I can't stand it any more."

"That's not the way it is, Mr. Frenchman. To make me his woman Bonfim gave me twenty pounds of gold."

"Have me..."

And Maruanda outside listening to that whispering. And I couldn't even think, getting more and more giddy.

"It can't be that way. I've already gone too far. My desire has to be a mystery. Just wait, Mr. Frenchman."

"No, Saraminda." And I squeezed her so she wouldn't leave my side.

"Don't use force, that's not how it is with me. Let me leave."

I relaxed. She loosened her arms, let her body go soft, and I began to caress her, kiss her, and threw myself with all my weight and madness on her. Then I saw my victory in that all-night struggle. But I really didn't see it. Like a snake she slithered out and stood up, a runaway rabbit. Dawn was breaking. The dogs began to bark softly, moaning, as if warning us that the light of day was appearing.

Poor Maruanda, who lost me, wanted to free me and I got myself caught. I didn't want anything more but slavery and feeling the knife at my throat, dead in that possession. From that night on I was dominated by an anguish of wanting Saraminda, whom I hadn't had. The next day the same thing was repeated.

I was always waiting for her to arrive at the brink of the waterfall and she would run away along the bank. No one ever underwent greater torture, and that's how seven nights were consumed.

Cleto arrived. Silence returned to my prison and the pleasure of living disappeared for me into the morbid urge of loving with the desire for death, since my passion had no way to exist. Along with imprisonment, despair. It was during that tangle of misfortune that Maruanda returned:

"Your escape has been arranged, Mr. Kemper. Tomorrow in the early morning Severino is coming to get you, to go with three more men on the portage to the Cunani."

"How can I go? I don't want to run away anymore. I want to rot here."

"They've discovered some new diggings and are going there."

"Cleto will come looking for me wherever I am. I'm not going."

"You can run away. They're going to a place that's close to the port for the ships that put in to Calçoene."

Those words didn't mean anything to me anymore. I didn't want to leave my prison, waiting for the miracle, the return of Saraminda.

Maruanda then brought me a note from Saraminda in rounded, childish writing:

Kemper, forget everything. Severino is coming for you tomorrow. My desire has left me.

I was humiliated. What remained for me, then?

"Did you tell Saraminda about your plan, Maruanda?"

"No, she guessed it. She knows everything. She doesn't read palms, she reads minds."

"Does she know that you slept with me?"

"She's the one who told me to. But rest easy. That's the way she is. Severino's coming tomorrow to wait by the big well and I'll take you there."

The next day, with no signal, distraught, my mind wandering aimlessly, not knowing what was going on, I waited for Maruanda. I wasn't anxious.

Dawn broke and she hadn't come. They brought me my meal early. I couldn't figure anything out. There was no news. That night I heard steps. It had to be Maruanda. I looked through the cracks. I only heard the voice of the other Saramaca woman who worked with her, Gedina, who leaned against the crossed boards and whispered between sobs and tears:

"They found Maruanda with her throat cut this morning."

23

The Way Out

I spent two days not eating or sleeping. How far responsible could I have been for bringing about Maruanda's death? Could Saraminda have done it out of jealousy? Could Cleto have out of vengeance? But Saraminda knew all about everything and had prepared my flight. I no longer meant anything to her and she wanted to see me leave. What about Cleto? Why would it have been he? These things were turning over in my head and I didn't know how I could have got mixed up in that web of passion and misfortune.

On the third day, around one o'clock in the morning, I heard steps inside my room. How could I have heard them if the door was locked and I hadn't heard anyone calling me? My heart beat faster. Was it my turn to have my throat cut? It was probably the invisible hand that feeds gold with blood preparing my end. I would be free of that other death that had been tormenting my days. My last thought was of Saraminda; I couldn't get her memory out of my head. Her body and her warmth wouldn't leave me. I couldn't see, but I knew that someone was beside me. I could feel the breathing, the presence. I didn't have the courage to ask. It was as though I was ready to be sacrificed. That was when Maruanda's voice rose up:

"Don't worry, Mr. Kemper, I've come to complete our arrangement."

I was terrified. My hair stood on end.

"Aren't you dead?"

"Everybody dies and lives in this place. It's Purgatory. My mission is to help you get away."

"Is it really you, Maruanda?"

"Yes, it's me. Severino will be here at five in the morning. I can't lead you on the road to the well because the dogs have been sniffing me out."

I felt her hand on my head. It was as cold as the water from the well and it stuck and yet didn't stick. It ran along like gelatin, dissolving in her gesture of giving me a tender pat.

That's all I know. An emptiness came on and I was taken by a feeling that I'd been dreaming without having dreamed. I clutched my own arm and felt that I was feverish, a heat entering through my eyes that suddenly got into me, and I began to sweat. The beetles were buzzing around and falling into the basin of water placed beside the lamp. It felt as if mosquitoes, locusts, blowflies, *sauba* ants, caterpillars, spiders and crickets were swirling inside my head. My body was turning to liquid that ran down through my armpits and over my legs. I only woke from that drowsiness when dawn began to break and there in front of me was a burly man wearing a wide-brimmed straw hat, with broad shoulders and little eyes that were hidden in a sunken face.

"I'm Severino Boião. I promised Maruanda that you could go with us to the new claim on the banks of the Cunani."

I don't know how I came out of my delirium. I only remember myself in the jungle after I don't know how many days of traveling, shivering with a cold heat in my body, my feet swollen. I ran my hand over my face and felt the growth of a wet beard. It wasn't tears, but sweat running down over my eyes. I could still hear Severino's voice:

"The French firebeard has monkey fever."

I heard them starting a fire and eating some boiled fiddlehead ferns, with *sago* palm stem flour, which they always carry on long trips through the forest. I listened to the stories of things that a person should know when he's lost in the mysterious and treacherous jungle.

"Only eat the fruit that monkeys eat. Grass and cooked plants. Stalks and the tubers from the roots of white lilies, coconut worms, bamboo shoots, bramble-palm fruit, wild papaya and snakes. They can all be eaten if you cut off the head and the tail. The middle part is all right and the meat is tasty and white."

But I didn't eat anything. My thoughts were far away. I followed along, dragging myself behind them. They would come back and then head off again. Saraminda was beside me, a snake that flicked its tongue in and out, showing its fangs and trying to bite my throat. And I was asking her to bite.

With the last light I managed to see a crab-tree, lifting up its arms and seeking the sun, trying to breathe.

24

A Frenchman From Britanny

A fine rain was falling from the tall trees in the dense jungle, reaching the ground after filtering through many leaves and branches. It was constant water, dripping down with the sound of the wind as it flees hidden through the open skylights in the forest trees.

The footpath along which Kemper was dragging himself was hacked out and hidden away among low-lying plants, imprecise and muddy, only visible to eyes possessed by the mystery for finding gold in streambeds. The clay-colored rotting leaves made the ground sticky, a carpeting of mud softened by the rain, coming down drop by drop from the snakewood trees to the *ucubas* and from these to the palm trees which sweated along their plump and weary trunks, also dripping onto the great stretches of shrubs of every species and sliding down bromeliads and creepers as they hung from vines and furrowed aerial roots that curled around in thin, snakelike stems, reaching down to the tree bottoms. The tiny yellow flower petals of the *copaiba* tree spread out upon the ground.

Kemper was a ghost inside his own body as it gave off filth and rot, the sticky, bitter sweat of a horse. His nostrils opened up like those of a colt running wildly in a field and gasping for air. The weather darkened the light under the trees, sadder and more somber than the jungle itself. His fever pulsed with the plants, his bones were twisted, painful, trembling with cold. His eyes and his dirty open mouth showed despair.

"Saraminda? Come closer, Saraminda."

Not even his own ears could hear his delirious voice, strangled sounds with no way out.

"Saraminda?"

The silence ran off endlessly into the rain and into the sounds of the bellbirds as they played their invisible marimbas that carried along for leagues and reached the startled ears of birds and beasts. It sounded like a tolling for the dead.

"Saraminda?"

Firebeard refused to die. Sprawled out on the ground, he didn't have any strength left to get up and move his body.

Why had he come to Cayenne? His head was all questions. Everything else had been consumed by misfortune. The remains of his consciousness were dead. They were no good for thinking about anything anymore.

"Do you think we love France?"

In his delirium he was bringing back the ships that had sailed out of Cancale, pirates and adventurers, and the weather was always dismal. Annie, his only sibling, would squeeze her tiny child's hand in his. It was the same squeeze they had exchanged when the man with the long blond mustache said in church that he wanted to marry their mother. Their father's corpse was still warm in the open coffin, his teeth slightly showing. And no one told him why.

His old witch of a grandmother hid the distant traces of her descent from the Caribbean Indian woman who'd been bound and thrown aboard the caravel because of the beauty of her breasts and hair and brought to Saint-Malo. She would prattle on morosely, always about men, money, pork lard, oils and oysters. Over two centuries her blood had been diluted by men and women, sperm and eggs, but the savage look survived in their Breton deportment: "Charlotte's still too young for widowhood, a black shawl, and a body without love." That old cretin of a grandmother, making *congre quessant*, *crêpes*, and sour buckwheat pancakes.

Six months after his father's death was a short time. Hate had taken root inside him and was growing and on that day it alit on the red flame of the candles burning in the bell tower of the village. He swore never to accept the intruder in his house, thinking about seeing him in bed with his mother and feeling her breasts, stroking her body. He never forgave anything that happened or that he imagined was happening. He had to run away, and the sea in front of his house with its dirty beach was his destiny. But it didn't justify his trip to Cayenne, the mysterious events that had gotten him into the miserable state of a fugitive and gold hunter. "It's the lowest level a man can reach—misfortune, misery, and sickness." The trip, the fight, the French flag torn down, the gold, *la couleur* of the Creoles and Saraminda. It was all over. There was nothing left but his questions.

"Get up, Firebeard, you filthy old Frenchman! Get going, you bum!"

And he was only twenty-five years old.

His stumbling legs could only take one week in the company of the group. At daybreak, after the night's stop, Crescêncio came to see if he was still breathing. He put his hands to Kemper's nostrils. The first signs of light were appearing in the jungle treetops with quivering sunbeams. He couldn't feel anything anymore. He'd arrived at a state of exhaustion and delirium, anxiety and feverish heat. Nobody knew how many days they'd been walking. Their salt sacks were empty, the flour was all gone, and there were only a few cartridges of lead and powder left. On a portage nobody knew where the end was or how many days were left to go or if they were going to find gold. Anyone who couldn't take it was left on the trail to be eaten by armadillos and ants.

The day they'd crossed the Oiapoque, had they found gold above Seven Rapids? The moment when Saraminda, with her dark body and green eyes stared at him for the first time and read his hand: "Your fate is thorns in flesh. I don't see flowers, I see blood."

"You can't make it with us anymore and we can't carry you on our backs. That's the way the jungle is. The only ones who'll reach the new claim are the ones the Devil has picked."

"What kind of a taste have you got in your mouth, you filthy Frenchman?"

Firebeard still had enough strength to run his trembling hand over his beard. They gave him some water. The taste was bitter, like a she-turtle's liver. His putrid saliva stank. His tongue was rougher than that of a *pirarucu* fish. Day was just breaking and they had to keep moving. The group came to a decision:

"He's going to die! There's no way out. He'll stay behind here."

So Gabriel picked up the machete and the old shotgun. Kemper's eyes opened wider. He'd been condemned. Cold and fever were taking possession of his blood and his head. Monkey malaria owned his body. The smell of his skin scared off the beetles and mosquitoes. But flies lighted on him.

"Saraminda, wipe my eyes!"

"He's raving," Crescêncio said.

His companions agreed. It was the end.

"And he's going to die pretty soon. That's the way life is. His time has come."

"Help me up, Saraminda. The stories they told me."

Was the tide going out on the Amapá River? Where were the rescue boats? That cripple with his broken legs, holding his rifle, shot at the bugler from his ambush hole: "Surrender your Indian body to me. Four pounds of gold for one night." And the early morning shot. The knife. Why this fate? The rapids with snakes that swallowed alligators? The anaconda on the River Carnot? All of it wrapped up in questions about the eternal flame, the fire of the fever lighting torches in his eyes.

Firebeard tried to stand up. Severino pushed and pulled his body into the higher foliage. He thought that death would be more pleasant there.

"Wouldn't it be better if we took him out of his misery so he won't suffer anymore?" Crescêncio asked.

"We haven't got all that many cartridges and we're not going to waste one of the last ones, which could kill a peccary for lunch," Severino replied, adding, "Let him go in peace."

They all crossed themselves. Day was breaking. They threw their belongings onto their backs and began cutting and clearing the way they were to walk.

No one looked back. But that's how it was.

25

Returned Passion

What happened with me was something that had never happened before. I started wanting Kemper again. Afterwards, as always, the desire passed and I was left with a feeling of repugnance for him. He'd escaped with my help. After the death of Maruanda I considered the case closed. But when I had those thoughts I began to feel growing inside me the love I'd had the moment I saw his blue eyes. And I became desperate, asking Bonfim to bring him back. My period, which had never been even a day late, hadn't come. I became suspicious. Never in my life had I thought I'd get pregnant. It didn't come the next day either. Another day and nothing. Then my thoughts went back to the Frenchman and the repugnance disappeared and I went out of my mind and began dreaming about his eyes and I called to Cleto, "Send somebody after the Frenchman."

I put on the whole act, something I was quite good at, but now I was repeating myself and remembering Kemper and I was happy that black Maruanda was dead because she'd gone to bed with him, and I, who'd never been jealous, was jealous of a dead woman. "Are you pregnant, Saraminda? Did you get pregnant from the Frenchman, Saraminda?" How could I have got pregnant? It had only been a virgin's kind of thing, petting and then doing it without doing it. They'd told me once in Cayenne that a virgin got pregnant from love play like that because the semen had gone up during her rut. Having never been pregnant but wanting to, as Cleto had wanted for me, I was now unfortunately pregnant without wanting to, without any reason for being so. I kept on questioning myself until I heard the dogs barking and Celestino Gouvela shouting:

"The man's back. But he's done for."

What knife pierced my heart? What stone crushed my head?

"Where is he, Celestino?"

"He's in the basket where I carried the equipment for the trip. He stinks worse than a chunk of rotten meat!"

Such anguish. I wept and thought that my passion for Kemper had returned and that inside me there was a piece of him, that it had happened. It was my misfortune, one I didn't want. I'd wanted him to go away, but when I heard he was done for I was done for, too. The ways of a woman like me.

When Celestino Gouveia put the basket down on the floor of the prison and laid Kemper out, he was paler than whitewash. If he was breathing nobody could tell, but every so often he moaned in a death rattle.

I didn't know what love was. I'd begun a life deprived of love. In the brothel I had to love the work, it was my way of life. I wanted to have a man, but I felt disgust for all men. They wanted me for one night, but they never really had me. If a woman wants to feel a man and give herself to him, she has to sense that he wants her, that urge in the body, that feeling in the body. Nobody can feel the soul without feeling the body, love is both in the soul and in the body. You can't love before or love afterwards, you've got to love right away. I don't have the brains to talk about these things. I was sorry I hadn't given more of myself to Kemper. My way of always leaving a little bit for later, to drive him crazy, hadn't worked out. You think you can wait. Then you wait and nothing else happens and the moment drops to the bottom of the well and time passes. I made myself a woman of the street and I only loved Kemper's eyes, not him, but afterwards I loved Cleto. I loved him as I'd never thought I could love him one day. All that's mixed up in my head. I felt it when I was afraid of being made pregnant by Kemper and not wanting to be, but I had never imagined that happening. I wanted to be pregnant by Cleto, but Kemper was the one who was left inside me. Disgusted with myself from that moment on, I discovered that I loved Cleto. He taught me how to be a female and now he was teaching me how to be a woman with a soul.

I learned then that the feeling that was making me Cleto's prisoner was greater than that of receiving him. It was no longer an obsession. He did everything for me, put up with everything, went along with all my wants. He deserved my having greater affection for him. Poor Cleto Bonfim! He suffered because of all the things I wanted and did. I felt pity at first, then affection, then friendship, then the habit of the obsession disappeared and I went on to feel the habit of living with him. Waiting for him to come home, running my hands through his hair, asking him about his day, asking for a kiss, afraid to think that he might leave me one day. I'd never thought that way before and I began to think that way now. That change came about after I felt I was carrying Kemper's child in my body. Common woman that I was, I could do anything to Cleto except get a belly that wasn't his. I suffered. I was disgusted with myself. When Celestino told me Kemper was done for I suffered, but I felt a kind of relief. God's destiny was freeing me of him. But my thoughts made me turn back to the child that was his. He was dying, but he was alive inside me.

Then I wanted to kill his child. What's the love I have or think I have? I began to think things through again. Thinking about Cleto, I discovered that he was everything to me, that without him I didn't even exist and with him I was already dead. Something I didn't understand. Betrayal and love. My soul was like those mysterious woods, tempting, beautiful, full of trees of all kinds and shapes, dangerous like the evils in me; ants, snakes, wild animals, swamps, thorns, and the loneliness that never goes away.

My woman's soul was like a jaguar, treacherous, fierce, hungry, strong, mistress of all ambushes. My soul was like a flower spreading its perfume, bringing joy, making beauty, but rotting away.

My soul was like a *tonka* bean tree, which only grows where there's gold. That's the way I was. Saraminda. My kind holds a woman to be independent, commanding men, giving herself to the one she wants and not to the one who orders her to. What I did with Cleto Bonfim was in my soul but it wasn't in my blood. A Creole woman likes her body, but she has a soul.

26

A Death That Doesn't Come

"Run, Gedina, go get a bucket of water and throw it onto the man. Hurry up, he's dying," said Ovídio, the man who took care of the vinegar plant garden. Everything was in an uproar, with workers running to see the dying Frenchman who wouldn't die. Lariel, the gardener, arrived and saw Jacques Kemper stretched out on the ground, pale, his mouth open, his chin drooping like that of someone who's lost control of his body. No one wanted to take his pulse or test his breathing. His feet were stuck into what was left of his shoes, all torn apart with his toes sticking out, and there were his swollen private parts which from the outside looked like dirty acorns, the skin and filth indistinguishable. His shirt consisted of nothing but loose pieces held together by what had once been sleeves, the ragged remains curled around his armpits. All that was left of his pants were the faded legs, all covered with gray filth and tied around his waist by knotted pieces of cord, evidence of his stumbling through thorns and vines in his path. A yellow sweat ran down his face. Everything stank. The people around were holding their noses. Every so often a deep moan would come out of his throat and give a quick gurgle in search of air and then sink into a sigh. Silence would fall again and everyone was waiting for his final death rattle.

Ovídio suggested they perform a Jesus-call to quicken his passing. That ritual to free a person from his suffering consisted of sitting on his chest, taking his hands and opening his arms strongly, closing them over his thorax, and asking him to say the name of Jesus. The gesture would be repeated several times until Jesus

155

came to take him. The candle to light his way to the other world was already burning alongside. But no one had the courage to do anything. The awful smell, the fear of catching the disease, the filth and the yellow spittle kept everybody away. Gedina said to Ovídio, "Hurry up and get a bucket of water and throw it on him, the way you do with a baby chick."

It didn't seem right to wait for other words or nods. There seemed nothing else to do. Ovídio ran right off to the well and came back with the can on his head. He put it down on the ground and only then did he notice there was no gourd and he didn't dare toss all the contents at once with the water coming down in such a rush like a waterfall. He sent someone to fetch a cup from the house. Then, like a lightning bolt, the thought of what Saraminda might be thinking at that moment struck him. Hadn't she sent to have him brought back? Everybody thought she was madly in love with the Frenchman who'd brought her the dress from Paris.

"Would she think I brought on his death quicker?"

Fear made his hands tremble.

"I don't dare throw any water on his face."

Kemper gave another moan. Ovídio hesitated again. That was when Celestino Gouveia entered to relieve him of his indecision.

"Is he dead yet?"

They all answered together: "He's giving off his death rattle."

"If he's dead, let's bury him right away. I'm going to pour this water on his face to get rid of that moaning."

Only a little at first, then he poured out all the liquid. Those present drew back, getting out of the way of the spray that splashed off because Celestino Gouveia had thrown the water forcefully from above. Kemper moaned and twisted about, raised his legs, thrashed with his arms, and contracted his face. He put on such a horrible grimace that Celestino Gouveia drew back in fear:

"I never saw a beast look that ugly when it was dying. It looks like the Fiend himself is coming out of him."

The convulsions lessened after a while and Kemper's face returned to normal, the white color replaced by yellow, then brown, turning pink and reddish, a red so strong that those around opened their mouths and clapped their hands in amazement: "My God, I never saw anything like it! It's the work of the Devil."

156

And they all began to pray. Gedina mumbled a plea: "Oh, Mother of Heaven, Mother of Earth, save the one who needs you, drive off the evil one."

And the chorus of those present responded, "Satan be gone."

The gardener Zeduco lit the candle and placed it between Kemper's hands. The rotten smell disappeared as if by magic. Kemper threw up his hand out of control, trying to push Zeduco's arm away. A dog barked in the distance. Kemper opened his eyes and everybody, terrified, heard from his lips a beseeching voice that almost faded away:

"Saraminda, Saraminda, Saraminda."

Celestino Gouveia, who'd heard it quite clearly, pretended not to and asked all around:

"What's that Frenchman saying?"

Nobody answered. And, to their surprise, the wet ground was drying up and giving off an evaporating mist as his body began to resuscitate and his breathing got better, becoming normal. Celestino asked again, and a great swarm of cockroaches poured out of the Frenchman's rags onto the floor.

"I'll be damned. What's that Frenchman saying?"

And nobody answered.

"The best thing would be to give him a deathblow and put him out of his misery."

He took his thirty-eight from his belt and aimed it at Kemper's face.

"Mr. Celestino, for God's sakes, don't do that. He's calling Dona Saraminda's name."

"Whose?"

"Dona Saraminda's," Zeduco repeated.

Celestino lowered his arm and said, "I'm going to talk to her and tell her what's going on. I don't know why Cleto didn't authorize me to kill this stinker during the trip."

He went out, the revolver still in his hand, and they all thought he was going to turn around and finish off Jacques Kemper from the door. But Celestino Gouveia didn't want to take that chance. He was afraid of the reaction of the others, the testimony of all those there.

"I never killed anybody in a prayer circle," he was thinking, because there were a lot of witnesses and he was afraid of the vengeance he might receive from Saraminda, whose thoughts concerning the whole situation were unknown to him. He felt hate for Kemper, who'd conquered Saraminda. He knew Kemper wasn't dead and that a deathblow would be a charitable act, but he had no charity to offer him.

Ever since he'd begun to suspect that Saraminda loved Kemper, Celestino Gouveia began to feel rancor, jealousy and who knows what else. When he saw him imprisoned on his arrival to the claim he'd actually been generous to him. The greatest proof of his loyalty to Cleto was following his orders to bring Firebeard back alive. And he only did so because he knew that he was dead or would die on the trip. When he saw the state the man was in, his intention was to bring in his corpse and throw it, stinking, into Cleto's yard, with the vultures eyeing what would soon be carrion. "But the bastard held on, survived the trip, and is still kicking now," was Celestino Gouveia's real thought. With that rage in him he went off to talk to Saraminda. He had to settle accounts with her, collect for everything she'd done, her seducing, her devilish plotting in which he was involved. He didn't forgive Saraminda for encouraging him to be a swine, agreeing to betray Bonfim, playing around with him, offering herself and toying with his reputation as a man's man. But she wanted to demoralize the lot of them, bind them to her will, dazzle them with her body, and get them to do all sorts of things. His memory roiled with all the things that had happened.

"Celestino, Dona Saraminda told me to give you a message to go to her house because she's got to talk to you," Ludgero the overseer told him.

"Did she say what she wanted?"

"She didn't say anything."

Celestino thought the summons was just something thought up by her to catch him.

"Have you got any *cachaça*, Ludgero?"

"I do."

"Get me a drink. I'm fighting off a cold," was the excuse offered for the occasion by someone who'd never needed to excuse himself for anything in his whole life.

What he really wanted, though, was to get himself all heated up, because he had a glimpse of what was going to happen. Then he thought she might want his services to cut someone's throat. But no, what she wanted was some screwing around. She wanted to make him suffer.

Now he decided to go to Saraminda and tell her that he was going to shoot the Frenchman, not out of pity, but because he was a man of courage and feeling, killing Kemper out of rage for himself and for Cleto. And off he went like that. He knocked on the door and the dogs ran toward him, like guards awaiting her orders.

"Saraminda, it's me." He clapped his hands, shouting, "I've got to talk to you right now!"

"Is it something urgent?" she asked from inside.

"It's something about yesterday. I've got to talk to you right away."

Saraminda was puzzled by Celestino's state of mind. She'd never seen him that way.

"I'm going to open the door. Leão, Leão," she shouted, "stay with Celestino."

And the big orangish lion dog with jowls and a black back, the size of a calf, looked at Celestino and went up the stairs to the verandah with him as if he were a slave. Saraminda was in the bedroom. Celestino was trembling. He remembered the day when she'd half-opened the door and he could see her naked. Then that other afternoon when she'd sent the message by Ludgero for him to go there and he had and when he arrived she told him to come into her room. He'd gone in all shaking and she'd been naked in the white hammock, her dark flesh shining and framed by the white hammock, like the decoration on an altar. Her breasts, and only then did he see them, were a legend throughout the claim, but no one who'd seen them ever talked about it. They were yellow like gold, not the dirty gold on the claim, but the gold that decorated women's throats and fingers. Celestino Gouveia had turned his eyes away, tried to lower them, but couldn't. He stared at her skin and ran his eyes over her form.

"I sent for you, Celestino, so that you could see me. Look at me, because you're always watching with a wish to see me."

"Don't do this to me, Saraminda. I can't betray Cleto. Why did you pick me for this, child?"

When he said "child" he felt the word revealing a hidden feeling of tenderness which might be the barrier to prevent him from going against his loyalty.

"No, Saraminda, no."

And she asked, "Kiss me, Celestino."

And weakened, Celestino kissed her. He caught a taste of poison and ran out, but he didn't get beyond the verandah, held back by a fierce growl from Leão, which he quickly understood. He would never forget that day. He was left with rage, love and jealousy.

"Leão, let him go and come here."

The dog withdrew and Celestino went on his way. He couldn't sleep anymore, he couldn't think about his work anymore, not even about gold. All he could think about was Saraminda's body. He planned how he would kill Cleto and take over the claim. And he thought that if Saraminda did with him what she was doing with Cleto, he'd have her throat cut and her head put on a stake in the middle of the settlement so everybody could see to what point a man can be led by a woman. He also thought about going away, but that wouldn't solve anything. He'd go away, but with the dead woman's head.

He remembered once more Saraminda's insistence, sending a message so he'd come and visit her, tempting his spirit as a way of driving him crazy, all mixed up between seduction, desire and loyalty, which was no longer to Cleto but to himself.

Now he was there with all those layers and layers of thoughts like sediment, proving that he, Celestino, had been an instrument for putting into effect her way of seducing men and bringing them to devastation and madness. It had happened to him, to Kemper, to Clément, as well as the young fellow with long hair, Ricardo, and Carlindo, a magician, jeweler and gold buyer who had to run away, and Cleto, the greatest of them all, who never dreamed that he was a slave.

Celestino wanted to tell Saraminda that Kemper had survived and was calling for her. It seemed he'd revived and was repeating her name in his delirium. He would have also said that he'd been afraid to kill him. Everybody thought that Saraminda was possessed by a great passion for him.

He wanted to tell her that he was going to kill Kemper. He wanted to see her cry, confess her weakness when confronted

160

with this situation, just to show her that everyone knew how she treated men and to let her know that her love for the Frenchman was out there in a chunk of rotten, stinking meat, finished. That he was calling for her and that she should go and see just what her partner was like.

He went in. Saraminda was dressed, standing beside the hammock with that look of disdain, still in the posture that he knew so well, one of mystery. There was no apparent emotion.

"Saraminda," he said firmly. "Kemper didn't die. He's coming back to life and is calling for you."

"For me?" she said with a certain fear, and repeated, "For me?"

"Yes, for you."

"What does he want?"

"I don't know, just that he came out of his death rattle to show that you'd led him to the edge of his grave."

"What's that, Celestino? Show me some respect."

"No, Saraminda, you did it to me, too. You made me suffer, you drove me crazy, worse than a dog, and I came back to life, but I didn't call for Saraminda."

"Show some respect, Celestino. Don't take any liberties." And she shouted in a loud voice, "Respect, Celestino!"

Leão gave a deep bark outside.

"Take off your mask, Saraminda. That Frenchman you made Cleto grab, let go and send for to satisfy your wants is on his last legs now. I was going to give him the *coup de grâce*, but when I heard him call for you, I came to take you there so you could see to what point your evil had reached, and then kill him in front of you."

"Have you gone crazy, Celestino? Show me some respect."

"No. You're coming with me right now. Your lover the Frenchman is calling for you."

"Show me some respect, Celestino!"

Celestino Gouveia took the revolver from his belt. Saraminda gulped in all the air in the room. She never thought she'd be killed by Celestino.

"Don't do that, Celestino. Put that gun away."

Leão growled again outside.

"Make that dog stop, Saraminda."

"Leão, stop."

The dog fell silent.

"Let's go, Saraminda. Walk. I'm going to kill the Frenchman in front of you. Let's go, Saraminda."

She remained standing, mute, a great look of terror on her face, and got a hint of the feelings that had grown in the men she'd seduced. She was in a state of perplexity and panic. She thought of Kemper, who'd shaken up her life.

"The Frenchman is calling for you, Saraminda. Let's go find him alive and help him die."

Driven by hatred and jealousy, Celestino thought he was taking his revenge on behalf of Bonfim. His eyes were gleaming, his hand was firm, not shaking as it held the butt of the revolver. He kept Saraminda in front of him and, knowing her power over the dogs, told her:

"Send them away."

Saraminda was pushed along. She came out onto the verandah, Celestino close behind her pointing the revolver, aiming at her with a steady hand. That was the way she started down the steps and put her foot on the path. The dogs retreated, except for Leão, still by her side.

"Send that dog away, Saraminda, or else I'll shoot him."

"Leão, go away..."

But Leão didn't move.

Celestino wanted to humiliate her by taking her to Kemper. He couldn't tell the dog, "Go away or else I'll kill Saraminda." During that dilemma he started to feel confused, unnerved by the presence of Leão, which wasn't acting like he usually did. He was neither barking nor growling. Saraminda was completely terrified.

"Saraminda, send that dog away. I'll kill him."

He quickly moved the gun from her back and pointed it at Leão. Like a bolt of lightning the dog grabbed the arm with the gun, knocked him down, leaped on him, and began to bite and tear him.

"Leão," Saraminda shouted, "Leão!"

Voracious, the dog was tossing Celestino's body back and forth. The other dogs joined in the attack. Saraminda shouted:

"Stop...!"

And they all stopped.

Celestino's days were ending before Kemper's. Saraminda ran up the stairs and locked herself in her room, sobbing.

There was great turmoil. The dogs went away. The yard was covered with blood and pieces of Celestino's body. Gedina, the first to arrive, felt no pity when she saw the scene. "A man like that who's caused so much evil could only die that way, by the mouth of a dog. It's God's punishment."

Everybody on the claim came over. When Cleto saw what had happened he bit his lips, tightened his face in rage and went to confront Saraminda:

"Did you see the awful thing your mania for dogs has brought about?"

"No, Cleto. He was to blame. He came here to rape me and this happened."

"Rape you?"

"Yes, Cleto. He broke into my room. I resisted. He threatened me and made me go with him. He was going to take me into the woods and attack me...taking advantage of the Frenchman's dying."

"Celestino Gouveia?"

"Yes, Cleto Bonfim. Him. The bandit who betrayed you. When he went down the steps I was saved by Leão."

"The swine!"

Cleto Bonfim went back down the stairs and shouted to everyone:

"He died the way he deserved, the treacherous swine!"

27

The Arrival of the Enemy

In the big old house of shadows, the memories never ceased. Clément and Cleto were chatting in eternity.

"The claim had already changed, Bonfim old friend. My fate was coming to an end. I could feel it in the air. It wasn't the gold. The gold continued coming out. You know that gold has a master who lives in the ground and is addicted to blood and *cachaça*. I never gave him any blood, but every morning I had them pour out ten quarts of *cachaça* onto my diggings," Clément recalled.

"Don't talk to me about gold anymore," Bonfim said with irritation. "I saw so much gold that it's beginning to make me sick now."

"I don't see why, Bonfim. Everything we've been talking about has come from it. Things like corn flour," Clément replied. "The mother of gold would get drunk and men could pull it out, and it was always there. But the poison of politics got into the men. People stopped looking at me the way they always had. There was mistrust and I began to be afraid. That visit Governor Charwein of Guiana made to the claim was a great mistake. He said the territory belonged to France and named Trajano as his representative. He picked a Brazilian, thinking in that way he was giving some kind of assurance, but it was a disaster." Clément rambled on: "The Brazilians considered him a traitor."

"And he was," Cleto put in.

"The only real reason we French went there was to get out gold."

"Come on, Clément, old friend," Cleto said, holding a cigarette in his hand. "I was the one who went there to calm things down and ask you to do what you did."

"I always put up the French flag in front of my store, the France de Calsuène. But it wasn't because of politics. I had nothing to do with that. It was a personal gesture by someone who wanted the products I imported from France to sell better. Eleutério was my friend. He'd been my carousing buddy in Cayenne. But on that day he was different. He came at the front of those men and told me angrily: 'Take down the flag of France, Clément! This here is Brazil!'"

Clément stopped speaking. He was staring at the wall. After a long pause he went on:

"I explained that I didn't want to own the land, but he wouldn't give in. 'Take it down or we'll take it down.' That was when I sent for you, Bonfim, old friend. And you came and saw how things were tense and advised me, 'Clément old friend, if Eleutério and his Brazilians consider that flag a symbol of government, take it down, old man, and let's stick with what's in our own interest— our work and our gold.' I went out and took down the flag, but I was upset and on that day I began collecting gold from the Frenchmen in order to buy weapons. But then I realized that I wasn't a member of the Gendarmerie, so I kept the gold and didn't arm anybody. I was already getting involved with Lucy at that time, Cleto. She wasn't young, but she was pretty and respectable. Cabral arrived with his people and they started that to-do. Reports came from Cunani that he'd arrested Trajano and his wife and children, tied their hands together, and taken them to Vila do Amapá. I heard that Trajano was crying as he left, and Madame Coudreau, the scientist's wife who spent her time making sketches of the river, was there when they left. Eleutério denounced me to Cabral. He said I was the leader of the French cause. All because of that poor flag I'd hung in front of my store. Merchants everywhere put out the flag of their country in front of their stores. But not there. It was disputed territory, a fight between governments. Then I decided to send all the gold I had to Cayenne. I bought eight barrels from Zaqueta, the importer of *cachaça*. He was a Creole I'd known in Guiana as a tooth-puller. I got ten or so kegs. I began to fill jugs and then lined the barrels with dry *guarumã* and wild arrowroot leaves, strong stalks, and wrapped it all up so that it wouldn't break. First I would roll up a jug in cotton sheeting and put it in a sack of thick cloth so that if it broke the gold wouldn't pour out. Then I closed up the barrels, which went first by ox cart and then by barge down the Calçoene River, going through the rapids to Vila do Firmino, and from there by ship to Cayenne and the warehouse of the Société Equatoriale. I didn't send them all at the same time. They went by twos and threes, accompanied by my men. But there wasn't any danger. Stealing gold was a waste of time there, with no place to hide it and no one to sell it to. It would only work if some lunatic stole it and mixed it back into the earth again. We controlled all commerce. Me, you, Pedro Nolasco and Teodoro Leal, who had a house on the claim and in Vila do Firmino. Genibaldo Pereira, from Belém do Pará, sold a thousand pounds of gold he sent out in the three years he did business on the claims on the Calçoene, where he died of fever. Life was peaceful and our business was good. But it took on a bad taste after the fight and the talk about a war coming."

"Clément, old friend, it was in the middle of that fight when I was living the hardest time of my life. The Frenchman had run away and Saraminda, planning it all out, jumped on me, saying that I'd killed him. I swore, me Cleto Bonfim, and I had to beg Saraminda not to accuse me of having killed the man. She hollered, cried, and called the dogs which were barking all around me, and me, revolver in my hand and that Rhodesian lion dog looking at me and me looking at him. Clément, old friend, do you know who cut black Maruanda's throat?"

"It was you, Cleto. Why do you ask me a thing like that?"

"No, Cleto, it wasn't me. I didn't do things like that. I liked the Saramaca. She'd even been my woman."

"Then who did kill her?"

"It's a mystery to me. Saraminda, as far as I know, would do anything, but she had nothing to do with a thing like death."

"Cleto, old friend, I don't want to know about any mysterious things that took place in anybody's house, but...when Celestino was around any sort of blood crime could happen."

"But, old friend, that woman called me and said, 'Cleto, if the Frenchman has run away, send somebody to bring him back. I knew that he was going to run away but he didn't. Then he disappeared. He disappeared, you must know that. Send after him. My dogs will go along. I'll only keep Tupã, Leão and Hot-Iron with me.' But Saraminda liked to make trouble. I'm not sure whether she wanted the Frenchman or just wanted to hurt me and make me submit."

"Cleto, that's something you'll never know, because it's a case of a man driven crazy by a woman. I got that way over a flirtatious Frenchwoman who'd been kicked off a ship. She'd been living with the captain and had got under his skin. I was crazy over her. She was a woman made for bed and knew how to drive a man mad. It lasted two months. But even today I can catch the smell of that woman. At night I rest my head on my hand, doze off, and the smell of that Frenchwoman comes on. It's infatuation."

"Don't talk about women, old friend, or mention Saraminda's name. She was my misfortune but she was my green field. I sent Celestino after the Frenchman and I told him: 'Bring the man back, but alive.' And Celestino brought him back, except that he was rotting away. Up till then Celestino had been a man I trusted. When the basket was set down by the prison shack he'd escaped from, he stank worse than a possum. And me, the fool, wanted to save him. But he wasn't saved."

"What do you mean, he wasn't saved, Cleto?"

"From her. Nobody was ever saved from her."

28

The Queen of Spades

"Where are you from?"

"I'm from Belém do Pará. I live there. I've got good work. But I was born in Ananindeua," Artônia answered.

"Where did you learn those spells?"

"It's a gift, one of God's mysteries."

Cleto Bonfim didn't look kindly on her, the witch woman he'd sent for, paying her in gold to treat Saraminda, who wasn't getting pregnant and who, after what had happened with Celestino Gouveia, was taken with a new love for Bonfim and asked, something she'd never done before, "I want to have a child of yours. Send for a cure, because all I can think of is filling my belly with you." It was a story that Cleto never got straight in his head and it only came up after he grew suspicious of her link with the Frenchman. Thus the need to send for Artônia. Rodrigo, a prospector who'd come from Pará, told him about Artônia, famous for her work at doing impossible things, and hiding the real reason Cleto said he needed a conjuring woman to bless away the curses in the house.

Artônia had a long, yellowish-white horse face, the look of someone who didn't sleep. Around the curves of her cheeks thick black curly hair fell down, covering her ears and part of her forehead, looking like a huge lion's mane over two long, dark eyebrows. Her dull eyes were always turned toward the ground. She came in the company of a robust mulatto woman with large buttocks who answered to the name of Querida and helped her, but didn't participate in her spells and activities.

Artônia was the most famous clairvoyant witch of those parts, lands that held many versions of indigenous witchcraft. Cleto sent for her, accepting her conditions of spending a moon, receiving two pounds of gold and having a hut of her own, boarded up with overlapping planks and slats to cover the seams so that neither light nor spying eyes could penetrate, because only in that way could she do her work. She also asked for the freedom to take care of other customers. The expenses and arrangements of her trip, coming and going, as well as the day-to-day costs, food and drink, were to be taken care of by the one who hired her.

"'Cleto, kiss me, Cleto. I'm pure. I've begun to be a virgin again. I can feel it. You can see. I want to have a child,' she told me and I believed her, Clément. I began to think about having a child with her, someone who didn't get pregnant. Could it be that she was pregnant and wanted to deceive me? Like I told you before, she never got pregnant, not from me, because I'd given a belly to lots of women, but I never took responsibility for any child. Saraminda told me that she'd come to have another big love for me. Her cousin Lorette, a swindler and big whore, kept her grandmother's four pounds of gold, but she brought and gave her the certificate of deposit for the sixteen pounds I paid because nobody could collect except her since the document was in her name and had been with her grandmother Balbina, who'd died.

"Saraminda made me cry. She called to me, shut herself up in the bedroom with me, and showed me the certificate. 'Bonfim, this piece of paper is everything I've earned in my life. It's the gold that bought me for you. A piece of stained yellow paper. Because of it I came here and began this Passion-week life.'

"I remember, Clément. I thought that Saraminda was a woman who wanted to be mine alone. She was repentant. I'd finally gotten into her soul.

"When the dogs ate Celestino, I was revolted. I saw that Saraminda was my misfortune.

"'Cleto,' she shouted painfully, begging me, 'Kill me, but don't send me away, Cleto. I can't live without you anymore. There aren't any more Frenchmen, there isn't anyone anymore. I'm a virgin again and I've menstruated, but I want to get pregnant.' I

169

was already crazy with that new bit about getting pregnant. Where had that urge come from?"

Dressed in checkered madras, Lucy began to hum the music of a *touloulous* from a Cayenne carnival.

"Saraminda opened her trunk, took out the certificate of deposit for my sixteen pounds of gold, and said, 'It's yours, Bonfim. I come to you now because I want to and not because of gold...'

"But I was already losing my passion for her, suspicious about her wanting to have a child.

"'The gold is yours...'

"'But it's not doing me any good, Bonfim. I want to belong to you...'

"Saraminda was showing her body with tears falling down onto her breasts, their yellow tips shining. Then I lowered my eyes and looked at what nature had given her. I weakened completely and gave in to temptation again. I began kissing her. She stroked my head and for the first time I said to her, 'Kiss me, Saraminda. Saraminda, kiss me...'"

Clément grew excited. He got up and wanted to leave.

"Stop it, Cleto, stop it. I'm starting to get all worked up. I remember the waterfall."

"What are you talking about, Clément?"

"Lucy, send for a painter. Have him paint this window here. This one here. This one, off the verandah. Black. The molding and the blinds. I want a black window that's always open. She'll come someday."

"She who, Clément?" Cleto asked, joining in the conversation.

"Nobody, nothing."

Cleto went back to his story and took up his remembrances again.

"On that same day Artônia asked me to come to her place. She wanted to start her work. I went in, half suspicious, because I'd never had any dealings with that kind of woman, the ones who uncovered mysteries. I'd never wanted to know the future and I wasn't given to incantations.

"Artônia looked at me and asked: 'What's the job, Mr. Bonfim?'

"'Saraminda wants to have a child.'

"'Then let's get to work. Do you want to know everything the cards are going to say?'

"'You can tell me.'

"'Look, Mr. Bonfim. I see things, but I only tell what the customer wants. The cards show things that a lot of people don't want to know.'

"'You can tell me. I'm not afraid.'

"I didn't like her face, the wily witch. She took a well-worn deck of cards from the pocket of her skirt. She placed a glass of water on the table and tossed a nettle leaf into it. She closed her eyes and opened the deck. She drew a card, took it in both hands, and lifted it up to her open eyes, saying 'The cards know where all truths lie, Mr. Bonfim. Your misfortune is here,' and she threw a queen of spades onto the table.

"I looked at the card. It was Saraminda.

"'Mr. Bonfim, you were born in Cameta and you've got the gift of gold, but you let a female devil into your life.' And she went on: 'I see a golden razor. That's what's going to save you. There's something farther away than you think.'

"I shuddered. How could she know that I was thinking about the razor? And what about that hidden mystery? She was a she-devil, too.

"'What should I do?' I asked.

"'Don't give up your plan with the razor. It's the only thing that can cut the cords around your neck.'

"'Don't draw any more cards, Dona Artônia. I don't want any more of your services. Pack your bag and get ready to leave.'"

29

The Night for Decisions

It was on that night, invaded by a strange silence, that the idea of
the razor came to him. The rain was pouring down. Then everything stopped. Bonfim wasn't asleep. In the darkness of the
bedroom he heard Saraminda, who was lying down, breathing with
a sigh that was almost like the night breeze. Her odor of lilies
spread through the darkness. A flash of lightning exploded in his
head and gave off quivering jabs. He was thinking about his life,
the emptiness into which it had been transformed, with nothing, no
children, no family, no wife. Gold had destroyed him. He'd left his
life behind and still he kept looking for it. Saraminda was the happiness he'd known, but she was also the unhappiness. "I made
myself and I unmade myself." That was when he first thought
about becoming free, after what had happened with Carlindo, the
magician. That case had brought him to the edge of the precipice.
What would the first step be? "Who tied me up in these cords?
Me. Then I myself will cut these cords and entanglements. Bonfim
is going to be Bonfim, the one who was born and grew up as
Bonfim."

He'd always had the courage to make decisions. The solution
was right there. He took the lamp from under the hammock along
with the box of matches next to the revolver. He arose, turned up
the wick, lit it, and then trimmed it so the flame would be low, a dim
light not spreading everywhere. He wanted to see the shadows,
the darkness. And he lifted it high over Saraminda's bed to light up
her body, moving the lamp slowly over it from her feet to her head.
He stopped at her throat, which was turned to one side and stretched
out as her head lay on its side. She turned over, as if feeling the

brightness. He put his hand over the beam of light, shutting it out. He waited and then let the beam out again. The light now partly revealed the back of her neck. Her throat was the path by which he would get out of the labyrinth. The idea was coming to him now bit by bit, pieces that he was putting together in his thoughts, an idea that no one but he himself could have or execute. He wouldn't allow anyone else to touch Saraminda. Only he could do her harm. The idea terrified him, but he had to free himself. Killing her wasn't his wish, but, through her death, finding the Bonfim who had disappeared. And on that day that blessed blood would overflow all the streams and the god of gold would reveal his mysteries and there would be so much that a thousand bottles wouldn't be enough to hold it all.

It was just that he couldn't bring off that awful thing with a barber's razor, the kind used on the claim for the usual services. "I'm going to Cayenne and have them make me a gold razor, one with precious stones and pretty designs." And he imagined a jewel of a razor, something into which the gold had never thought of being transformed. All aglow, full of labyrinths, neat, incapable of growing dull. It would be like the sun.

That seductive thought had passed through his mind many times. It always horrified him. Gold couldn't demand such pure blood of him, that red dew which fell on mornings of love. The monster was a mystery growing inside him, especially after he'd grown suspicious of Saraminda's belly and how she gazed at him. It was a matter of increasing hallucinations. They never settled, always vacillating, shifting, as though they were hiding a secret. Those green eyes that leaned over his face and crossed their arms, waiting there, afternoons and nights, the color of the jungle, the sea, the leaves, the mosses, the rapids at Grand Dégrad.

It had to be a secret that no one could ever suspect, one that she never could have thought of, that he had never imagined. That razor would be a jewel that had never before existed, made of gold and wind, dreams and nothingness, for no one to touch or see or suspect.

But along with her I'll be killing myself, killing what I loved most. All men kill the thing they love, I've heard said. I'm a coward because I'm going to kill someone who doesn't love me. I'm going to kill my love, which doesn't die.

He heard the song of the birds waking up the day. Night had passed without his noticing as he talked to himself. Bonfim to Bonfim.

Dawn broke.

30

The Decision on the Trip

The *Evangelina*, an old English steamer making the run from the Calçoene to Cayenne and from there to the Antilles, stopped at many ports. Coming from Europe, it was casting off now from the Firmino docks. It blew its departing whistle and everybody was on the quarter deck waving goodbye. There were a lot of passengers, most of them heading for Cayenne, many of whom were people involved in the business of selling supplies to the stores that stretched out along all the paths demanded by the claims, not only on the Lourenço, but on all the rivers and streams in the region where gold had been found. Others were ill and going to Guiana for treatment. As soon as the ship began to move, Bonfim went to his cabin. He was traveling in the company of Ricardo, a young fellow who'd studied in Belém do Pará and who, after a nursing course, had come to the claim to earn some money. He grew close to Bonfim and soon abandoned his profession in order to fill a position of trust with him, helping him in his dealings, keeping him company, and taking care of the books. He was a typical man from Marajó, broad-featured and short, with straight reddish hair. Ricardo was with the second-class passengers, in the lower part of the *Evangelina*, where in accord with the rigid hierarchy of the region subordinates traveled. Bonfim didn't discuss his personal matters with him, even though they did have long conversations about people, business and life in general.

Bonfim went into his cabin. The narrow bunk had been made up. On top of a tiny bureau was a tray and a pitcher with a wavy rim. In the corner was an iron washstand with a round porcelain basin and a simple cast iron frame holding a square mirror. In the other corner was a door painted white, also made of metal with rounded edges. It led to the small bathroom, where a white Williams toilet bearing the prestigious Manchester-England guarantee occupied half the space. Overhead was the flush box, which worked with a small cord that had a wooden handle at its end. On the room side, matching the width of the bathroom, was a small space for suitcases and clothes. It was a very concise miracle of saved space, all done up in naval paint. For light there was a porthole that opened onto the narrow companionway going around the upper deck of the modest ship. Up front was the bridge.

He lay down, took off his loose jacket, and remained in his shorts, continuing the monologue that never left his head. He stopped thinking a bit to lament the fact that he had to travel on an English ship, without understanding anything being said, even though there were some people he knew with whom he could converse in Creole.

"Do you know what you're doing, Bonfim?" said the one.

"I do. I know that I've already made the decision," replied the other.

"So, then, Bonfim, continue on with your martyrdom," said the first.

"It's got nothing to do with martyrdom. I'm going back to being you, who ran away from me."

In the open sea the voyage to Cayenne confronted the waves at Cape Orange.

31

The Funeral Procession

I came out of the sleep of death without knowing it. I looked around and all I could see was an ox-blood dove cooing on the slatwork. I was on the floor with nobody around and the door opened wide as though they had run away. There was nobody on guard, nothing. Everyone must have run off. An immense silence remained, filling my ears. I got up, tapped my knees to see if I had any feeling. I rubbed my hands to warm them and went out. Nobody stopped me. There was nobody in the yard, no sign of the dogs or the pigs or the chickens. I remembered when my escape had been arranged, Maruanda's voice: "Severino will come for you before dawn." I realized that I was permanently deaf. No sound penetrated my ears, neither the rustle of the wind nor the song of the birds.

I was awakened from my fear by a kind of distant murmuring, a whispering that was vaguely lost in the distance, as though coming from anxious voices. I slowly got the impression that the sounds were getting closer and I felt at once that they were coming for me in a group, carrying clubs, shotguns, stones. But it was only a feeling. Nothing appeared. The whispering stayed in the distance and I was the only one who heard it. It wasn't a buzzing or a ringing in the head, it was real sound, something taking place quite far away.

I didn't know how to run away nor did I want to. Where could I flee to? I was free, but I was a prisoner inside myself. I walked away, I don't know how, and was foolishly heading into the woods along paths that went nowhere and saw I was heading in the direction of the Lourenço settlement. I caught sight of Jacu hill and saw a procession. The men were walking along in silence. There was what looked like a dead person in a hammock in a bamboo frame. No one was saying anything or weeping. I remained up there watching the procession as it squeezed itself in and stretched out in order to make its way through the overgrown path. They were heading in the direction of the old abandoned cemetery through the Oh-My-God Marsh and its mire. The cemetery had been abandoned because it used to flood and remain under water when the stream overflowed, covering high spots and getting into the woods, where it stagnated in low places and brought on mosquitoes and fevers. Spooks would appear there. "Why are they burying him in the old cemetery since it's been all forgotten?" I wondered when I saw the procession go down and disappear from view. Then I put two and two together and was certain they were burying Celestino Gouveia. No one had dared bury him in Limão or Lourenço. As far as Bonfim was concerned, he would have left his remains there to be devoured by dogs and vultures. But Bonfim was nowhere around to make any decisions. He was silent, shut up in the house for a week, he and Saraminda. But it wasn't because of mourning and nobody knew or would ever know what they were talking about during that time. Gedina, who saw them, said that they weren't talking at all, locked up in silence day and night. It was Gedina who remembered to go look for me, finding how I had revived. She came in and saw it was all empty.

"Kemper! Kemper!" she shouted.

Inside the prison a black sloth was hiding. He'd come in through the open door and stayed there.

"You ugly critter. I don't like seeing you dragging along."

Noting Gedina's presence, the animal curled up and huddled its body together, remaining motionless. Gedina felt a chill.

"The Frenchman had the devil in his body. He's turned into a soul from the other world. He disappeared. In the state he was in he couldn't have walked." And she went out saying a prayer and crossing herself.

She went to the kitchen and said to Zeduco, "The Frenchman's disappeared, vanished, without a trace!"

It had all happened so quickly and magically that it didn't seem true. It was a dream, like some kind of spell having to do with the evil one. Things had happened so fast. No one could have thought that Celestino's death would have come before mine.

"That Frenchman arrived and brought all kinds of bad luck. Let him go to Hell and keep the Devil company. That's who his father is."

Famished and out of my mind, I walked along aimlessly. I had no knowledge of the law of survival in the jungle and didn't dare show myself. It was then I entered a deserted hut and found Domingos the ring seller there.

"Who are you?"

"Kemper. I've lost track of time and any memory of who I am and when I came to be here."

"My name is Domingos. I'm running away. I was done in and will never come back. I saw the Calçoene be born and I saw it prosper. It's started to die. It's got fever. Dogs are already eating people."

"I don't know who I am, just my name. I came out of the grave. Take me away from here."

He felt pity for me. I was whiter than the milk of wild cotton. My eyes wouldn't close. I was a sight.

Domingos lifted me up. I only remembered being put aboard a ship at the Cunani post with a piece of paper on which the name of the Société Equatoriale was written. I was supposed to look it up in Cayenne.

He gave me a ring, the kind he sold, and instructed me, "Don't take it off your finger. It will take you along in peace."

I looked at the ring. It was small and had a smell of body odor, but it was enchanted.

179

32

An Old Goldsmith

"How many days will it take you to make the piece of jewelry I'm ordering?"

"A month. It's got to be a work of art, you know. I still have to get the stones and the diamonds. Nothing's easy here. I've got to go to my professional colleagues for help. I have the emerald, from an old ring I bought years ago that I couldn't find a buyer for. I haven't got the other things."

"Don't hold back because of money. I'll pay whatever's necessary. What I want is for the work to be done and for it to be a thing of beauty."

"It will still take the same time, Mr. Bonfim, because for a jewel of that kind I'm the only one who knows how to handle it. There's no jeweler better than me here in Cayenne. I've been working at my craft for more than forty years now."

Cleto looked at Jean-Baptiste, a white-haired man around seventy, with round-rimmed glasses a bit twisted by age resting on the tip of his nose.

"The problem is with the blade, Mr. Bonfim. A gold edge, no matter how much it's worked, isn't the same as steel. Unless you only want the razor as a piece of jewelry and not for use in shaving. Gold won't keep a cutting edge, only steel."

"I want it with the best cutting edge possible. It's got to be used without causing any irritation, just doing the cutting in a single stroke."

"But you have to know that gold can't be compared to steel."

"Can't you use a steel blade, like the ones on German razors, which are the best, and plate it with gold?"

"That I can do, but I'll leave the cutting edge free. It's a job for someone who knows how."

"Then make it that way. I want a razor that cuts, the best for what it'll be used for."

"It isn't a gift, then, Mr. Bonfim?"

"No. It's for something holy."

"Well, then, you can come and pick it up a month from now. I'll only be able to tell you the price after finding out what I have to spend on the materials, as well as accounting for my time."

"That's fine. I'll pay whatever the cost."

The razor remained in my head from the moment I left the jeweler's and it didn't leave my imagination until I got it. I couldn't stay in Cayenne for a month. It was the seat of the Société Equatoriale and I found out what had happened with Lefèvre there, his trouble with Laurence. The agent was new and asked me for the whereabouts of that young fellow Jacques Kemper, who'd gone down bringing the carriage and hadn't been heard from since.

"I don't know," I answered simply. "He arrived four years ago. That's a long time to remember things."

"He must have gone off on some gold-hunting adventure. I've already received four letters from our president, Mr. Foucaud, and the boy's family is asking where he is."

"I only saw him on the day I got the carriage."

"I'm sending someone to look for him and I've already made several inquiries to the French police."

"I'd like to have a look at my account. I've brought Ricardo with me. He has my complete confidence and he's going to stay and look over the books."

"Mr. Bonfim, you know that we have the greatest consideration for you. My orders are to take care of you in every way. Make use of our facilities any way you choose. It's all yours."

"Thank you," I answered quickly, with the story of Kemper in my head.

"Mr. Bonfim." I heard the request as I was leaving. "If you get any news about Kemper, please let me know."

I didn't answer. My hate for the Frenchman was still in me. He was handsome and blond; I was ugly and a half-breed. Saraminda chose him because even with all my gold I held no enchantment in her eyes. Stinking Frenchman. Nothing can repay the hate of a man who's been betrayed. My years have been heavy with Saraminda's falseness. She never told me anything, but I've had my feelings, which she hasn't noticed.

One Friday they came to tell me that a messenger from Cayenne was looking for me.

"Who is it?"

"A man bringing something you ordered."

"Have him come in!" My heart was pounding, knowing that it was the razor.

"Here he is."

I got a package wrapped in paper with a box inside. I went into the back room of the warehouse where the burlapping was stored and began to open the package. When I saw the razor I didn't dare touch it, but left it lying in its case lined in red velvet. It was on fire. It had a glow that didn't dim. The emerald in the middle looked so much like the green of a person's eyes that I remembered Saraminda's stare. All around were diamonds and other stones I didn't know. A mermaid and a woman's curves decorated each side. I plucked up my courage, picked up the jewel and opened the blade. It was gilded, but the edge was still steel, thin, cutting, cold. Jean had turned out a work of art. I put the razor back in its case.

I wrapped everything up, put it under my arm, and left. The sun was hiding. I asked Taíta, "When will the moon be full?"

She answered me, "On Wednesday."

I had the feeling there were no roots in my path for me to stumble on. The razor was like finding a new claim. Saraminda must be turned to dust.

33

The Lights of Le Havre

I didn't cry. I no longer had the means to weep. I never again found out what it was like to have tears. They had all fallen during what happened to me in the Guianas. I had really been there. I watched the horizon as it disappeared with the day's last sighs and what I saw was the great fog bank over the hills of Saint-Laurent. Dim kerosene lights began to appear. It was a small and facile gleam, occasional and fugitive, fading away as it passed along on the horizon.

I was relaxing on the quarterdeck of the *Belle de Martinique*, my eyes turned back into the past. I couldn't remember anymore when I left the harbor of Le Havre on my way to Cayenne. How much time had passed? It was impossible to calculate. I was left with only a pleasurable feeling of eternity and resurrection.

The lights were different ones now. They were growing. The ship was approaching and night along with it. I was in the tomb of my hopes.

The ship went along slowly, languidly, and I counted the twenty-eight days of the crossing, one by one. From the moment I got off the gangplank at Vila do Firmino and took a last look at the gullies I had once leaped over into the unknown. So many years and they might have been so few. I had a feeling of flight, of liberation from a hell, with a touch of heaven and purgatory thrown in. I had in me memories of Cancale, trees, forests, animals, Paris, gold and women.

When I awoke from my dream I'd lost the notion and memory of everything. I rose up like a ghost, unable to put what had happened together again. I remembered the moment when

Maruanda told me, "Severino will come to get you before dawn," and nothing else. My imprisonment was over; I'd been resurrected. I got up. Everything was deserted. It seemed that everybody had run away all of a sudden, unable to carry off anything, not even the shadows. The door was wide open and the wind blew in freely. I went out. I was floating. I thought I'd lost my hearing as an undisturbed silence entered my head. There was an absence of sound all about. I went off walking through the trees. I didn't know the jungle. I didn't know how to survive in it. I walked and walked as best I could. I went up and down hills. I saw the horizon approach and then hide away. Behind the hills were the roads. I was drawing close to them. It was a brutal feeling I had. The walls of silence broke and I began to hear. My ears were flapping like fans, bringing in a distant murmur. It wasn't the movement of the wind or leaves or air or animals. It was a sad sound, like some sort of enchantment calling me. I climbed a hill and saw a procession in the distance.

Then at night when I was awake Maruanda appeared and confirmed what I already knew.

"It was Celestino Gouveia's burial, Mr. Kemper."

"Did he die?"

"He was eaten by the dogs. Cleto wouldn't let him be buried in Limão."

"Celestino Gouveia? No, I can't remember anything. My head is clear of thoughts."

The lights of Le Havre were getting close. They were brighter now and rows of them could be seen along the land. "There's France, Jacques Kemper." My head was filled with empty terrain. Sharp whistles close by and others distant and deep could be heard. Where could my sister Anne be? All the memories of childhood came first. Why did I abandon my mother? She was there, present in my memory, beautiful, with pink cheeks and long hair, asking me to be tolerant. Tolerant of what? I didn't know.

The lights were getting larger. My eyes began to be shadowy and those lights weren't like the ones in Cayenne, weak, casting beams onto the cold ground of the pavement through the windows and spreading out on the irregular sidewalk punished by the rains.

The crossing had been rough. A storm prevented everyone from sleeping and the ship rode the seas the way boats ride the rapids between the banks of the River Carnot. In the morning I went out onto the portside companionway. Another memory unfurled in my head. I remembered that I'd taken a different trip before and there, at that spot, had been a girl named Geneviève with her mother, whose name I can't remember and who introduced me to her. I remember her from the nape of her neck as she disembarked at the docks in Martinique.

I kept on walking in the jungle, stung by wasps, horse-flies, fire ants and bees. I didn't know where I could spend the night or what to do. I saw an abandoned hut where I lay down. When I opened my eyes there was a short, stocky man beside me, a suitcase in his hand, and just as startled as I was.

"Who are you?"

"Kemper."

"I'm Domingos and it looks like the two of us are leaving Lourenço."

"I'm lost. I don't remember anything."

Domingos Eleutério de Barros was an adventurer, like all those who traveled those seas of trees and rivers and gold. A merchant in Belém do Pará, he'd come to Calçoene in search of Ricardino Merenda, a man he'd grubstaked who hadn't appeared for six months, owing him a pound of gold. Domingos had a goldsmith's shop in Pará with four craftsmen, two helpers, and a cashier. He was going through the claims buying gold and selling jewelry. Then he would return home and set to work transforming the gold into rings, chains, bracelets, tiaras, earrings and charms, and he would go off with them, trading on the claims and in the settlements. He always traveled as part of a troop of itinerant merchants, his friends, who carried cloth, clothing, footwear, medicines and perfume for barter, as was the custom in those parts. He sold a medicine called Electric-Oil, an unguent recommended for pain, Kemp pills for dizziness, antacids like Ostrog, and nitrate pills.

I don't know why Domingos appeared. His story seemed like an aimless direction.

He went to Lourenço trying to collect on an old bill. As was his custom, he financed the supplies, tools and expenses of a digging, receiving in return a percentage of the gold collected. For three years he'd partnered with and had loaned money to Ricardino, an old acquaintance from Pará like himself who was involved in the business practices on the claims. It had been six months now and he hadn't come back to settle accounts, as he ordinarily did every two months. They told him that Ricardino had left Lourenço for Cunani, where Domingos didn't find him. There they told him that he'd gone back to Lourenço, where Domingos was looking for him at that time.

Domingos arrived on a Saturday. The people on the claim left work at four in the afternoon and were starting their break, which lasted until Monday. It was a time to wash clothes for the week's change. Saturday was party day, when naked feet put on raw leather boots bought in Belém, canvas shoes from France or low-cut regular shoes. Neatly shod and wearing clean pants, zinc oxide deodorant in their armpits, they went to the bars in the settlements with their grams of gold. The women there were worse off than animals and were picked up to go with them into the woods, because the dance halls were sheds without walls.

The ship maintained its speed. The boilers powered the propellers, weary from so many crossings. The lights were getting closer, clearer and clearer, brighter and brighter. No one would be waiting for me on the dock and no one even expected me to be still alive. Domingos had brought me to Vila do Firmino and, taken with compassion, had put me on board for Cayenne. When the agent of the Société Equatoriale saw me, he shouted, "You're dead. The firm has already paid your family for your death."

"I don't know if I'm dead or not. I just want to get back to France."

Maruanda had told me, "Leave Guiana, Kemper, get away from the Contestado, go away. I can't cross the ocean because spirits from the claims can't get free of the gold."

Domingos knew that life quite well. Recognized by some, unknown to others, he inquired about Ricardino.

"He passed on his claim about four months ago and went off to Cunani."

186

"He's not in Cunani, I've just come from there."

"Well, he's not here anymore. What do you want with him?"

"It's just that we're partners and since he hasn't come back yet, I've come after him so I can find out what's going on."

"Yes, he got to be a big man in this region. He struck it rich three times and it seems he went away because he had a run-in with Cleto Bonfim and left for the River Carnot sector," said one of the many people he questioned.

"And where's Bonfim?"

"Three days ago something hellish happened to him. Celestino Gouveia, his right-hand man, was killed, torn to death by his wife's dogs. He's been shut up in his house and nobody knows what's going on with him."

Domingos remembered the last time he'd been with Bonfim two years ago, when he was invited to dinner at his residence, a Creole house that looked like a palace hidden away in the jungle. He'd met his wife and remembered the pack of dogs outside.

She was a pretty woman, a well-shaped Creole with a suspicious look. He remembered quite well the conversation when she saw him with his black satchel, the kind that everybody knows is carried by jewelry salesmen, and right away she began questioning him.

"Do you sell jewelry?"

"I buy and sell gold, Dona Saraminda. It's been my life's work."

"Of course. I could tell by your suitcase. We women are nosy creatures."

"But I didn't come here for that purpose, ma'am. I came because of the pleasure of an invitation from Bonfim."

"But I'd like to see your jewelry."

"I can't refuse your wish. If my friend Bonfim will permit me."

"Go ahead and show it, Domingos," he answered. "Gold is ugly, but it turns pretty when goldsmiths make it into rings, earrings, bracelets, watches and necklaces. And women like all that a lot."

Domingos picked up the case, which was divided into rectangles, lined in red velvet and filled with those gewgaws sold everywhere. Nothing that could catch the eye of the wife of the biggest claim-owner in the Calçoene. But his duty was to show things, half-embarrassed.

She picked up a medallion and asked, "What saint is this?"

"Our Lady of Nazareth, the patroness of Pará."

"Of Belém do Pará, isn't she...?"

"Yes, ma'am..."

"Did you know that Cayenne was the name of an Indian prince who married the Princess Belém? My grandmother told me that story..."

"No, I didn't know that, Dona Saraminda."

"I've already asked Cleto to take me to Belém so I can attend the feast day of that saint..."

"The Círio pilgrimage in Belém, ma'am, is a beautiful procession, with people passing before Our Lady's eyes for half a day and throngs of penitents attached to ropes that pull the floats. It's a pretty sight, a great demonstration of faith."

"So Cleto promised we'd show up there someday..."

"There's plenty of time ahead of us, Saraminda," Bonfim put in.

"That's true. In Cayenne, Mr. Domingos, the biggest gatherings of people are on July 14th at the Place des Palmistes and in September during the festival of Majuri, with dancing. They have a whole garden filled with flowers, Japanese lanterns and gas lamps next to the Carrefour de Jean-Paté-Banane, with sack races, donkey-runs and stilt races. There's another good time at Carnival and another sad one, *La Nuit de la Toussaint*, when everyone takes lighted candles and flowers to the cemetery for their dead. It's sad, but it's like it was a dance of the souls. The cemetery was famous, with its chapel and an old bell at the entrance. The first tomb is pretty, like a column of split marble, where Governor Louis Massin lies. He was Captain of Land and Sea and died during the plague of 1851. And there's the tomb of Sister Norbert, who did charitable work in Cayenne."

Recent memory was better. Kemper could see Domingos's eyes, his hard, calloused hand squeezing his shoulder and saying, "Go. Don't come back again. I won't be coming back either."

He picked up his reminiscences again. Everybody he'd met on his arrival had disappeared. Lefèvre was dead, he'd killed himself. Laurence had run away, chasing after a new love, freeing herself from "the Guiana heat."

The fear of being pursued and found. The thoughts in his head had dimmed and ideas were tumbling about. There were huge empty gaps, mostly about his time on the claim. He remembered his arrival and there were a few windows still opened on his memory. He couldn't understand clearly who Saraminda was, or Cleto Bonfim. Nor did he remember his fevers and the gold. With great difficulty he opened the doors of memory to recall the walk he'd taken in Cayenne with Laurence. Everything was hazy. It gave him a wish to see the giant anteaters on the shield of Guiana once more. He went to the fort of Saint-Michel de Ceperou and in his head was Laurence's story of how the bell at the fort had rung for eight days and eight nights in 1888 during the great fire that had destroyed the commercial part of the old city.

"Look at the Palace of Government and the Hôtel de Ville. In the beginning they formed part of the old Jesuit monastery," she would repeat because she liked to do that in order to pass the time, to stroll along with the help of the city landmarks.

Kemper remembered Laurence and his visit to the city. He saw once more the huge palm trees at the end of the ancient Esplanade, now called the Esplanade of the Palms, transplanted from Guizambourg, brought God knows how, gigantic as they were, to that locale.

"Look at this palm tree. There's not another like it in the world. It's got two trunks! A palm tree with two heads. Only in Guiana..." It was Laurence's voice in the wiles she had for his seduction.

All those images were references coming into bloom like bubbles escaping from the depths of the sea and rising to the surface. Everything he remembered began with Laurence in a full skirt. She was dancing, and after that her taking him to his room, resolutely undressing him, kissing him all over, shoulders, chest, legs, sides, his whole body, with her perfumed mouth, her saliva filling him with pleasure. She was excited by the dress that was supposed to be for the other and then and there it belonged to her.

Cayenne was a mystery that kept revealing itself, a modest city with the beauty that small things have. Its people were merry. There was an explosion of a diversity of races on the streets, with a predominance of beautiful black blood, a color that showed itself to be dazzling to the east wind and the mystery of the northern forests.

The long days of waiting. The expected quarantine. Internment in the Civil and Military Hospice, the General Hospital, which had taken care of the sick ever since the 18th century. The compassionate eyes of the Sisters of Saint-Paul de Chartres because of his intense, pale yellow color, something leftover from the illnesses of his resurrection in the prison on the claim.

In a confused spin, Kemper began to get his memory back, bit by bit, dim, dark, with a vision shaded by the stains that still covered his eyes.

He got on board. The crossing, the tossing of the ship, the storm, the lack of appetite, and, worst of all, the loss of any desire to see the land from which he had first departed.

The lights of Le Havre helped open his eyes.

34

Saraminda's Night

Cayenne was waterlogged from the rain. Thick drops gathered in bunches and tongues of water filled all the spaces in between, carrying off the leaves and refuse, all the filth from the streets running along the narrow channels in the gutters that sought out the deep storm sewers built to receive great seasonal storms.

Clément Tamba was wandering vaguely, strolling through the shadows of the house made of old wood that the years had eaten away. The trees in the gardens and flower beds that faced the rooms were all taken by rot and the tree trunks bore whitish spots, leaving the leaves curled up and full of holes. The jasmine vines grew legless; the weight of passing years had knocked them over into shrubs that stretched along the ground and hid the Bermuda grass which became slow-growing and rotten. Only the scent of the star lilies had resisted, penetrating the bedrooms with a sweet and bitter odor.

"Lucy, my dear Lucy, when could I ever imagine that you would accompany me through this life that never ends, these years so full of mildew?"

"I'm neither happy nor sad, Clément. I'm following my destiny of being at your side. There are things we have no control over. Your presence doesn't bother me, but it doesn't comfort me either. We share the same chimes of time."

"Have you heard the cathedral bells, Lucy?"

"Yes, when they ring the Hallelujah and on the days when they announce the funeral of some Christian."

"Where is Father João, who tried to convert me once, asking me to be baptized and to ask forgiveness for my sins?"

"I don't know. I remember Father José, who took my confession for the first time. 'How have you fulfilled your duties to the commandments? Have you known the sin of the flesh yet? Have you denied any aid to the poor?' 'No.' 'Say three Our Fathers and two Hail Marys, promise to repent your sins and never turn to the temptations of the Devil.' I've never been tempted by the Devil. God for me was the sort of father who would protect me and who wasn't going to throw me into the bottom of Hell. Father José's God scared me..."

Cleto Bonfim said, "I never went to confession in my whole life. I always resisted matters of the Church. I always believed more in the Devil than in God. The Devil made me afraid, but God never threatened me. The spells of witch doctors were the Devil's work for me, like *piaille*."

Lucy, in a soft voice, made some revelations:

"Tamba, I suffered when I had to confess to the priest about the first time I gave myself to a man. He was a schoolmate. I was seventeen and he was eighteen. He took me for a stroll behind the building and then we went into the woods. I'd been walking out with him for six months and he already knew all the pathways of my body, covered by his child's fingers. Until one day he fondled my breasts and told me that he wanted me. I refused. I was always shy. I don't know how it happened. He broke down my defenses. I accepted passively. Father José asked me how he reacted when he saw me. I told him that I didn't remember. 'Was he all excited?' 'I don't know, Father José.' 'What do you mean, you don't know?' 'I don't know if he was.' 'Tell the truth. Was the Devil inside you?' There were so many questions and I only remember that I went out with a feeling of terrible guilt, which didn't drain off in the confessional. 'Was it the first time?' 'Yes.' 'What did you feel?' Father José was asking me too many questions. My boyfriend wasn't crude. He treated me with tenderness. He caressed me. He loaded me down with compliments and we became lovers like that for two years. Afterwards, I don't know why, we didn't continue, but I thought I was sinning and asked Father José to advise me. He answered, 'Abandon your sin.' I abandoned it. Today I'm not sorry about giving myself to Juvêncio."

"Don't talk to me about the men you've had, Lucy. I don't want to know about your past. When we got together you were a new life for me. This is an ancient love that I had no desire to know about. A beautiful house, but I didn't want to uncover who built it," Tamba muttered.

"My past is today, it's here on this big verandah where there's no breeze, empty, next to you, with no children, no memory, ruminating on time."

"One of the happiest moments I had in Cayenne was when the square landau I ordered in Paris arrived. It was a classy carriage, manufactured by the Million Guiet Cie and designed by Alfred Gabriel Count, the famous carriage-maker. The outside was black with silver trim. The door handles had my monogram on them. The interior was silk satin. It had studs on the roof with gilt rosettes. The steps could be folded up and were made of Morocco leather, and it had two lamps, one on each side. It cost me twenty thousand eight hundred pounds, a small matter with all my Calçoene gold. It had four wheels, good springs, and was drawn by a team of white horses I acquired. I had them rubbed with oil and harnessed their sheen for going through the streets of Cayenne. It was a nice carriage, with crystal windows. Everybody went to the door of their houses to see me inside with friends and lovers. Then the people began to think it was vanity on my part, that I was ridiculous and wanted to look like something I wasn't. Nothing but envy. No one had ever seen a carriage from France in Cayenne. I ordered a uniform with gold buttons for the coachman, who wore a kepi and would get all ready to go out with the carriage. In time people began to lose their curiosity and everybody got used to it. It was no longer a novelty. It rotted away in my backyard. There it is, falling to pieces, faded, wounded by old age. I survived better than it or the horses did. It was much better than the one Cleto had brought to Lourenço. Cleto's shame, getting a cabriolet for Saraminda."

"Don't speak that woman's name, a tramp who didn't even know how to pray," Lucy said.

"No, Lucy, she was a phantom in the center of the claim. Even today she torments our heads."

"Stop all that, Clément Tamba."

The rain went on and on. Every so often a thunderclap could be heard and lightning cut the darkness.

"Clément Tamba, old friend," the shade of Cleto Bonfim reap-

193

peared. "I'm in need of talk. Free me from these other memories of mine."

He was standing there wearing his famous old hat, with a goatee and long arms full of veins reaching out, stretching his long hands.

"Clément," Cleto said. "The French were bandits. They themselves were ashamed of what they'd done. They invaded Vila do Amapá and killed everyone, set fire to the houses, and didn't leave anything. They pillaged, sacked, and the land belonged to us."

"But it wasn't us," Clément answered. "They were soldiers sent by Charwein. We, the Creoles in the Contestado, were French but we had nothing against the Brazilians. It was the governor of Guiana. And later on, Bonfim, he showed his perverted generosity by sending the widows of the victims of Mapá two jugs of Saint-Julien wine. Cabral wasn't Brazil."

"Show some respect, Clément, Cabral was Brazil. Cabral was a hero. He gave up everything, risked his life. Charwein is hated in Guiana. Cabral is a hero in Brazilian territory."

"You're hearing the shouting, the horses galloping, the dust rising, the diggers cheering, and Cabral, Winchester in hand, with his captains, invading Lourenço and shouting, 'Freedom…' I was hiding there on the mountain, looking down."

"Yes, Clément. I was at home and there I stayed, sunk in my misfortune. After I'd talked to the witch woman and she'd had her throat cut, the claim began to dry up. I saw the mother of the claim bar the doors to the gold. The pans began to come up with mud and muck. A lot of water turned into blood. Many diggers ran away afraid. The sheds were collapsing, the roads were filling with brush, everyone was leaving. The curse fell upon Lourenço but it didn't fall on other claims. Everything started when that Frenchman arrived. Saraminda fell into a passion for him and for that dress infected with witchcraft."

"I wasn't there at the time the claim dried up. I'd run away. You're getting things mixed up, Bonfim," Clément said.

"For me, everything is mixed up."

"My last day was that one. Cabral parading on the streets of Lourenço, all the people backing him up and shouting, 'Where's that man from the House of France?' And they surrounded my house, went through everything and took out the flag hidden in my trunk. Bonfim, when I saw that cloud of smoke my heart began to split in two. And the house was burning and in it my things, my memories, my past. I could hear it when the fire made my table crackle," Clément sobbed deeply, as if getting a new look at the fire. "I almost threw myself down the slope. But I couldn't do anything, I didn't have the strength. My road led to exile in Cayenne. I hadn't known that so much love for Lourenço had grown in me, that I had so much love for the Calçoene. But when I think about it clearly, it was Cabral who made me leave that hell. Those people dying, the swollen feet, the fevers, the poverty, and us stealing food from the poor devils with fraudulent weights and doctoring the books. We paid for the evil we did to those people, Bonfim. My escape wasn't difficult, I knew the people, the roads, and I had a lot of fugitive Creoles along with me. Cabral had no intent to chase us. He only wanted to get rid of us."

"But, Clément, I died twice over. When they saw that the claim had come down with fever the Brazilians ran away, afraid of the death of the gold. The pannings brought up blood, my storerooms were empty. I couldn't even bring back the merchandise. I was alone with Ricardo, who they said was Saraminda's lover. I left the lower warehouse and stayed on the land I owned near the mine. On that day I made my decision. That day. I left everything and walked home. I filled my pockets with nuggets and hit the road. I was tired, my head was in rotten shape. I began to cry. I sobbed as I walked. I was going to kill everything I loved most.

"A rooster crowed. Six in the afternoon. When I went through the swamp those frogs were croaking. Among the *mururu* palms, on the top of the water lilies, I saw the head of the witch Artônia asking, 'I want my body for my head that was thrown here,' and she repeated, 'I want my body.' I looked up at the mountain and there on top was her headless body with its arms open. A woman who'd brought me nothing but bad news. Then I looked at the underbrush and there on the dry trunk of a snakewood tree was Artônia's head, two heads. I closed my eyes. She was everywhere. An ugly business. And she was laughing. She was the one who'd cast a spell over the claim."

"You saw that, Cleto, and didn't run away?"

"I saw it. I saw it, but I already had the decision in my head."

"What decision, Bonfim?"

"The one I knew I was going to make someday."

"You thought about the cock's crow."

"I thought about getting away from those rivers of gold, I swear it."

"Swear what?"

"The cock crowed three times."

"Why?"

"It was the cock's crow that confirmed for me what I already knew. Betrayal."

"Cleto, old friend, did you cut Saraminda's throat? Tell me. Until this day nobody knows."

Bonfim disappeared. Lucy came on the run. Tamba was sweating and breathing hard. He was pale, on the verge of fainting.

"Lucy, call for the landau with four white horses. Clap your hands, make them gallop. Have them open the black window so she can come in. She's coming..."

"Clément...," Lucy sobbed. She repeated, "Clément?"

He didn't answer.

"Raimunda, bring the candle that's in the cupboard drawer. Light it. Bring it."

Again he didn't answer.

The room was filled with the strong yellow-clove smell of a dead person. A silence was bleeding and dissolving in space like smoke.

It was broken by a neighing coming from the street at full trot and stopping at the door. Firm footsteps leaped down and could be heard on the porchway. The horses were silent.

"Monsieur Clément Tamba, *je suis prêt*, I'm ready. Where are we going?" the coachman asked.

196

35

The Winding Cloth

"What have you done with your life, Cleto Bonfim? How could you have found so many thorns to walk on? Where is my body, Cleto? My head rolls from place to place. Why did you slit my throat, Bonfim? Did I come at your call in order to lose my head?"

"No, Artônia, don't accuse me."

The shouting of the ghosts was like a buzzing of bees in his ears. The claim in Roraima, where he'd begun this life of his, the painted Indians hooting, arrows and bullets going back and forth. So many dead. Running away from gold and searching for gold. The pathways of the Calçoene, rapids galloping along over stones, the river hiding here and there as it passed through the narrows, and us struggling with the empty canoes. Always the same agonies, treading back over memories. The new claim, houses springing up, the arrival of the French, the trails, the ships, everything smelling of money and whatever he wanted done everywhere. The nights in Cayenne. The arrival of the women. His meeting with Saraminda:

"Oh, my misfortune. Bear with me in this final decision. What's the use of living? What's gold good for? I didn't eat gold, I didn't drink gold, I dug gold, and it tormented me night and day. Lie down here, Saraminda, I want to hold you. I want to run my hand down your thighs. I want to lick your breasts, kiss you, and then feel your otter body rubbing against mine, all curled up as I breathe on you, sweating and feeling the warm pleasure of a single body, one on the other, two in one in the quiet of our moans and the drool of our pleasure. I want you, Saraminda, and you betrayed me, you loved the filthy Frenchman and gave yourself to him. The claim's dying, the panning's drying up, the veins, the woods and even Salomoganha Mountain are all dry. The roots of the *tonka*-bean tree, which flourish where there's gold, with their sweet-smelling beans, stink ranker than goats now. All that's left are your yellow breasts and your green eyes. Where's my razor, a piece of jewelry made for just this night? Only that rare piece of gold and diamonds could take you to the sleep of the dead."

Cleto Bonfim picked up the case, opened it, and took out the razor. The stones glittered and the gold gleamed.

The room was deep in shadow. The windows were open and the opaque light of the moon, hidden behind clouds, came in. Cleto looked at the bed. Saraminda was sleeping; the Calçoene heat was heavy. She was the way she liked to be, in the magical simplicity of her nakedness. Her body was resplendent, her gilded breasts and bare sex in full view. Her breathing was like a soft sigh. Her head, fallen to one side, was resting with the abandonment of her soul to sleep and dreams.

Cleto Bonfim brought the lamp closer. Saraminda was sleeping. His hand was shaking, his lips quivered from fear, his eyes blinked nervously. He had constructed that moment, a prison without bars.

He opened the razor and gripped it tightly, firmly, his right hand resting on his left, all the muscles of his arms contracted. He trembled as he looked at Saraminda. He wanted to prolong that moment in his life. He wanted to have her one last time. Saraminda wasn't moving. Her eyes, even when closed, gleamed mysteriously with fear and terror. Bonfim drew back, went to the window, breathed a little deeper, couldn't hold back his sobs, and returned with the razor in his hand. He wanted to see her all illuminated. It was like the first night. The blade of the razor was giving off rays of green light that sparkled on Saraminda's strange closed eyes.

He went closer and knelt down. He shut his eyes.

The dogs were running about and howling desperately.

Cleto Bonfim's hands weakened and his eyes began to rain tears.

A smell of lavender and brimstone hung in the air.

The dogs suddenly quieted down. There was nothing but the silence of the pack disappearing into the woods.

"Saraminda! Saraminda!"

198

36

The Dead Claim

The sky filled with a flock of black-wooled sheep, clouds that had come from far away, tossing dust into the infinite. Everything grew dark. Day turned into night. The claim was dead and exhaling a smoke with the smell of lilies of the valley.

Birds, animals, disoriented, were running and flying in confused circles. A cold wind was blowing, punctuated by explosions of sparks from the burning stands of bamboo.

"It's the flood tide droning like that. It's like a tidal wave and when it reaches the coast it gets into the woods and its thunder scares the animals, who've had their ears to the ground far off and hear the thunder brought in from the sea and the insides of the earth," Ricardo commented.

Cleto wasn't to be seen. Everyone was asking about him. What had happened in the shadowy house wasn't known. The wintry rain broke out and went on for three days.

"It's Cleto Bonfim's tears. Saraminda was sleeping," someone said.

The thunderclaps were sobs, monotonous, deep, sad, long.

The water ran in channels to the pond formed among what remained of the claim. People were abandoning the sheds and running away. The yellow rivers had turned red. Dogs were barking and howling all around. There seemed to be thousands of them but nobody saw a single one.

"What mystery lies in this wet afternoon? Has Cleto disappeared?" Taíta asked with her eyes open, eyes that hadn't been closed or weeping for three days.

"The claim died of melancholy," declared Crescêncio, the same one who'd run away on the portage to the Cunani with Jacques Kemper and later returned.

"All the gold has run out. Now staying here means hunger, fever, the madness of the heat of summer months, and nothing else at all," a shadow added.

They all looked at the sky and in the midst of the rain they saw a bonfire. The clouds were burning like wooden embers.

A shape with a broad hat and a suitcase of jewels crossed paths with the gold diggers who were fleeing in disorder along the road to Oh-My-God Marsh. He looked familiar.

"Isn't that Domingos?" asked Manira, the last woman from the brothel who'd remained there.

"Yes, but he was murdered," Taíta said.

"I came looking for Cleto Bonfim. I want to buy gold."

"Domingos, it's been raining for three days and nobody knows what happened to him."

"Some throat-cutting maybe?"

"Nobody knows."

"What about Saraminda?" Domingos asked again.

"She disappeared, too."

The claim is dead, black *tonka*-bean palms burned into old brushland.

37

A Light on the Docks of Le Havre

Kemper went back to his cabin. The whistles in the harbor came one after another from all sides. A grinding of chains and engines invaded his ears, a trumpeting of shouts: Port, starboard! And the lights of Le Havre drew closer and closer. Passengers were carrying their bags onto the deck and in the companionways of the *Belle Martinique*, weary from so many crossings.

Kemper picked up his wooden suitcase, painted yellow with black reinforcements at the corners and iron clamps to close it. It contained articles of clothing, all bought in Cayenne. No memories of his misadventures, no object to remind him of those years.

Kemper was the carcass of himself. His colorless hands were a reflection of the paleness of his face. His head was like a chessboard where the pieces had fallen over, one used by a player who didn't understand the pieces or the rules of the game. His memory consisted of cut-outs that didn't fit together. He was the last prisoner returning from an invisible *hagne*, a hellish prison colony in Guiana, his body reduced to bloody cuts of meat. The facts he remembered were concentrated in a mysterious box, which he broke open and inside found another, broke that one open and another appeared, and he never reached the end.

It was in that anguish that he became aware of a cold sweat pouring over his body, freezing his soul. Confused, like an expurgated ghost, he picked up a cotton shirt he'd bought on the rue Pichevin in Old Cayenne and paused with it in his hands. His eyes grew dim, an earthquake was taking place in his head that was spinning, knocking everything down, shaking his memory and reconstructing that array of ruins which never came back together. His thoughts and his legs were trembling, his eyes were leaping out of their sockets as though they wanted to leave his face in order to see everything, only to return back inside twisted. It was as if he were feeling once more the malaria of his night of flight, with his sweat all bubbling out. When he came to, the ship was close to the dock. The nearby lights were bright and clustered together. The hubbub was growing. Commands were given: Drop anchor, tie up, and the engines slowed, floundered, with the propellers in reverse, and the mooring ropes were thrown into the broken waters. Kemper was trembling, overcome by an acrid commotion.

His memory was jumbled, returning little by little, hastened by the end of the voyage. His past became clear, the weft of his life was being reconstructed: his departure, the claim, Cleto, Celestino, Maruanda, Laurence, the dress, his flight, his fever, his death, his resurrection. Everything was coming back, like the rains of Cayenne. He remembered the passion, which like a volcano in eruption was spreading lava in all directions: "Who made the decision for me to return? I want to stay with you forever, Saraminda."

The smooth dark body, a water-snake coiled up in the hot vapors of the steamy jungle. The storms, her body immersed in the water of the falls, in the scented baths, the dogs all around her, gold in everything.

The delirium broke.

He heard the order to disembark from a sailor tapping him on his sore back.

Jacques Kemper picked up his suitcase. He was trembling and could barely lift it. In his head he carried the dementia of a love lost forever. Stumbling, he stood at the gangplank, moving clumsily among the other passengers and the strangers waiting for them.

Kemper cast a glance at the lonely space hovering over the port of Le Havre, open to the world, from where he'd left for that dream. He put his sad little suitcase down. He raised his eyes and came face to face with the Calçoene and Salomoganha Mountain. The crowd was descending, growing into an avalanche, with the waters of the rivers and the rapids that he'd gone up and ridden down so many times, heavy currents that lashed the rocks, risen

202

with the rains, turning everything gray, but glistening like a rainbow in the sunlight.

No one was waiting for him. No face. Only the water, the rocks, and the whirlwind of his memory.

A ghostly call filled his ears, invading the whole dock where people disembarked. It was a voice distant and near, with the strength of a bell-bird, that chimes of the jungle.

"Jacques Kemper from Vila do Calçoene! Jacques Kemper..."

He lifted his hands to his face, covered his ears. He couldn't figure out the meaning of the sounds. He opened his eyes. In the middle of the vestibule, making her way through, was a woman. She stopped in front of him. The enigmatic beauty of her green eyes, the mysterious nakedness of her golden breasts:

Saraminda.

Table of Characters

Alexandre: The owner of the claim in Roraima.

André: Kemper's stepfather.

Annie: Kemper's sister.

Arthur: The dead leader of French expedition to Amapá.

Artônia: A witch.

Astrolábio: Cleto Bonfim's representative in Vila do Firmino, a port on the River Calçoene.

Augustin Ruppert: Clément Tamba's father, a French soldier.

Baibina: A Créole brothel madam, Saraminda's grandmother.

Bizene: Kemper's hospice mate in Cayenne.

Carlindo: A jeweler.

Celestino Gouveia: Cleto Bonfim's foreman.

Charlotte: Kemper's mother.

Charwein: Governor of Guiana in 1895.

Clément Tamba: Guianan, a Frenchman born in Cayenne who went to the claim in the basin of the Calçoene River.

Cleto Bonfim: The boss of a claim who bought Saraminda at an auction.

Coudreau: A scientist who spent some years in the Contestado studying the course of the rivers.

Crescêncio: A claim worker.

Denara: Clément's cousin.

Descoup: Saraminda's father.

Domingos Eleutério de Barros: A traveling jewelry salesman.

Doriques: Raída's husband.

Edith Mourreau: The first wife of Rent d'Orville, who was murdered by him.

205

Esode: A saxophone player at Cleto Bonfim's funeral.
Foucaud: An official of the Société Française de l'Amérique Equatoriale in Paris.
Father José: A priest who heard Lucy's first confession.
Gabriel: A claim worker.
Gedina: Saraminda's maid.
Genevieve: A passenger on the ship Gazelle.
Genibaldo Pereira: A merchant on the Calçoene claim.
Greba: Gertrudes's mother, Clément Tamba's aunt.
Jacob Biarritz: Clément's grandfather, a Jew who brought his grandmother from Africa as a slave.
Jacques Kemper: Nicknamed Firebeard, a Frenchman from Cancale and an employee of the Société Equatoriale.
Jansen: A Dutchman, Balbina's father and Saraminda's great-grandfather.
Jean-Baptiste: A goldsmith.
Jean-Louis Lefèvre: An agent of the Société Equatoriale who killed himself because of his wife Laurence.
Jean-Mann: A pianist at the Tour d'Argent.
Jean-Pierre: A merchant in tobacco and sugar in the Ceperou district of Cayenne.
João: A gate guard on Cleto's claim.
Joaquino: A claim worker who disappeared with Raída.
Jules Gros: Founder of the Republic of Cunani.
Julienne: Saraminda's mother.
Juvenal: The owner of the shipping house in Vila do Firmino.
Juvencio: Lucy's first lover.
Juventino: A claim worker from Pará.
Koron: A cousin of Sarminda and Lorette.
Lariel: A gardener.
Laurence: The wife of Jean-Louis Lefèvre.
Leão de Rodesia: Saraminda's dog.
Ledério: A fugitive from Surinam, Clément's employee.
Li Yung: A Chinese man who discovered a thirty-seven pound nugget in the Calçoene River.
Linderfo: A friend of Clément.
Lorette: Saraminda's cousin.
Louis: A pianist in the bar Chez Martin.
Lucienne: A woman auctioned off at Marie Turiu's brothel.

Lucile: Kemper's aunt with whom he went to live in Paris at age fourteen.
Lucy: Clément's wife in his old age.
Ludgero: A bookkeeper.
Maruanda: Saraminda's maid.
Nicomedes: Saraminda's monkey.
Ovídio: Saraminda's orchard keeper.
Pedro Nolasco: A gold buyer.
Possidonia Biarritz: Clément's mother, who was Jewish and black.
Querida: A witch and Artônia's helper.
Raída: A half-breed from Maranhão who ran away from the claim.
Raimunda: Clément's servant.
Raimundo: A claim worker.
René d'Orville: Clément's stepfather.
Ricardino Merenda: A claim worker.
Ricardo: Bonfim's assistant.
Ritinha: A washerwoman in Cayenne who taught Creole to Saraminda's parrot.
Rodrigo: A claim worker from Pará.
Roger: Lorette's husband.
Saraminda: A Creole woman from Cayenne, Cleto Bonfim's wife.
Severino Boião: A claim worker.
Taíta: A cook on the claim.
Tatie: A prostitute on the claim.
Teodoro Leal: A gold buyer.
Terêncio: An employee of Bonfim.
Trajano Benítez: A representative of France and delegate of the governor of Cayenne in the Contestado.
Wiabo: A woman auctioned at the brothel.
Xaxá: Saraminda's parrot.
Zacarias: A gold buyer who took part in the auction of Saraminda.
Zaqueta: An importer of *cachaça*.

208

Desire and Its Shadow
Ana Clavel
ISBN 0-9707652-5-8 ISBN 9780970765253 list $14.95
"A magical, terrible, dazzling Mexico..."
Vuelo (Mexico City)
"An Alice-Lolita trapped between Wonderland and daily life...magical language..."
Siempre (Mexico City)
"Ana Clavel...part of [Mexico's] new literary pack."
Publishers Weekly

And coming in 2008 by Ana Clavel:
Shipwrecked Body

Die, Lady,Die
Alejandro López
ISBN 0-9707652-6-6 ISBN 9780970765260 list $12.95
"A story full of madness that combines Almodóvar with Latin pop, fan clubs, soap operas, and lonely hearts magazines."
Página 12 (Buenos Aires)
"Such is the brutal truth of this dizzying novel: there is no reality beyond that of an alienating mass media."
Tres Puntos (Buenos Aires)

Jail
Jesús Zárate, translated by Gregory Rabassa
ISBN 0-9707652-3-1 ISBN 9780970765239 list $14.95
"In its static setting and absurd slant, Zárate's approach resembles Beckett's *Waiting for Godot*, in its questioning of cruelty and power, Kafka's *Penal Colony*...Zárate's novel is something special, and its arrival in English is a welcome gift."
San Francisco Chronicle
"This amazing novel assumes nothing about freedom; as a consequence, *Jail* gives the idea of freedom a tangibility unparalleled by contemporary discussions of the term."
Rain Taxi

Luminous Cities
Eduardo Garcia Aguilar
ISBN 0-9707652-1-5 ISBN 9780970765215 list $16.95
"Juxtaposes scenes of decadence and splendor, vulgarity and exquisiteness, creating a dizzying mosaic of urban life."
Américas

Magdalena: A Fable of Immortality
Beatriz Escalante
ISBN 0-9707652-9-0 ISBN 9780970765222 list $12.95
"A fable of feminine ambition that alludes as well to other genres and traditions: biblical and Borgesian parables, alchemical treatises, fairy tales, and contemporary feminist fiction."
Delaware Review of Latin American Studies

Mariana
Katherine Vaz
ISBN 0-9707652-9-0 ISBN 9780970765291 list $15.95
"*Mariana*'s evocation of life in seventeenth-century Portugal glows with colour...in its lyrical descriptions of ordinary lives transfigured, in its detailing of everyday routines and beliefs, and in its account of spiritual and emotional struggles."
The Times Literary Supplement (London)
"Dialogue and descriptions that transport us to the turbulent Portugal of the seventeenth century..."
Activa (Portugal)
"With intensity and erudition, Katherine Vaz has written about the 'forbidden love' that has long fascinated such brilliant minds as Stendahl, Rilke, and Braque."
La Vanguardia (Spain)